Praise for Lisa Marie Rice
and the Me...

"With a tightly-w... ...r of
engaging second... ...will
easily satisfy fan...
—RT ... ...nce

"Lisa Marie Rice pulled me in from the first page and
kept my attention to the very last word of *Midnight
Promises*... I'd highly recommend *Midnight Promises*
to any romantic suspense reader, you won't be able to
put it down!"

—*Harlequin Junkie*, Top Pick

"This book delivers with the crackalicious elements
of a sweet romance, sexy tension and a cute heroine
who knows her way around a computer."
—*The Book Pushers* on *Midnight Promises*

"This book is hard to put down once you start
reading, so my suggestion is to carve out some alone
time, because this book hooks you and doesn't free
you until the end of the journey."
—*Harlequin Junkie* on *Midnight Secrets*, Top Pick

"Ms. Rice weaves her story seamlessly, with strong,
well defined characters. I will be going back to read
the rest of the series. If you are in the market for a
fantastic hot suspenseful romance—*Midnight Secrets*
is fantastic!"

—*Bitten by Love Reviews*

**Also available from Lisa Marie Rice
and Carina Press**

Midnight Vengeance
Midnight Promises
Midnight Secrets
Midnight Fire

LISA MARIE RICE

MIDNIGHT FIRE

carina press®

If you purchased this book without a cover you should be aware
that this book is stolen property. It was reported as "unsold and
destroyed" to the publisher, and neither the author nor the
publisher has received any payment for this "stripped book."

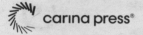

carina press®

ISBN-13: 978-0-373-00324-2

Midnight Fire

Recycling programs
for this product may
not exist in your area.

Copyright © 2015 by Lisa Marie Rice

All rights reserved. Except for use in any review, the reproduction or
utilization of this work in whole or in part in any form by any electronic,
mechanical or other means, now known or hereinafter invented, including
xerography, photocopying and recording, or in any information storage
or retrieval system, is forbidden without the written permission of the
publisher, Harlequin Enterprises Limited, 225 Duncan Mill Road,
Don Mills, Ontario M3B 3K9, Canada.

This is a work of fiction. Names, characters, places and incidents are
either the product of the author's imagination or are used fictitiously,
and any resemblance to actual persons, living or dead, business
establishments, events or locales is entirely coincidental.

This edition published by arrangement with Harlequin Books S.A.

® and TM are trademarks of the publisher. Trademarks indicated with
® are registered in the United States Patent and Trademark Office, the
Canadian Intellectual Property Office and in other countries.

www.CarinaPress.com

Printed in U.S.A.

This book is dedicated, as always,
to my husband and son.

I'd like to thank Adam Firestone
for demolishing my original plot,
though he replaced it with a better one.
All the cool stuff is his, all the mistakes are mine.

MIDNIGHT FIRE

ONE

Washington DC
National Cathedral
Memorial service for Hector Blake

FUNERALS BROUGHT OUT the worst in everyone, Summer Redding thought. Particularly when the man being buried was universally hated.

Well, maybe not everyone hated him, but certainly no one loved Hector Blake, former US Senator, survivor of the Washington Massacre, the man who would have become the Vice President of the United States if Alex Delvaux had lived.

But Alex Delvaux hadn't lived. The entire Delvaux family—a huge clan—had died except for Isabel Delvaux. Even Jack Delvaux had died—and he'd been so beautiful, so full of life, so amazingly charming you'd think he could outcharm death itself.

But no.

Hector Blake, however, had survived. Like one of those proverbial cockroaches that would survive a nuclear apocalypse.

Summer had never figured out how Hector had survived when so many others had died in the Massacre the evening Alex Delvaux was supposed to announce that he was running for the office of President. By all accounts Hector should have been in the stone cold ground six months ago instead of mysteriously drowning in the Potomac two days ago.

His funeral service was amazingly long and tedious. Just about everyone who was anyone had climbed up on that podium on the mosaic hardwood dais and droned on and on about how wonderful Hector Blake had been. Not one person who spoke believed a word they were saying.

Hector had been a mean, nasty piece of work with no redeeming virtues beyond being a childhood friend of Alex Delvaux, who'd been a good guy. Hector had also been a relative by marriage of Summer's, for about fifteen minutes a million years ago.

The National Cathedral Chorus started up "I know that my Redeemer Liveth." Beautiful piece of music for such a miserable asshole.

Summer was there professionally because there was a lot about the Massacre that made no sense to her and she'd always felt that Hector was the key to unlocking the mysteries. For just a moment, though, she allowed herself to get caught up in the gorgeous music. She let it run through her, the harmonies reverberating in her, the genius of the music lifting her soul.

She found herself doing that more and more often lately. Switching off for a moment to listen to music, to read a poem, to take a walk in the park. Because more and more it felt like mud was seeping into the world from some secret putrid underground source, making everything filthy, tarnishing everything that was fresh and clean.

Her political blog/webzine, *Area 8*, was highly successful. It was incredibly successful because political wrongdoing—her specialty—was so popular lately.

These past years it seemed you couldn't turn around without a congressman or senator or cabinet secretary taking money from the wrong people, diddling a teenager or crashing cars while drunk or high. Sometimes all three.

It was like some kind of epidemic of crazy.

Area 8 covered these in loving detail. When you took the long view, and squinted and put a little Vaseline on the lens of life, it was funny-grotesque. But Summer took a closer view and was often heartsick at the blatant wrongdoing, the betrayal of the public's trust.

She found herself seeking out concerts of all types, whether in small churches or large concert halls, and she'd sit at the back, close her eyes and let the music wash over her, through her, like she was doing right now. More and more, she would take time out from her busy schedule to drive to Rock Creek Park and walk for an hour, two. Breathe in the fresh air, watch the squirrels, bask in living things that weren't cheating each other and cheating on each other.

She'd re-read all of Jane Austen four times last year.

Even she recognized she was on the verge of burn-out.

But she had to keep going because there was something even nastier than usual swelling underground and the Washington Massacre was part of it and Hector Blake had been in the middle of the Massacre.

Summer didn't have any hard data, nothing she could take to the authorities, or at least to authorities she trusted. No documents, no files, no videotape, no recordings. Just gut instinct and a few signs of blood in the water.

The last lingering notes of the choral music shimmered in the air, rising to the immense coffered ceiling, then dissipated. The music was over, alas. Now for some more fragrant bullshit.

Marcus Springer, the CIA's Deputy Director of Central Intelligence, took the podium. Fussy and prissy, he shot his cuffs, carefully placed a sheet of paper on the podium and slowly withdrew his reading glasses from a fancy steel tube in his front jacket pocket, movements slow and deliberate. Expression serene, the very opposite of grief-stricken.

"We're here to celebrate the life of a great American, Hector Blake," Springer intoned and Summer tuned out. Another fluff piece.

Blake's life was of little interest to her. She knew the highlights. But there was something really wrong with Blake's death. The coroner's office had been extremely terse in its findings after the autopsy.

Basically, Hector Blake had drowned. Somewhere.

Maybe the Potomac, maybe not. Maybe in his car, maybe not. That was the sum total of the info given in the coroner's report. The full report was unavailable for reasons of national security. Summer had a really good informant in the coroner's office—coroners saw a lot of mischief and her informant could be bribed by tickets to concerts—but this time her informant, James Hadson, who had a secret crush on her, was completely mute. He gave her zip. Nada. He could not put his hands on the report, which was in a separate file that required a password James didn't have. And James hadn't assisted in the autopsy. Strangely enough, for the autopsy of such an important man, it had been carried out solo by the coroner of Washington DC herself, who had since taken unpaid leave and was nowhere to be found.

It all stank to high heaven.

Summer had no problems imagining someone whacking Blake—but who?

In her head a very long imaginary line formed of people who'd like to off him.

Her Aunt Vanessa, for one. Aunt Vanessa had been briefly married to Blake, so there was a connection to Summer, though not a blood one. Sharing DNA with Hector Blake…eww.

When her parents had died she'd landed on Aunt Vanessa's doorstep for two months, waiting to go to boarding school. Aunt Vanessa and Hector had been going through a vicious separation that would lead to a hotly contested divorce.

Those two months would have been unbearable if it hadn't been for the Delvauxes who stopped by often and invited her over often. She ate a lot of meals at their house and would probably have gone hungry otherwise. No one at the Glades ate in the house and they didn't care whether she was eating or not.

Isabel Delvaux had been two years older than her and had been kind and fun. And Jack—when Summer first saw him, her jaw had dropped, the first time that had happened to her in all her twelve years. She was sure he jump started her puberty.

He'd been fifteen and drop-dead gorgeous. From his sun-bleached tousled blond head down to his perfect feet which she spaced out on when they spent the afternoons at the backyard pool, he was beautiful boyhood incarnate.

She'd lost sight of Isabel but had met Jack again her first week at Harvard.

He'd done a double take when she'd shyly said hello to the dazzling senior, even more gorgeous than before. A handsome man instead of a beautiful boy and oh, just looking at him was such a pleasure. He'd been really nice to her and then he'd bedded her and it had been as if her life were finally coming together. But Jack was like a sun god, too magnificent to stay with a lonely freshman. He'd seduced Summer, her dorm roommate and two other girls on the floor in one month and then he'd disappeared.

He'd been her first and her last for a long, long time.

He'd given her blinding pleasure, she'd so foolishly thought it was true love, and he'd shattered her heart. All in a few days.

And then he vanished into smoke. She never saw him again. And now he was dead, too, in the Massacre.

He'd broken her heart but he'd also been brimming with life and joy—the golden boy who should have had a long and happy life, now dead in the cold, cold ground.

Summer shivered and shook herself.

Hector's funeral was affecting her too much. She was here as a reporter, an observer, searching for clues to the Washington Massacre, she wasn't here to reminisce. Springer's droning voice came to an end and the entire audience seemed to wake up.

Summer looked around at all the well-coiffed heads atop elegantly clothed bodies. More or less anyone who was anyone in Washington was here. They had even set up a Jumbotron outside for those who wanted to follow the memorial service but hadn't been invited.

Summer hadn't been invited either, but there was a section set off for journalists and she'd found a place to sit by coming an hour early.

The funeral was over and a hidden organ began playing leave-the-church music. A huge perfumed rustle of expensive clothes and everybody rose, chatter buzzing immediately.

"One more wanker gone," a sour British voice said next to her. "Good riddance." She glanced to her side, recognizing the man. Billy Atkins, formerly of the *London Times* until he was fired for uncovering one too many royal scandals. Now he freelanced in Washington and drank. She could smell the beer coming off him.

"So what do you think of that coroner's report?" Summer asked, curious. Billy was a cynical drunk, but he had a first rate journalistic nose.

"Cover up, lass," he replied and moved away before she could question him any further. Maybe sometime this week she could invite him to a beer or two or seven, loosen up his tongue.

Someone somewhere had to know something.

People were shuffling out of the pews, spilling into the huge aisles, heading for the big open doors at the back. Sunlight streamed in through the blue and pink stained glass windows but all of a sudden, like everyone else, Summer craved the real thing. Craved sunlight and open air.

She made a beeline for the big open doors, uncaring that there were a thousand contacts for hundreds of possible stories all around her. She didn't care, the air in the cathedral was stifling and she couldn't breathe.

Everyone wanted out. The line moved swiftly to the exit, propelling her out onto the large cement porch.

It was chilly but sunny, the cold sun turning the hill-top lawn a bright green, the buildings down below as white as snow.

For some reason it made her think of the Delvaux compound in Virginia. Bright green grass, white build-ings...

Unsettled, Summer turned to snake her way through the throngs pouring out the doors and down the stairs. Hector Blake's funeral was stirring up things she had put in a box long ago. The bewilderment after her par-ents' deaths, her heartbreak at Harvard when Jack had dumped her like an ice cream cone he'd licked and found decent but not special. At Harvard there had been so many tastes for him to savor.

It had taken her *so long* to get over him. An em-barrassingly long time. Good thing he had essentially disappeared and she didn't have to see him on cam-pus with a different girl every week on his arm. She'd been so shaky at the time, it would have broken her heart even more.

Good thing she was strong now. No man would ever—*could* ever—break her heart again. Certainly not Jack or anyone like him. Too handsome for words, utterly charming, a lightweight.

Around her, several people pulled back quickly, al-most violently, one woman stepping on Summer's toes. The woman didn't even turn around to excuse herself. She was being crowded by the person in front of her.

Summer wasn't tall, so she had to go on tiptoe to see what was going on.

Oh. A homeless guy. A tall vet, dressed in filthy, tattered BDUs, smelling of urine and body odor, long lank greasy dirty blond hair hanging in dreadlocks over his face, down his back, an unkempt beard covering half his face.

Well. Though her own heart swelled with pity—with the economic downturn there were a lot of homeless vets on the streets—she understood the people in front of her jerking away from him. Homeless vets didn't fit into the elite's mindset. They shouldn't exist and when the elite came across them, they shied away.

The vet turned his face toward her for a second and that's when their eyes met. Sharp, bright-blue eyes. Eyes she'd seen in her dreams a thousand times. Eyes that had stared into hers when they'd made love.

He turned immediately and ran. Though Summer pushed through the crowd brutally, stepping on toes and elbowing people aside, she lost him.

The vet was nowhere to be found.

Summer stood, frozen, unable to believe her eyes, yet knowing exactly what she'd seen.

Jack Delvaux, dead these past six months.

FUCK! SHE MADE HIM!

Jack Delvaux vaulted down the great stone steps of the National Cathedral, pushing people out of his way. But they parted for him anyway. He looked bad, he smelled bad and Washington's elite simply broke ranks to let him through because the alternative was him touching them and their skin crawled at the idea.

Good.

Pretending to be homeless had kept him alive these past six months since the Washington Massacre. Everyone thought he was dead, which was just fine by Jack.

Because the Washington Massacre hadn't been carried out by jihadi terrorists. No, the Massacre had been carried out by homegrown monsters, masquerading as terrorists. The Massacre hadn't been about terror, it had been all about money, and dear departed Hector Blake had been right in the middle of it.

Jack had been present when Hector had really died. Had been part of it, actually. Hector had drowned in the Willamette River in Portland, Oregon four days ago while trying to abduct Jack's sister, Isabel. Like him, she was one of the few survivors of the Massacre that had taken the lives of their parents, their younger twin brothers, their aunts, uncles, cousins and about seven hundred other people in the Burrard Hotel.

Jack's heart still burned when he thought of it.

He wished Hector were still alive so he could kill him all over again.

But Hector had left a lot of secrets behind. A deep conspiracy that reached into the upper levels of the American intelligence community, including Jack's former employer, the CIA, and Jack wasn't going to rest until he unveiled it all and saw the conspirators in jail or in the ground. Preferably the latter.

Everyone thought Jack had been killed in the Massacre. Jack had stayed off the grid by pretending to be homeless, while living in a hidden safe house no one else knew about, set up by his former boss, who was now dead.

Pretending to be a homeless vet made him invisible. People didn't want the homeless around at all. And homeless *vets*? No way.

Jack had bought old BDUs from the Salvation Army, pissed on them a couple of times a week and kept them out on the safe house's little balcony where they got rained on and snowed on and grew more and more filthy.

He showered but took care to never wash his face. He shaved his head regularly and wore a filthy dreadlocks wig and pasted a scraggly beard on his face every time he went out, to confound the facial recognition bots. It worked. He didn't even recognize himself.

For the entire funeral, Jack had watched from the edges of the crowd outside, keeping an eye on the Jumbotron, looking for clues, looking for *something* and wasn't once recognized in the city he'd grown up in.

Except for Summer.

Damn.

She'd always been too smart for her own good.

He vaguely remembered the summer she'd been around at Hector's place—she was some kind of relative of one of Hector's wives—after she'd lost her folks. She'd been a funny looking little thing, eyes and mouth too big, a messy mass of reddish-brown hair sitting on her head like a bird's nest. Stick-thin and quiet as a mouse. It was the summer he'd had the crazy idea of training for the Olympics as an archer but it had turned out to be too much work and interfered with his social life. Life had been really good back then. He'd been pretty busy all that summer training and competing and partying and hadn't really paid her much attention.

Then she disappeared. People were appearing and disappearing from his life constantly in those years because he was too clueless and self-involved to pay attention.

And then in his senior year at Harvard he'd run across her and—whoa. Her face had grown so the eyes and mouth were sexily big without looking weird. She didn't have a rat's nest at all, but a smooth auburn bob and had filled out nicely. Very nicely.

He'd barely recognized her and had been able to place her thanks to her voice. She'd grown up abroad, dragged to a thousand places by her hippie parents. She spoke beautifully but with a tinge of an exotic accent that had made him smile when she'd been twelve and made him sweat when she was eighteen.

And then he'd fucked her and left her. Which was what he did on a massive scale in those years, thinking with his little head and not his big head.

It felt like ancient history, something you'd study in a textbook. The Years of Fucking Around: 1997-2001.

He had to get out of here, fast, because Summer would follow her instincts and try to catch him.

His years in the CIA's National Clandestine Service had taught him to walk really fast without appearing to hurry. He just lengthened his stride and made sure he wasn't pumping his arms.

He didn't really have to worry about anyone other than Summer, because no one noticed him, except to draw back or even cross the street to avoid him. Down the hill from the Cathedral and four blocks away was a black SUV with mud on the license plates and smoked windows. It looked exactly like every other official vehicle in the city.

Jack jerked the passenger door open and sat down.

"Well that was fun," Nick Mancino said as he started the engine. Nick wrinkled his nose. "Man, you smell."

"That's the point," Jack said. "Now drive."

The SUV pulled out and headed for Jack's safe house. "So?"

"I think I was made," Jack said sullenly. Six fucking months without being made in a city full of intelligence operatives and government agents and one girl—woman—made him in an instant.

"Well…fuck," Nick said, driving fast. Nick, a member of the FBI's elite Hostage Rescue Team, was under unofficial cover. Only one person knew he was here investigating the Massacre, the Director of the FBI. With possible CIA involvement, it was the hottest of hot potatoes and so far, the investigation was off the grid.

Officially, Nick was on leave from the FBI and would stay on leave until they unmasked the conspiracy. He was almost as driven as Jack to find the fuckers responsible. Almost.

Jack had lost his entire family except for his sister, Isabel. He was going to find out who was responsible or die.

"Who made you?" Nick's eyes swept the side view mirrors and the rear view mirror in a constant rotation. Jack was a good driver but Nick had taken combat driving training at Quantico.

Jack clenched his teeth. "Summer Redding."

Nick's eyes widened and he flicked a glance over to Jack. "Summer Redding? The blogger? *Area 8?*"

Jack nodded.

"Well, hell." Nick shook his head. "That is very bad news. Redding is one sharp lady. Are we going to read about you being alive after all in today's blog? If so, we're fucked."

They *were* fucked. If Summer posted that he'd been seen today—alive—the entire mission was endangered. It wasn't just a question of himself. Jack knew that forces inside the CIA were working against the country. The Massacre was just the first of what he felt might be more attacks coming soon.

A drumbeat of dread thrummed through him.

Just before the Massacre, Jack had stepped on some kind of trip wire. He'd first come across whispers in Singapore, where he'd been posted for the past four years. An informant had contacted him about a secret plan at the highest levels of the Chinese government to destabilize the United States with the help of a few very highly-placed American citizens, including a few in the CIA. When Jack heard that, every hair on his body had stood up.

The plan had several steps and the first one had been the Massacre and the second one was going to be an attack on US soil. He had nothing more than that. No timetable, no indication of where.

And then the informant had disappeared and reappeared as a floater in the Singapore city morgue. The corpse had been so bloated it had taken the coroner an hour to discover the slit across the informant's throat.

But it had been serious enough for Jack to fly home to talk to his boss, the head of the National Clandestine Service, Hugh Lownie. He'd been meaning to fly home anyway because his dad, against the entire family's advice, had announced his intention to declare his candidacy for the presidency. His mom had gone into panic mode, frightened to death that someone would assassinate him. Rumor had it that they were fighting, close to a divorce, but that was bullshit. His parents loved each other deeply.

His dad was an idealist, wanted to run, and Jack had come home.

He'd met with Hugh in a park with no microphones

anywhere because he didn't trust anyone or anything at Langley. Hugh had promised to start an in-house investigation.

That night, the night his father was slated to declare his candidacy at the Burrard Hotel, Hugh had called him. Jack had been on the podium because whether or not he agreed with his dad about running for President, he loved the guy and would swing his support behind him.

Everyone he loved had died that night with the exception of his sister, Isabel.

Nick wrinkled his nose. "Dude, do something. You fucking reek."

Jack unfastened the seat belt, took off the stinking jacket and slid out of the uniform pants. He also snatched the smelly wig off his head. He hated it almost more than the sweat-and-piss-soaked BDU. The wig itched and was heavy as fuck. Underneath, Jack kept his hair shorn and did it himself. Looking at himself without the wig, he looked like a prisoner of war. He pulled the beard off, too. The beard was stuck on by a miracle glue like that on Post-its that he could apply and tear off without pain.

Nick kept his eyes firmly on the road. Jack reached behind him for a hoodie and sweat pants, put the stinking homeless uniform in a plastic bag, tied the handles together, and put the bag in a gym bag. The funk factor in the vehicle dropped by about a thousand.

"Thanks," Nick said, sighing with relief. "So, what are we going to do about Redding? She made you, she's going to put it in her blog. We have to stop that, stop her. It would be a disaster. She can't write about it. Not now, it would put the entire mission in jeopardy."

"Whoa." Jack shot up in the seat. "We're not touching her. The hell you talking about?"

"Calm down, bro." Nick clutched the steering wheel harder. "I don't mean hurt her, Christ, what do you think I am, CIA?"

Jack let that slide. A couple of years ago he wouldn't have taken any abuse from an FBI puke, no sir. The CIA wasn't perfect but he'd been proud to serve. At least in the beginning. Then later…

And now? Now someone in the CIA had killed an informant, carried out the Massacre and moles—he had no idea how many—were plotting to bring his country down. So he kept his mouth shut. Slumped back into the seat. "We're not touching Summer," he repeated. "She won't post anything, she never posts anything without some kind of proof. So we're okay."

He hoped.

Nick narrowed his eyes at the road and slapped his hand against the wheel. "You fucked her. That's what this is about."

Jack sighed. "Yeah. About a million years ago. I fucked a lot of the women who were at the funeral. I was a man slut. So what?"

"So you were imprinted on her, that must be it. Because no one else noticed you. And if that's the case, she'll be like a dog with a bone. Must have been some fuck."

Jack stiffened. Nick was a good guy but no one could talk like that about Summer. Jack swiveled his head and glared. "Say anything like that again and I'll rip you a new one," he growled, meaning every word.

Nick's eyes widened. "Dude. Sorry. Whoa, didn't mean it that way. Hell, she's an incredible woman. She followed the trail of Senator Rowland's abuse of the family au pair like a terrier with a bone. If we have one less shit in the Senate, it's thanks to her. I read *Area 8* regularly, love it." He blew out a breath. "So—now that we've got that out of the way—we still got a problem. A big one."

Jack clenched his jaw.

"Problem. We've got a problem. You see that, don't you? Talk to me, Jack." They were at the safe house and Nick pulled into the covered alleyway in the back. "What are you going to do about it? One of the most well-known bloggers in America knows you are not dead. How do we remedy that?"

Silence.

"Jack?"

"I'm going to go talk to her," Jack said finally.

TWO

Jack Delvaux is alive!

But... Jack was dead. He'd died in the Washington Massacre.

There'd been a memorial service for him and she'd cried bitterly over the golden boy who was no more.

Summer sat in her cute yellow Prius in front of her apartment in Alexandria, shaking hands still on the steering wheel, mind whirling.

Jack Delvaux, alive.

Most people would shrug the thought off as a figment of their imagination. Most people, knowing Jack had been dead for six months, would have told themselves that they were mistaken.

So anyone else who thought they'd seen a man who'd been dead for six months would have said to themselves—*that homeless man really looked like Jack Delvaux, but...nah. He's dead.*

But Summer couldn't do that because she had irrefutable proof that she'd seen Jack.

Her body. Her body had told her.

The week they'd been lovers at Harvard, her body hadn't been her own, it had been connected via some magic spell to Jack. Everything about her had changed. Her skin had felt different—too tight. Every time she saw him heat flashed through her, head to toe, an unstoppable blast that made her breath stop in her lungs.

Her fingers and toes and breasts tingled and heat blossomed between her legs, as if seeing him threw a switch that made her body change. It had never happened to her before and after he'd dumped her, it had never happened to her again.

And this afternoon, right outside Washington National Cathedral, her body had bloomed alive, like she'd been zapped by something. She'd channeled her 18-year old self.

Her body had recognized Jack before her head did and it freaked her out

For a second there, outside the National Cathedral, she'd wondered if she was having a stroke. She hadn't connected the boiling sensations under her skin to the tall homeless vet. And then...then she'd recognized him. First by his effect on her—the only man who'd ever made her feel as if she had an "on" switch and knew how to use it—and then by those intensely blue eyes.

Crazy as it sounded, she believed she really had seen Jack.

So—how could that even be possible? The only way it would be possible would be if he'd survived the Massacre but had been so badly injured in the explosion he was unable even to say who he was.

If he'd been so concussed he couldn't communicate, if he was disoriented, he'd end up living on the streets.

The thought was disturbing. It was disturbing for anybody, but for Jack Delvaux...he'd been destined by DNA to lead a long, happy, golden life. Isabel too, and yet look at her. She'd been in a coma, had lost her entire family, had quit her food blog. Her life shattered.

Isabel. Isabel had been so nice to her that summer.

Then they'd lost touch, of course, as people do. But if Isabel, who'd disappeared from view, thought her brother was dead, and he was alive...

Summer had to tell her. It was a moral obligation, wasn't it? Except how could she do that unless she were certain? It would be cruel beyond words to tell Isabel that her brother was still alive unless Summer were absolutely certain.

And just because a man made her tingle wasn't exactly proof of life, was it?

She dragged the groceries out from the back of her Prius. It had been a long sad, startling day. A nice meal at the end of it would put her in a better mood. After eating, she'd tackle the Jack problem, though it was going to be hard to find one homeless man among so many others.

Maybe check video footage at some shelters, to start. Since the Massacre ten new ones had opened for the masses of men and women who had suddenly lost everything in the economic shock. So...shelters. And then?

The security at her door was, as always, reassuring but balky. Keypad and deadbolt, which always meant putting on the floor whatever she had in her hands. What an English friend had called "belt and braces." It did make her feel safe, though.

Finally, she was through the door and in the calm, fragrant quiet of her apartment. Her refuge. She loved coming home to her pretty apartment, where everything was orderly and clean and sweet-smelling, so unlike the kind of places her parents had lived in. They hadn't cared that they lived in squalor. Why not? It was a question she still couldn't answer.

But she wasn't her parents. In no way was she her parents.

Shaking her head, she put the groceries on the kitchen counter, intending to cook and eat because she knew she'd be awake until morning doing research and would need her strength.

She moved into the living room to switch on a few lights and froze.

A man. A very big man was standing there, unmoving.

Oh God! A nightmare! Somehow someone had gotten past her layers of security. That took knowledge and focus and that meant nothing good.

She kept a loaded gun in a small safe on the opposite wall. The man was standing between her and the safe, so the gun could have been on the dark side of the moon for all the good it did her.

He was huge, shoulders a yard wide in outline, head shaved, enormous hands loose at his sides. With the bookcase lights at his back, his face was in shadow. All she could see were hard planes. She felt, more than saw, the intensity of his gaze. It was like being in a dark beam of light.

She'd taken self-defense courses and could hold her own against a normal-sized man but this guy was not only huge but built. Those enormous shoulders tapered down to a lean waist, the neck muscles strong even in shadow.

Summer's heart hammered as she ran through the options open to her. It went fast because she had none.

The gun was behind him. She had plenty of sharp knives but they were in a butcher block at least ten steps behind her. He could cut her off in a second if she made a dash for the kitchen door. And foolishly, fool-ishly, her cell wasn't in her pocket as it usually was. It was in her purse, on the kitchen counter, out of reach.

About the only thing she could do was scream, even knowing that one of the selling points of the condo was noise insulation. Her throat was closed up and she could barely breathe, like those nightmares where you couldn't scream, couldn't run.

She took in a deep breath and it froze in her throat.

"Summer," the man said in an unusually deep voice.

Her hand went to her throat where it felt as if some-one had grabbed her, was throttling her. She couldn't breathe.

He knew her?

This was personal then. Not some random stranger who'd broken into her home.

"Don't be afraid," he said and stepped forward.

Something about that voice…

Another step and the light from the kitchen illumi-nated his face.

Summer gasped.

Jack.

Summer stared, rooted to the spot, heart hammering Jack. And yet…not Jack. The man standing in front of her had nothing in common with the golden boy she'd known. The man-boy who'd bedded her and then disappeared, a creature too fine to settle to earth.

This man was bigger, bulkier. The Jack she'd known had had a refined, swimmer's physique. Muscular and lean. This Jack was huge, defined muscles that had been hidden by the homeless man's baggy uniform now clear under his black sweater. He didn't have straggling filthy dreadlocks. His head was crudely shorn, like a prisoner's, uneven and brutal-looking. His long, dirty-blond biker's beard was gone, too, leaving a bare chiseled chin with the jaw muscles working.

He was staring at her, narrow-eyed.

Summer was really glad he didn't look anything like the Jack she knew, that he looked so dangerous. If he'd been an older version of the friendly, charming boy, she'd have rushed to embrace him, hugging him tightly, happy he wasn't dead.

The Jack she knew would have hugged her back, maybe made a crack, pulling away from the hug because you didn't cling to Jack Delvaux. But he'd have been friendly and utterly harmless. The old Jack wouldn't have hurt a fly.

But *this* Jack?

She didn't know about this one. He could swat her away with one swipe of that huge, powerful hand. This Jack had been on the run, staying under the radar, for six months—which in this age of surveillance she'd have said was impossible. She had no idea why he'd stayed hidden, letting everyone think he was dead, but he had to have powerful reasons. So. Now she'd discovered his secret. How was he going to react?

"Hello, Jack," she said. "I thought I saw you at Blake's funeral." Summer kept her voice steady. Inside she was trembling, but long years of experience as a political journalist, showing absolutely nothing, served her well.

He frightened her, instinctively, but he couldn't be allowed to know that.

"Hello, Summer," he said, stepping toward her.

Summer forced herself not to step back. That would show she was intimidated. She was, but damned if she'd show it. He was very close to her, so close she had to tilt her head back slightly to keep her eyes on his face. He'd somehow grown in the past fifteen years. She didn't remember him being this tall.

Pointless pretending she didn't know why he was here.

"So I guess the reports of your death were exaggerated?" she said, trying to keep her voice light.

His huge fists closed, then opened. Summer's mouth went completely dry. Was he going to attack her? No. Besides the closing of his fists, he remained completely and utterly still.

"Yeah. So now you know." He stared at her unblinkingly.

She swallowed and nodded.

"So, I guess the question is—what are you going to do about it?" Jack's voice was low and deep and emotionless. But he was watching her keenly, gaze as intent as a blue-eyed hawk's.

Summer tried to keep it light. "I'm not too sure anyone would believe me if I wrote about it. I imagine the security cameras never caught you? I'm sure you're in a lot of facial recognition databases, even if you are certified dead."

"No. Never been caught."

Washington DC had thousands of security cams. If he'd been here all this time, he'd been extremely clever in avoiding identification.

"Just like my security system didn't stop you." Somehow evading the two security guards and the security cams around the perimeter of her complex plus cameras on every floor seemed even more difficult than evading security around the city.

"Your security system is crap," he said dismissively.

Summer drew in an outraged breath—her security system was *not* crap!—then clamped her jaw shut.

And then it occurred to her...if he thought her security system—which was top of the line, thank you very much—was crap, he was used to breaking into places. Into places with a better security system than hers.

"Listen, Summer," Jack growled, stepping forward.

Startled, she stumbled, trying to scramble away from him, then at the last minute turned it into a smooth pivot and said the first thing that came to her mind.

"So," she said crisply. "It's been a long, lousy day and I haven't eaten. I'm hungry. Do you want to talk about this over food?"

The surprise in his eyes was genuine. He nodded and followed her into the kitchen. In the bright light of the kitchen Summer got her first good look at him and oh, God.

He was gorgeous. In a totally *Prison Break* kind of way. How could he possibly be more attractive than he'd been as a boy and a young man? This man didn't have anything classically handsome. His blond hair was shorn to stubble, the only hint of the color a glints of gold under the overhead lights. His face was filled out, all hard angles and planes, weather-beaten skin showing lines around the mouth and eyes. Cheekbones hard and chiseled, the skin hollowed out under them. He looked older than his thirty-four years, like he'd been a prisoner of war in a far off land.

In all these years, she'd dreamed of encountering Jack again. She'd be polished and successful, courted by many men. He'd look dissipated and puffy, all those years of partying finally catching up. Unrecognizable, paying the price for years of debauchery. She'd squint, saying *Hey Jack? Is that you? Nice to see you.* And feel absolutely nothing at all.

Not like now, where she felt strong fear and an equally strong attraction to this man she barely recognized.

Summer began preparations for the meal, movements brisk to keep her hands from trembling. She caught glimpses of him out of the corner of her eye as she pulled ingredients from the fridge and the cupboards, the way you catch glimpses of a solar eclipse. Because it hurt to look at it directly.

Disturbingly, Jack came closer to her, leaning his back against her counter, watching her. She could feel his body heat, smell him. He smelled of soap and nothing else. He'd washed the homeless vet off him.

She chopped zucchini and onions fast, put them in a pan to sauté, took out fresh farm eggs from her shopping bag, whisked them with some grated parmesan. Not speaking, aware every single second of Jack watching her.

She pulled out romaine lettuce, shredded it and washed it under the faucet. There were a thousand things she wanted to ask but held off. How would he react to questions? Would he think she was interviewing him for an article?

An article. What a kick ass article it would be, too, headliner stuff. She could almost see it, could write the article in her head.

Jack Delvaux Found Alive Six Months After the Massacre. She'd have a million clicks, be on every talking head show, maybe be nominated for the Pulitzer.

Then again, maybe Jack would kill her before that happened.

"Nice," Jack said finally.

"What?" Startled, Summer looked him full in the face for the first time since he'd scared the hell out of her. She saw him through the scrim of time, the beautiful boy superimposed over the potent, frightening man, then she blinked and the scrim disappeared and all she saw was this Jack, in the here and the now, powerful and intimidating.

As she stared at him, the corner of his mouth turned up. He wasn't smiling but the expression lightened up a fraction.

"I said it's nice, someone cooking for me. That hasn't happened in six months. Since even before the Massacre, as a matter of fact."

For a second, the veil ripped away and she saw yet another Jack—weary beyond belief, a man who had lived on the streets for six months. Or at least in hiding. And of course the huge question was—why? Did she dare ask him? This Jack was so formidable she was almost scared of him. But her curiosity was greater than her fear.

How had he remained hidden for six whole months? He belonged to one of the most famous families in America. Had he been in Washington all this time? Had he actually been living on the streets or was that a disguise? And above all—*why*? Why let everyone think he was dead?

Was it possible that he was in some way responsible for the Massacre? The instant she thought that, she jerked it right out of her head.

No. The one thing she knew about Jack, over and

above anything else, absolutely integral to his personality, was that he loved his family. The idea that he
could hurt a family member, cause the death of a family member—no. Simply wasn't possible.

But killing someone else? This Jack Delvaux looked
perfectly capable of that.

Summer had never liked beating about the bush.
She put down her knife—she didn't know whether to
be happy or angry that Jack didn't seem to even notice
she had a very sharp knife in her hand—and turned
to face him.

"Why?" she asked. "Why did you let everyone
think you were dead? Why have you been living on
the streets these past six months?" And then a horrible
thought occurred to her. "Did *Isabel* think you were
dead? Did you let your sister mourn all these months?"

Isabel and Jack shared a special bond. Had he let
Isabel grieve the loss of her entire family when her beloved brother was still alive, but in hiding?

Nothing moved on Jack's face. Nothing. He'd had
such a mobile face as a young man, flickering through
ten different emotions in so many minutes. That had
gone. His face right now could have been carved out
of stone.

"She knows now," he said finally. And said nothing else. If Isabel had recently discovered he was alive
after all, surely…surely that must have been an incredibly emotional moment. And yet you wouldn't know
anything of that from Jack's expression.

"Why?" Summer asked again, everything she was
feeling in her voice. "Why disappear?"

Jack didn't answer. He simply stood there and
looked at her. So intensely his eyes were tracing her

face as if they were fingers, touching every tiny muscle to trace out her intentions. She stared right back, memorizing this new Jack, with lines in his face and hard blue eyes and a grim mouth.

The entire summer she'd spent with Hector and during the brief whirlwind affair she and Jack had had at Harvard, she had never seen Jack not smiling. Right now, it felt like the face she was looking at had never smiled and never would.

"Are you going to write about this?" he finally said.

"What?"

"Are you going to write about this in *Area 8*? That you saw me, that I'm alive?"

Well of course, she wanted to say, but held her tongue. It was the biggest story imaginable. Jack Delvaux alive.

He tilted his head, studying her. "You'd be crazy not to. Be a big story."

She said nothing. There was a *but* coming.

He stared at her, intense blue eyes unblinking. "But I'm going to ask you to wait. An article now would ruin everything, but I can't say more than that. Don't run it."

Summer blinked. This sounded very much like a command. From a very big, rough guy who was undercover. A man she realized now she didn't know at all.

She swallowed. "Don't run it or...what?"

An impatient gesture of one of those huge hands. "I'm not going to hurt you, if that's what you mean. Jesus, Summer. You know me better than that."

She slowly let out the breath she'd been holding. "I'm not a fool, Jack. Something big is at stake and it concerns a terrorist attack that claimed over seven hundred lives, including the man—your father—who was supposed to be our next president. Whatever is going on must be very serious if it forced you undercover for six months, and forced you to let your sister think you were dead."

Those sky blue eyes were intent. "It is. Very serious."

"And you don't think people have a right to know?" It was the bedrock philosophy of *Area 8*. *Area 8* didn't have a political viewpoint. She was no ideologue. The only philosophy *Area 8* followed was that citizens had a right to know what was going on with the people in power. They had a right to know what was being done in their name. And she also believed with all her heart that sunlight disinfected. Shine a light in the darkest corners and it got cleaned up. "This is big stuff. There are a lot of questions surrounding the Massacre. None of what happened made sense to me and I've been doing some digging of my own."

"You have?" Jack passed a big hand over the stubble on his head. "Tell you what, you show me yours and I'll show you mine."

Oh *God*.

He'd meant it in a completely different way but the image that blossomed in Summer's head was sexual. Him showing her his. That big, tough body, naked. From the powerful shoulders, the broad chest, the long, long legs down to the beautiful feet. She knew what he'd looked like naked fifteen years ago and he'd been dazzling, in a lean male model kind of way. Now, a naked Jack would be pure male power, unadorned and raw. Scarred and tough and mouthwatering.

Heat streaked through her—fast, explosive, unstoppable. The reaction only Jack had ever coaxed from her body. A conflagration from the top of her head to her toes because the truth was—she'd seen his. She remembered it clearly and it had been the source of blinding pleasure. She'd never known anything like that pleasure after him.

God forbid he realize that.

And what business did she have, getting all hot and bothered when he was standing there like a glowering lump of stone, surly and unshaven and he was supposed to be *dead* for heaven's sake!

Get yourself under control, Summer.

The thought was unusual, because as a rule, she was nothing but control. She was a highly disciplined investigative journalist who took her work extremely seriously because it had consequences. She was not supposed to be hot flashing on the man who had turned her on to sex, then disappeared from her life without a word, but not before seducing every female in her immediate vicinity.

He'd broken into her home for a reason. To stop her from writing about him surviving the Massacre, which was major news. He was here to persuade her and it was to his credit he wasn't using his sex appeal, which had always been off the charts.

Though, to some, maybe now his sex appeal would be a little…faded. Switched off. If you liked youthful good looks and playful male charm, this Jack was not for you.

It was an enormous pity that the mature Summer found the mature, beaten down but clearly powerful Jack even more attractive than the golden boy of fifteen years ago.

She turned off the flame and put dinner on the table.

The omelet, naan bread, a salad and four French soft cheeses on a wooden board.

"Sit down," she ordered. "Eat."

A corner of his hard mouth lifted as he sat. "Yes, ma'am."

He waited until she had her fork in hand. "Eat," Summer said again.

Maybe he actually had been homeless because he ate like it was going to disappear from his plate at any moment. Mary Delvaux had hammered manners into her kids and he didn't spray food and didn't use his fingers. But he inhaled the food, staring down at his plate and not making eye contact with her.

When he'd used the last bite of naan bread to pick up the last molecule of omelet, she said, "I have some homemade ice cream, if—"

"Yes," he said, lifting his eyes to hers. "Please."

Suppressing a sigh, Summer went to the freezer and took down a big container of homemade peach ice cream. Jack demolished it.

When he put the bowl back on the table, Summer lifted an eyebrow. She'd stopped eating half an hour ago. "We good?"

He wiped his mouth with a napkin and sighed. "Real good. Thanks."

She sat back, crossed her arms, looked at him. "Now that we've got that out of the way…"

"Yeah." Jack placed the napkin delicately next to the plate, taking his time. Gathering his thoughts. As well he should, because he was going to have to explain why she shouldn't go with a major story. And while he was at it, explain why he'd been in hiding for six months. And what the deal was with Hector Blake.

A *lot* of explaining.

Jack flexed his jaw.

"What happened to your beard?" It came out without any thought.

He sighed. "Really? I'm not dead after all, and that's what you want to know? What's with my beard?"

Stupid, stupid question. But Summer doubled down. "And the dreadlocks. What happened to those?"

He looked at her for a long moment. "I wear a wig and a false beard when I go out. They're in that gym bag, as a matter of fact." He jerked his head to the living room and Summer noticed the gym bag for the first time. Stupid. Usually she was more observant than that. Another sign that having Jack pop up had unsettled her a lot.

"There are security cameras everywhere. And though my face has been removed from official records, I had to be careful. So the wig falls over my face and distorts the faceprint. The beard is fake, too. It would be easier to just grow a beard, but a fake beard doesn't follow the natural contours of the face and makes facial recog even harder."

"Someone...*removed* your image from facial recognition databases?" Summer tried to think how that would be even possible. Whoever did it had to be extremely high up in the security community. Like the director of the CIA or NSA something.

He nodded.

"Sounds like...you've done this before. Evaded discovery."

Silence. "Not quite like this, but yes, I've done it before."

"For?"

More silence.

"That's classified." He sighed. "It's crazy. I'm no longer operational. As a matter of fact, I'm dead. But I took an oath and I took it seriously when I did."

She digested that, thinking it over. "Okay. Let me tell you what I think. Word had it that you were making money and chasing girls as an investment banker in Singapore. But I'm guessing that's not what you were doing. If whoever you work for has the power to wipe your photos from official databases, I'm guessing you're in some intelligence service. But you were never really sharp at analytical courses at Harvard, so I'd say not in the analysis department. You'd be an operator, not an analyst. Not to mention the fact that you cut right through my building's security and my apartment's security, which is top of the line whatever you might say. So—not special ops because they don't operate with official covers. My guess would be CIA. How'm I doing?"

Jack's face gave nothing away. But he wasn't saying no.

Summer looked at him, really looked at him. Seeing him as he was now and remembering him when he was a boy and then a young man. She'd been so in love with him she'd made him an object of study. She'd had a PhD in Jackology, though she'd made sure no one knew anything about her obsession.

But she'd known him pretty well back in the day and some things did not change in people.

"Like I said, you're not particularly analytical. You were smart but it was a gift that you never polished. I'm guessing you got into Harvard as a legacy and because you were a gifted athlete, not because of your grades.

Your grades sucked. So I'm ruling out the Directorate of Intelligence. You liked your gadgets but you weren't a nerd so I'd rule out the Directorate of Science and Technology and I definitely do not see you in the Directorate of Support, fussing about with logistics and supplies. That leaves the National Clandestine Service. And if you're pretending to be an investment banker that would leave you plenty of time to go on missions."

The silence stretched for a full minute.

Jack stirred. Blew out a breath. "I got decent grades," he said mildly.

Bingo. She smiled.

"Any good grades you got were strictly because you charmed the teachers. I never saw you open a book all that summer I came back to the US. And not once while we were—"

She stopped. Fought a blush. She was about to say he'd never cracked a book while they were dating but they'd "dated" for about a week. Enough to stoke her infatuation and introduce her to world-altering sex before he disappeared.

So *dating* wasn't strictly the right term.

And this walk down memory lane had had the unfortunate effect of reminding her that they'd essentially spent that one week in bed, having sex so incredible it should have been classified as a controlled substance.

"You're blushing," Jack said.

"Am not," she answered sharply. And then, because she'd sounded like a child, she said, "So—how close did I get?"

"Nailed it. Except I'm not CIA anymore."

"No. Because you're dead. So let's hear this story and I need to know why it has to remain secret because there's been more than enough secrecy around the Washington Massacre. I'll hold off if there's a really good reason, but not for long and you'd better be pretty convincing."

Jack drew in a deep breath and for a moment she was startled at how wide it made his chest. *Focus, Summer!* She told herself. This was important and she couldn't be distracted by a gorgeous male chest. She wasn't eighteen anymore.

Jack leaned forward, shifting away the plates with one strong forearm. "Why were you at Hector Blake's funeral?"

He wanted to ask questions first? Okay. "Well, he was sort of a relative. For a little while, anyway. Remember? But mainly because the whole thing stinks to high heaven."

His face gave away nothing, but his fingers curled up in a *gimme* gesture.

She sighed. "First of all, the reports state that he drowned in the Potomac but everyone is real vague on exactly where in the Potomac. And it is unclear whether he was in a vehicle or just sort of fell in. Like you'd trip and fall into a pond. It's really hard to do that. Either he committed suicide, diving in from a bridge, or it was homicide and he was thrown in, or it was an accident and he drove off the road into the river. The coroner's report is unavailable, which is the first time that's happened to me. The authorities didn't exactly invoke the Patriot Act, but they might as well have. I applied for a copy of the report and got a sharp email from the coroner's office. The office, not the coroner herself. She's on indefinite leave. Starting yesterday. And no one has been appointed to replace her. And the DC morgue itself has been closed for 'scheduled repairs' though no such schedule has ever been published. I can't figure out what happened to Hector but something did and it wasn't what the reports say."

Jack held her eyes. "Hector Blake drowned in the Willamette River in Portland, Oregon four days ago. I know because I was there."

He dropped that bombshell and watched her reaction. She kept her face without expression, but her hands itched for the iPad, because this was the story of a lifetime. *What were you doing there in Portland? What was Hector Blake doing there? How did it happen?* The questions bubbled up inside her.

When she felt a story start to happen, it was like a fisherman feeling a big tug, knowing he had a whopper at the other end of the line. That was exactly what she was feeling right now. A huge tug from a momentous story.

"You're going to have to explain that to me," she said steadily.

Jack nodded sharply, as if happy at her cool reaction. "Well, the short version is that Hector kidnapped Isabel, who had moved to Portland. I was there and, together with three other men, we followed him. Isabel says he told her the plan was to fake her suicide in a motel, because she'd called him to tell him she knew something. Knew he'd been involved in the Massacre. That scared him enough to come out to Portland and kidnap her. She fought back and the driver of the van drove off a bridge and one of the members of my team, a former Navy SEAL, dove in and rescued Isabel. Hector was dead."

"Is the long version available?" Her mind was furiously trying to shape a picture from these small pieces of the puzzle but it wasn't working. Too many pieces were missing. Kidnapping *Isabel*? She was a lovely woman who was a gifted food blogger, nothing political about her. "Why on earth would Hector Blake try to kidnap Isabel? And why were you in Portland? None of this makes any sense."

Jack rubbed a hand over the stubble on his head. "Hard to know where to begin."

"At the beginning, where else?" she said and rolled her eyes.

He huffed out a breath. "Okay. I was running an informant in the Chinese PLA, who worked in their Fourth Directorate. He was found dead after passing some intel on to me."

"Fourth Directorate," Summer murmured. "Cyberwarfare."

"That's right." Jack narrowed his eyes at her. "How'd you know that?"

Summer took a deep calming breath, letting the first hot words that bubbled to the surface go. "Please. I majored in political science and I run an online blog dedicated to politics. Domestic and foreign. Of course I know what the Fourth Directorate of the PLA is."

Jack held big hands up, palms out. "Whoa, whoa. Sorry. I'm used to dealing with civilians who don't have a clue."

"Well, I'm a civilian, and I do have a clue."

"I guess you do." An expression flashed across Jack's face, intense and fleeting and Summer had no problems at all deciphering it. It was pure sex, just a flash of it, like an oven that popped open then closed again immediately.

Heat shot through her. She tingled down to her fingers and toes and it lit her up, exactly like walking in front of a blast furnace.

Or stepping into hell.

Because getting hot and sweaty with Jack would definitely put her in hell. That moment fifteen years ago when she realized that bedding her had been life-changing for her, but just fun for Jack? And there was a lot of fun out there in the big wide world and he was moving on? That moment had nearly crushed her. She'd been convinced he was the man for her, that all her years of girlish yearning hadn't been in vain, that he'd been secretly waiting for her, just as she'd been secretly waiting for him. What had rocked her world had been a great roll in the hay for him and she watched miserably as he took her dorm roommate out a week later. She'd cried herself to sleep for months.

So. Been there, done that. Not going there, ever again. *Focus.*

She had, potentially, the story of a lifetime sitting at her dining table, looking like an ex con, scruffy and rough, with explosive knowledge in his shorn head. There was no bigger story than the Washington Massacre and Jack had unknown information. She could ride this story for weeks. It could bring *Area 8* to an entirely different level, make it more a newsmagazine than a political blog.

This was important, so she needed to pay attention.

But oh, God. The man himself was such a distraction. Summer was used to bringing total focus to bear when it came to her job. Being thrown off-course by a source of information was new to her. But how could she focus when this big man sitting across from her was so fascinating?

He shared features with the Jack she'd known. His eyes were still that amazing ocean blue, the nose still straight, mouth beautifully defined. But everything else about Jack the golden boy was gone. Those blue eyes were bloodshot, the flesh beneath bruised-looking. Though he was much heavier than when he was young—and it seemed to be all muscle—his cheeks were gaunt hollows, as if he'd recently lost a lot of weight. That thick mass of sun streaked hair—often gathered in a careless ponytail—was light-colored stubble. Even his hands were completely different. No longer elegant, long fingered, beautiful—almost works of art. Now they were still long-fingered but not beautiful. Not works of art. They were something a physical man used a lot—huge, callused, tough, scarred.

Before, women looked at Jack and thought of trysting in a sun dappled field. Now, if anything, he evoked thoughts of being taken brutally, against a wall.

Summer mentally shook herself. Sex with Jack was something she no longer thought about and sex with this new, tough Jack? Impossible.

She leaned forward and looked him straight in the eyes. "So tell me how you're still alive and roaming the streets pretending to be homeless. Tell me why you never announced that you'd lived through the Massacre and pretended to be dead. Tell me everything. And if it is truly important that I not write about it, I won't. I will hold off. But remember this. Every single day I have people telling me that I would harm national security if I write about something, but usually it's them covering their asses. So if all of this is you covering your ass, then you're shit out of luck with me."

Jack's jaws clenched. "Not covering my ass, believe me. And I want all of this to come to light just as much as you do, but at the right time. The people involved are ruthless. So far, a number of very good people have died after the Massacre and I don't want any more on my conscience."

"Fair enough," she said. "So convince me. You said you had an informant who died on you. From the Fourth Directorate."

He nodded sharply. "That's right. There's a separate power structure in the Fourth Directorate, headed by General Chen Li. From what my CI told me, that power structure has put in place a plan for a soft takeover of the US. Military forces are only tangentially involved in the planning. This cabal inside the Fourth Directorate developed a plan to destroy us, or if not destroy us, weaken us to the point where we'd be easy to pick off. According to my informant, the plan involved minimal violence, not a full scale invasion, certainly not applying major military power. Conquest by stealth. So my mole was sending me intel over an encrypted line and we were beginning to get a feel for the plan. It was supposed to unfold in several stages or phases and stage one was coming up. Then my informant's body was found in the Huangpu River. Right after sending a message that the first attack would be in Washington DC."

Summer had trouble breathing. Washington. "The Massacre," she whispered.

"Yeah." Jack lowered his head without taking his eyes from hers. "The file was corrupted but there was enough intel to indicate an attack on Washington was imminent. My boss and I thought—the White House. The Pentagon. Congress. We passed on word to appropriate channels and security was beefed up in those three places and the airports. I was coming back to Washington anyway. My boss and I were keeping our eyes and ears open."

"You came back because your father was announcing that he was running for president. Your undercover career was over."

"Yeah." Jack's face tightened. "It was. I couldn't even tell Dad that he was messing me up because my family didn't know I was CIA. But it was Dad's dream and he would have made—" Jack's voice grew thick and he looked to the side.

"He would have made a great president," Summer finished softly.

Jack nodded and swallowed heavily. He drummed his fingers on the tabletop. "I think Blake was behind the Massacre," he said finally.

"But—but he barely escaped the Massacre with his life. And he was there supporting your father! And I had it on good authority that your father was going to choose Hector Blake as his vice president."

Summer had found it hard to believe Alex Delvaux would have chosen Hector Blake as his Veep but that's what her sources told her. Didn't make much sense to her, given that Hector was universally disliked, at least among Washington insiders, people who knew him personally. Outside the circle of people who knew him personally, however, he had the reputation of being a thinker, an innovative politician. Respected, even. And of course, Hector and Alex had known each other all their lives.

Jack shot forward, a ferocious look on his face. With difficulty, Summer managed not to jerk back but she could feel her heart slam inside her chest, an animal reaction to a powerful, angry male. "That man was responsible for the extermination of my entire family, for the deaths of over seven hundred people and for the chaos that followed. I know this but I don't have enough evidence to bring to court."

She swallowed. "I understand what you're feeling, I really do. I loved your family, too." *And for way too long, I loved you as well.* She didn't say that, though. "But to feel that Hector was involved in the Massacre, you have to have something to go on. Do you have any proof?"

"Nothing that would stand up in court." Jack's mouth twisted. "More like circumstantial evidence. I've been trying to gather evidence for a while. That's why I'm here in DC, to get hard evidence against Blake and whoever is backing him. But now he's dead and the leads are gone."

As she'd said, Jack didn't have sharp analytical skills. He was bright and intuitive, but she needed more order in this story. "Go back to the beginning," she said. "Tell me in order what happened, starting from the night of the Massacre."

"In the days right after the Massacre there was pure chaos. No one has written a comprehensive account. But you were there. Tell me how it went down. And tell me how you think our guys might be involved."

Jack's eyes widened. "I never said I suspected American involvement. Just Hector Blake's."

"Jack." Summer was used to being underestimated. And certainly in their short time together as a couple, she hadn't given Jack a reason to admire her smarts. She'd spent their entire week together having explosive orgasms and being tongue-tied around him. "You had, by your account, prior warning of the Massacre. If you weren't afraid that there was home-grown involvement you wouldn't have disappeared. And since you did, you think that someone in the CIA was involved."

His face tightened. "I do. I think Hector had backing from rogue elements in the CIA, an agency I dedicated my life to."

That was the part she found almost impossible to believe. She'd spent her entire adult life in politics and thought she could no longer be surprised by anything but…this surprised her. Shocked her, even, though she'd have said she was unshockable.

Maybe if Jack had said that the Washington Massacre was organized by purple aliens from Aldebaran, she'd have believed it. But the CIA?

If that was true, she was about to get the scoop of a lifetime, but it didn't excite her. If it was true, it made her sick to her stomach. If it was true, it made her want to take a month long shower then move to a remote hilltop and take a vow of silence.

Jack shook his head sharply, as if getting rid of unwelcome thoughts. "My boss analyzed the data I sent and was quietly carrying out an internal investigation. I stayed in Singapore as long as I could, but of course I had to come home. Dad was announcing his candidacy. I arrived the day before the Massacre. Mom was a little miffed that I cut it so fine, but not too much."

Jack smiled sadly and Summer understood. Mary Delvaux had spoiled Jack rotten. She wouldn't have stayed mad at Jack for long. She couldn't.

"What did you tell her?"

He lifted a massive shoulder. "That I was in the middle of negotiations of an important deal."

"And the truth?"

His lips tightened. "The truth was that we had just lost our informant as I said, and we were trying to backtrack his movements. I infiltrated Shanghai, stayed as long as I could and flew back on a CIA private jet, though officially I was on Singapore Airlines flight SA 327."

"So you landed and went straight to the Burrard Hotel?"

"No, I landed and was debriefed by my boss at a safe house. My informant was clear that the Fourth Directorate had moles in the CIA so we had to operate outside the lines of command."

"You trusted your boss?" Summer asked.

"Absolutely."

That was good enough for her. Jack might not be an analytical thinker but he grew up in a huge family network and he understood people on an instinctive level. Much better than she did, actually.

"Okay. So you holed up in a safe house. What then?"

"We went through a list of people who could conceivably be moles. Traitors."

"What were the criteria used?"

"I guess the same for every traitor since the beginning of time. Money. And ideology. Money was the easiest. We found a list of people whose lifestyle had suddenly taken an upward swing."

Summer frowned. "They spent off-the-books money openly? That's not smart."

"No, it's not." Jack sighed. "And in most cases, with

a little digging we found that most of them inherited some money when their parents died, or they married someone richer than they were or they'd made some decent investments."

"Not too many good investments in this climate," Summer said. She had some money from *Area 8* she wanted to put in a safe place and she couldn't find any. Not one. Not one place where she could swear to the investment not being rigged.

"No. But we found people whose extra money made sense. Flipping a good piece of property. Bought shares just before a successful IPO." He shook his head with a half-smile. "One analyst had starred in five bestselling porno films."

"Whoa." Summer tried to wrap her head around that. Around a CIA analyst good-looking enough to star in pornos. Most looked really nerdy—pale and hunched and furtive. Not porno material at all. "How much was she paid?" She bit her lips. "Purely out of curiosity."

"He." Jack smiled into her eyes. "And a cool million."

"Wow. I'm clearly in the wrong business."

"No." Jack's big hand shot out and covered hers, squeezed lightly, then let go. Crazily, her heart gave a massive thump. "It's a terrible world, like a swamp."

"As opposed to the good clean fun at the CIA," she replied testily, angry that her heart would thump at a touch of his hand.

"Touché." Jack hung his head for a moment and suddenly he looked a thousand years old. Summer was ashamed. He'd lost his family and he'd been through hell. And he'd dedicated his life to an agency that might have betrayed his country.

"Okay." She blew out a breath, preparing herself for whatever was coming next. She had no doubt that it would be devastating for her and even more devastating for Jack. "So tell me about that night. You and your boss—I'm assuming that would be Hugh Lownie. D/NCS."

Jack sighed. "The name of the Director of the National Clandestine Service is classified info."

Summer rolled her eyes. "Jack. Please." Just because the D/NCS wasn't on the CIA website didn't mean that everyone and his dog didn't know his name.

He sighed again. "Yes. Hugh Lownie."

Summer nodded. "He died the day after the Massacre. Of a heart attack."

"He was *murdered* the day after the Massacre," Jack responded angrily. "I never got near the body so I don't know how they faked it, but there was absolutely nothing wrong with Hugh's heart, in any sense of the word."

Wow. If Hugh Lownie had been murdered... "The Washington Massacre. Seven hundred dead. And the next day the Director of the National Clandestine Service, who presumably is always well-protected, is killed. This is scary."

He shot her a glance. "Yeah. Why do you think I've been in hiding these past six months? Do you still want to investigate this?"

"Yes." And she did. "It burns to think of people getting away with the Massacre and with all that followed."

"The blackout." Jack nodded. "Going to Defcon III."

"Yes, but that's not all of it. Over three trillion dollars were drained from the US economy after the Massacre. That's not well known, but it almost collapsed several major industries and plunged us into another recession. You've been undercover and probably missed it."

"I haven't missed it," he said grimly. "If ever there was a time to go undercover as a homeless person, it's now. You have no idea how many formerly middle class people are begging on the streets. The couple of times I slept in shelters I slept next to teachers and nurses and office workers who'd lost their jobs and couldn't find another one."

It was another reason she couldn't let go of the Massacre story. Not only had so many died, but so many suffered economically. "Okay. Let's backtrack a second. Whatever your Chinese CI told you wasn't enough to stay away from the rally?"

Jack stiffened, sitting up ramrod straight, staring narrow-eyed at her. "Do you honestly think that if I'd had a clue, even the slightest intimation, that they were going to shoot down everyone at my father's rally and then blow up the Burrard, I wouldn't have stopped the whole thing? Forced my father to call it off?"

She was ashamed of herself. Of course. Any idea at all of the real plans—plans that included his family in the crosshairs—and he'd have intervened. "I'm sorry, Jack," she said sincerely. "That was amazingly stupid of me. Of course you would have."

He blew out a breath and narrowed his eyes. "You're still seeing me as the skirt-chasing asshole who wasn't thinking much beyond the next woman and the next beer. I hardly remember him."

Bingo. Well, he certainly looked different from the

lightweight womanizer she'd known. Different gaze, different vibe. Almost a different person. "So tell me about that night," she said quietly.

"My parents fought right up until they arrived at the Burrard. The rumors that they were fighting were right. But they were fighting because my mom was terrified of losing my dad. The parallels to Jack Kennedy were startling."

Including the enormous, attractive family. Summer nodded. "But on the podium your mom looked thrilled."

He smiled faintly, sadly. "She was a real trouper. Once he declared, she was going to ask for leave from her job and work like a mule for him. She said if she couldn't change his mind, then she was going to do her damnedest to see he got what he wanted. And she would have smiled every minute of every day of his presidency and then heaved a huge sigh of relief when his term was over."

Alex Delvaux, President. Summer was more aware than most of the forks life took and she'd trained herself to never look back, ever. So with Alex Delvaux dead, she'd simply carried on. But now she took a moment to imagine him as president. He'd been a good man, an honorable man. But really smart with it, too, and deeply dedicated to the protection of the environment. It wasn't just lip service. He'd have battled the coal and oil lobbies with every fiber of his being and he'd have swayed people. He had the gift of communication. He'd have left the country a better place. Right now, the loss of his presidency shook her.

"He'd have made such a great president," she said quietly.

Jack nodded, eyes glistening. "He would have, yes. And the country would be a different place. So believe me when I say that I will find who was behind the Massacre if I have to die trying, because I lost not only my father and my entire family except for Isabel, but the country lost a great leader. A man who would have made a difference."

"That night," she reminded him, throat tight.

He nodded. "Okay. That night. I arrived late. My mom had called twenty times. I ended up just switching my cell off. But not my work cell. Hugh and I had spent the day going over possible traitors and it was sad how many people in the Company I wouldn't put a hand to the fire and swear that they were loyal. At the last minute, I called a cab to pick up me a few blocks from the safe house. I knew they'd be running late at the Burrard anyway. My dad was many things, but punctual wasn't one of them."

"The announcement was slated for 7:30." That had been in the press briefing.

"Yeah, but like I said, they were running really late. I got to the podium, hugged my parents and Isabel and the twins and my phone started ringing."

"Presumably the one Hugh gave you and not the other one."

He dipped his head. "The one Hugh gave me. I felt it vibrate and I knew something was up. I'd left him less than an hour before, why would he be calling when he knew I was at my dad's rally?"

Summer could see it. She leaned forward on her elbows. "He'd just found something out. Something that you had to know as soon as possible."

"He'd discovered something, that was for sure. I

walked out of the auditorium because I couldn't hear him. There were people shouting and the rally music was playing really loud on speakers. Not even my goddamned ear buds could filter out the noise. We couldn't hear each other, so he switched off and sent me a text."

"You remember what that text was?"

He speared her with his glare. "You think I could ever forget? He texted *Get out of there. Run. Hide. Now.* And then the phone went dead. But whatever Hugh thought was going to happen, I wasn't leaving without my family. I was running back to them when I heard shots fired. AK-47s. A lot of them. A firefight, in a crowded auditorium. Hugh had insisted I attend unarmed. I broke land speed records trying to get back to my family."

Summer was watching his eyes, brilliant blue, blood-shot whites. "So you saw—" she whispered.

"Everything." His jaws clenched. "I saw fucking everything. They doused the lights but there were candles everywhere. I saw. Men in ski masks opening fire on the crowd, working from the back to the front. They took care of security first. Amateurs, I don't know who hired them. My dad wouldn't have Secret Service protection until he declared so some bozo on his staff hired some clowns. They went down immediately. The attackers just mowed them down. They were the first to go. The rest—it was like shooting fish in a barrel. Ridiculously easy. The fuckers met with no resistance at all."

She held her breath. She could almost see the scene, smell the blood.

"People were screaming. The assaulters were efficient. In the time it took me to run into the auditorium, their work was almost done. I was running flat out when they got to the podium."

The podium. Where his family was. Not only his close family but aunts, uncles, cousins. God.

Jack's head hung down. She saw the stubble on the top of his head, the sharp blade of nose and jutting cheekbones as he stared at the tabletop.

"In a few minutes it was over. I couldn't see Isabel. I saw my father and mother turn to shield my brothers, arms outstretched. But it was useless. They fell in a heap. A bloody mass of flesh and bones exploding. Dead in an instant."

He stared at his hands, still and calm, though a vein beat fast in his temple.

He was silent so long she finally spoke. "And then?"

"And then the whole place blew up. I found out later charges had been placed around the ballroom. No one knows how that could have happened."

Summer knew. "Hector Blake was a silent partner in the Burrard. He owned a controlling share. Personnel later testified that there was a lot of unscheduled maintenance work the week before."

Jack's head lifted. "Is that true?"

She nodded somberly. Something else to lay at Blake's door. "It was hushed up. One of the waiters spoke to me and I recorded his testimony but when I checked back with him, he was nowhere to be found. When I asked, no one knew where he was and there was no record of his ever having worked there. The Burrard staff was let go, of course, the hotel simply shut down. Someone said they thought my waiter had gone back to Costa Rica but no one was sure. I don't publish supposition. The rule of *Area 8* is that nothing is published without two pieces of corroboration. And all I had was the video of the interview. I didn't even realize what I had until later, when I started putting the pieces together."

Jack's jaw tightened. "When I woke up in the rubble it was pitch black and I was completely disoriented. I couldn't remember where I was, *who* I was. At first I thought I'd died, but not gone to heaven." A corner of his mouth lifted. "It didn't occur to me that I might have gone to heaven, not after the last fifteen years in war zones. And it felt like hell, too. Hot, black, stinking of cordite and blood and death."

Her heart hurt to think of Jack stumbling in the darkness, covered in rubble, disoriented, grieving. "Were you wounded?"

"Concussed. Broken wrist. Lacerations and contusions. I'd inhaled a ton of cement dust." He looked down at his left arm and for the first time she noticed scar tissue and a slightly crooked wristbone. Had he had no medical treatment at all?

She had a sudden vision of him, having watched his family mown down by machine gun fire, wounded in the blast, lurching out of the Burrard into darkness. Tentatively, she touched his wrist, feeling ropy scar tissue and hard muscle.

Jack sighed and put a big hand over hers. He looked weary beyond belief. She remembered in a rush that just a few days ago he'd been in Portland, that he'd been there as Hector Blake had drowned.

So many questions.

Jack had gone silent, staring at his big hand over hers, a million miles away.

Summer understood trauma, understood bad memories. They had to work their way through your system, like shrapnel works its way out through the skin from deep muscle tissue. She said nothing and waited.

Finally, Jack stirred.

"What happened after the Massacre?" she asked quietly. "How did you get away?"

"There was the blackout." Jack's mouth tightened. "And our cells were jammed. You had to get a hundred yards away before reception started. It was total chaos outside the Burrard. The only lights were the ambulance headlights but they had overestimated the survivors."

"They had to ship body bags up from Fort Detrick," she said. A source had told her that. There had been pitifully few survivors. "Did you see Isabel?"

He nodded. "Yeah. With that last message from Hugh I knew I had to get out, but first I made sure that the medics loaded Isabel onto an ambulance. I was covered in dust and I kept my head down. Security cams had been taken offline." He pinched the bridge of his nose and swallowed. "I thought—" His voice had gone tight and he waited a moment. "I thought at first she was dead. She was on a gurney and she was so... white. And still. God."

He'd seen his entire family killed. Isabel would have been his last family member. "I can imagine how you felt," she said quietly. She herself had never had anything like a family structure around her and her parents had never paid her much attention. They'd been feckless druggies. But she'd lived among the Delvauxes and she'd seen happy families. They were like multiple organisms with one beating heart. The Delvauxes had been closer than most families. "But she wasn't dead."

"No." Jack shook his head. "She wasn't. Though she was badly injured. The medic said her pupils were unresponsive to light. I made sure I knew where she was being taken and left her in the ambulance. Hardest thing I've ever done in my life."

"You needed to investigate," Summer said. "Particularly when you knew something was coming and the Massacre was it."

"Yeah. I needed to disappear. No one looks for a dead man. Once out of range of the jammer, I called Hugh and he said to meet him at the safe house. That he had proof of who was behind the Massacre."

"Proof?" Her journalist part of her brain pinged. "He had proof? Why didn't he—"

"Because he was killed," Jack growled. "With the blackout and all traffic lights out, the streets were jammed. I ended up running to the safe house through the dark city. Took me four hours. When I got there I waited for Hugh, but he never showed up. He was killed right after the Massacre, right after talking to me, in fact. They said it was a heart attack but it wasn't. His body was never autopsied, either."

Summer had kept her ear close to the ground but she hadn't heard about any of this. "So, among many other things, we're talking about the murder of a senior officer of the CIA."

"His body was found two days after the Massacre, in his basement. Nobody came looking immediately. All law enforcement was tied up in the aftermath of the Massacre and dealing with the blackout. But I knew something was wrong when I got to the safe house and Hugh wasn't there."

"That's when you decided to disappear?"

Jack's face tightened and a dangerous shadow passed over his features. "There was nothing on earth that could have kept Hugh from meeting me there except death. And I was Hugh's protégée. So being presumed dead at the Burrard was a gift. If it was known that I'd survived, I'd have had a target pinned to my back. I'm good but I'm not good enough to evade the kind of resources the CIA can bring to bear. Whoever the mole or moles were, they'd have enough autonomy to fake evidence that I was involved in the Massacre and put out a hit on me."

"Evading them for six months is amazing."

"Not if they thought I was dead. The bad thing was I couldn't be with Isabel. I had some off-the-record credit cards and hired private detectives to stay in the hospital while Isabel was in a coma and to watch over her apartment when she was released. When she decided to move to Portland it was a huge relief. I kept an eye on her via computer."

Six months underground, posing as a homeless vet. Not many men could pull that off. "Have you found anything in these six months?"

"Yes." His jaws clenched. "Hector Blake was definitely involved. He made a vast fortune off the Massacre and parked the money in offshore accounts. He could never have made that much money without prior knowledge. I was keeping an eye on him. I was terrified when Isabel called him. In Portland, she fell in love with a good man, Joe Harris. Former SEAL. He works for a security company and one of their IT people found out that Blake had made a shit ton of money. Isabel called him to accuse him. I was in Portland already. I was there when Blake showed up." His mouth twisted. "I arranged things with Isabel's fiancé and his security company. They called in a good guy from the FBI. The FBI is the only agency I would swear is not involved in the conspiracy."

Summer studied him. "So you saw Hector Blake die. In Portland. That's a huge story right there."

"It is," Jack said steadily. "But not one I'm going to tell you, not yet anyway. But I'll make you a deal. Work with me and at the end, you'll be the one to break the story. But not before we figure out who the moles are in the US government. Any hint that you have some information and you won't live out the day, Summer. And I won't have your death on my conscience. So we work together and you stay under the radar and we crack this thing. I have allies in government. There's that clean FBI agent we're working with and to a limited extent we can use FBI resources. So let's team up. What do you say?"

And he held out his hand. Huge, long-fingered, scarred. Not the long, slender flawless hand that had once stroked her to ecstasy.

Summer stared at that hand. *Teaming up with Jack Delvaux.* It would have been her fondest dream fifteen years ago. Something she'd secretly hoped would happen. That the Golden Boy would choose her to be his partner.

And here, fifteen years later, that not-so-golden man was asking her to partner with him. Not romantic partner, of course. Summer was never going there, ever again. But he was asking her to team up with him to break the biggest story ever. Pulitzer Prize material.

But more than the career boost, Summer wanted in on this because her country had been attacked. And if what the darknet said was true and what Jack said was true, her country had been attacked by *Americans*. For money. And the plot wasn't over. More was to come.

The Massacre had nearly brought the country to its knees.

The streets were teeming with the homeless, unemployment was just below Depression-era levels, there was talk of Social Security going bankrupt. The country was dispirited, worn down, having absorbed blow after blow.

They had done this, whoever they were. Americans had conspired to bring her country low.

Summer loved America. She'd grown up in hellholes around the world. The only criteria for her parents for settling in a place had been cheap drugs, and Summer had seen hopeless despair, chaos, dictatorships. Coming to America as a teenager had been like walking into paradise. Not because it was richer than other places but because it was *better*. With all its problems, the underlying ideal held. Of the people, by the people, for the people. They weren't empty words. She'd embraced America with all her heart and she was prepared to fight her country's attackers with all she had.

Jack was still holding his hand out, waiting for her. "Deal?"

She took it, trying not to react to the feel of him. Such a different hand from the one she'd known. Hard and callused and hot.

His hand felt electric in hers, a massive burst of energy and heat.

"Deal." She pumped his hand then let go, happy not to be touching him. Pleasure at his touch had absolutely nothing to do with the pact they had just sealed. She had no business being affected by his touch, none. "We start by you showing me all the information you've gathered."

Jack's mouth turned grim. "It's not much, unfortunately. A lot is rumor and supposition. We were expecting to catch Blake, not bury him. We were going to make him talk and then we'd have enough proof to go to the Attorney General with the intel. We weren't expecting a corpse. Now I don't know where to go, how to follow the thread."

"Well." Summer stood and, startled, Jack stood, too. "It's a very lucky thing you have teamed up with me, Jack, because I do know where to go next."

"Where?"

"Hector's house. I have the keys."

THREE

WHOA, JACK THOUGHT. Breaking into Blake's house. But it turned out he wasn't going to have to break in, he could simply walk in.

"So, I can get us in his house, but once we're in we might need to crack into safes. Do you have your safe-cracking kit?" Summer flicked a glance at him.

"I'm good," Jack replied. He was. He was loaded for bear with surveillance equipment and the suppressed Glock 19 and MP5 Nick Mancino had given him in his gym bag. Plus of course his set of picks, a powerful autodialer and some C-4. Summer didn't have to know how well equipped he was. She was already a little spooked at knowing who he'd become.

Summer. Summer Redding.

The funny-looking girl had turned into a beauty by the time she hit college. Jack's head had definitely been turned and he'd made his play immediately. But then a lot of girls had turned his head back in the day. Beautiful girls were thick on the ground at Harvard. Healthy, wealthy American girls with twenty thousand dollars' worth of orthodontics in their mouths, years of dance lessons and tennis lessons and a lifetime of eating excellent food. They'd all had glossy hair and white teeth and it had been like a male cornucopia. All he'd had to do was reach out his hand and there they were.

Summer had been stunning, but then they all were.

Now…not so much. Not many of the Harvard girls had aged well. Oh, they were perfectly well maintained. Lots of gym time, lots of beauty salon time. Some had already gone under the knife, sometimes multiple times.

Summer hadn't. That was a natural beauty he was looking at. A very pissed-off natural beauty.

Well, after bedding her fifteen years ago, popping her cherry then walking cheerfully away without a word, then seducing her roommate and two other girls on her dorm floor, only to crop up after being declared dead and break into her home…pissed off seemed pretty reasonable.

"That's his official home," Summer said. "And we'll search it top to bottom. But he also has a luxury apartment that no one knows about. He brings—brought—his mistresses there and did drugs. Or at least he did according to my aunt, who hated him."

Pretty Summer Redding. Surprising him. "Do you know where it is? The secret apartment? And do you have keys to that, too?"

She smiled. "I know where it is, and I have the keypad code."

"Wow." Surprise after surprise. "How did that happen?"

"It's a long and unpleasant story." She sighed. "So, the no-frills version is that my aunt used to send me in to obtain evidence against him for the divorce. He didn't know that she knew about the apartment. She blackmailed one of his mistresses for the code."

"Let's hope he hasn't changed the code," Jack said.

"I seriously doubt that. At least in my day, Hector was tech-challenged. And he thought no one knew about the apartment. My aunt said it wasn't registered in his name but in the name of some corporation. We're bound to find something either in the mansion or in his bachelor pad."

A secret hideaway where Blake might have kept records. Exactly what he needed. "Blake was part of the conspiracy, no question about it. He helped the plan that killed my parents and he wanted to kidnap and then kill Isabel to shut her up. Let's go. We're going to break into both places."

Summer stood. "Okay. We'll take my car. Where's yours? And how can you have a car if you're dead?"

"You'd be surprised at the things dead people can do. I bought myself two rust buckets and had the chassis strengthened and the engines completely overhauled. One's in Portland and one's here. I bought them under one of my identities and have the ID ready if I'm stopped. Never have been, though."

Summer looked up at him, frowning.

"What? Do I have lettuce in my teeth?"

"No. I'm wondering whether you need to put your wig and beard on. You've survived this long as a dead man, I wouldn't want to be the one to out you."

He balked suddenly at putting the beard and wig on. He hated wearing them. They itched and made him feel confined. More than that, they made him feel like a non-person, which was, of course, the fucking point. But suddenly, with Summer here, knowing full well that it was a security breach, he couldn't stand the thought of wearing his homeless costume. Particularly the BDUs that smelled of piss. He didn't want to be an unperson. He wanted to be Jack Delvaux again, in the worst way. Seeing Summer again…seeing what an incredibly beautiful and fascinating woman she'd become, the man in him rebelled at going back into hiding, like a cockroach scurrying back under a rock.

But he couldn't say that. "Your car's in the garage, right? And you have an elevator that goes to the garage?"

He knew because he'd checked.

"Yeah, so? This place is still surrounded by security cameras."

This is where it got tricky. "Not any more, it isn't," he said gently.

Her eyes widened. God she had gorgeous eyes. A light silvery gray, bright and intense, alive with intelligence. He could almost hear the gears engaging in her head. "You disabled the security cameras in my building?" she asked, appalled.

He nodded.

"I don't know whether to be mad at you or admire you."

"The latter?" Jack ventured. He'd wanted to switch the cams off temporarily but it would have taken a ton of time so he'd ended up just disabling the damned things.

She stared, wide-eyed, hovering between anger and admiration and finally gave a half laugh. She'd opted for Door Number Two. Good.

"When you broke into my apartment you didn't do permanent damage, did you?"

"No," he said truthfully. But the building's security cams were all gone. Probably about $20K worth of damages.

"Whew." She shook her head ruefully. "So I guess

it'll be okay if you don't go into Full Homeless. What about at Hector's place?"

"I'll disable his system, too. At both places."

If she wondered why he was so hot on not going Full Homeless, as she put it, she wasn't saying it. Jack was aghast at himself because he was breaking opsec, big time. He thought for a second about putting that beard and wig back on and then—nah. Not going there.

The hell with it.

"Looks like you gave yourself over to a life of crime," Summer said as she gathered her coat and purse.

Jack grunted. Yeah. There had often been a very fine line between being undercover and being a criminal during his fifteen years with the National Clandestine Service. But if it kept the enemies from America's shores, it was fine with Jack. Until he realized that he'd been working for the enemy.

Summer was quiet in the elevator going down, which suited him. She stared straight ahead, lost in thought. Jack positioned himself slightly behind her so he could look at her without her noticing. He didn't want to perv on her but, man. She'd turned into an *amazing* woman.

Slim but without that skinny look he hated. He'd spent long periods in places where people were skinny because they didn't have enough to eat. He hated that look in fashionable women, all bones and sinews and hollows. All those underweight women looked deprived and unhappy. It was unnatural. Summer was slender, but strong, toned and healthy looking.

And...gorgeous.

Amazingly beautiful women were rarer in their thirties than in their twenties. Good looks were often a free gift to the young. After that, how you lived your life showed. And Summer lived her life well, it was apparent in every cell of her body.

And she did important work.

Jack had been reading *Area 8* for the six years of its existence, and he hadn't read a stupid article yet. *Area 8* hosted journalists of opposing views, but unlike many publications, the tone was always respectful, which he imagined she set.

And she was so fucking hot.

Maybe because it had been such a long time since he'd been with a woman. His last mission had been sexless because he couldn't afford distractions. Being undercover was dangerous. He could handle the danger to himself but he couldn't drag a woman into that life. He'd be painting a target on her back.

And of course the past six months had been absolutely sexless. Who was going to bed a homeless guy who smelled of piss? He'd barely been seen as a human being let alone a man.

So he was a little out of practice here with being in an enclosed space with a beautiful woman. A beautiful, accomplished woman who was definitely smarter than he was and whom he'd wronged. A long time ago, sure, but she hadn't forgotten. There was wariness and distance there, not good things in a former lover. Jack had liked to leave them smiling back in the day.

Fuck. What had he been thinking? He hadn't been thinking at all. Summer had been like an ice cream cone, all creamy and delicious. But vanilla. And then chocolate and strawberry and double fudge ice cream cones had presented themselves, readily available.

That week with Summer had been amazing. She'd been incredibly sweet and after that first little shock at her virginity—who the hell was a virgin at eighteen at Harvard? How the fuck could he have known?—it had been absolutely great. If Jack could rewind the clock, knowing what he knew now, he'd have grabbed onto Summer with both hands and never let go.

But—he'd been twenty-two and full of hormones and the party was never going to end. And then 9/11 and the CIA had come calling and his life had split into two.

But that week with her…it had been really great. His eyes roamed down her slim, straight back, from her strong shoulders to the ridiculously tiny waist to the full hips. God. He'd held her down while he—

Summer sniffed and wrinkled her nose, turning her head slightly to glare at him. "What's that *smell*?"

"Homeless stuff, sorry." He held up his gym bag. "Never leave home without it."

"Well put it in the trunk when we get into the car."

"No can do, sorry." He shrugged. "Have to keep it with me at all times. The best I can do is keep it on the backseat but I have to be able to reach it quickly. I can put on the piss-soaked jacket, beard and wig fast. Fourteen seconds. I practiced and timed it. Takes me fourteen seconds to get my homeless on."

"Oh." Her voice softened. "That might have saved your life. If Blake would go after Isabel who is harmless, he definitely would have come after you if he suspected you'd survived the Massacre."

Jack nodded. "I'm not easy to kill, but yeah. If I hadn't gone underground, if I'd openly investigated

LISA MARIE RICE75

the Massacre, I'd be dead. Arranged traffic accident, mugging gone bad…these guys don't fuck around."

"No." Her beautiful face tightened. "They're willing to kill hundreds of people and plunge the country into near bankruptcy. They don't play around."

The elevator stopped with a soft ping and the doors opened onto the garage. Summer didn't move. She stared ahead then turned and cupped his bristly jaw with a soft hand. "I'm glad you're still alive, Jack." And then she walked out.

Well, damn. What the fuck was he supposed to say to that? Did that mean she still—no. *Don't read too much into it.* She was a good person and of course she was glad he hadn't been shot in the head or nudged off a cliff. Though considering how he'd treated her in college…she'd have been justified to shoot him in the head herself.

She was halfway across the garage and some primitive instinct made him hurry to catch up. He'd long ago learned how to cover ground fast without running. He was at her side in an instant.

Nobody knew he was here but it wasn't lost on him that if someone knew he was alive and that he was with Summer, she wouldn't be safe. And that was like a cattle prod to the chest. The idea that someone could hurt Summer… God. Because whoever was behind this conspiracy, both in the CIA and in China, if it originated there, whoever was pulling the strings, was ruthless. Would kill without hesitation and Summer's beautiful light would be blown out. Jack shivered and caught up with her, stepped past her and opened the driver's side door without thinking.

"Thanks," she said and slid in. "You're riding shot-gun."

He had to clench his jaw to keep it shut. He wanted to drive. Needed to drive. But it was her car, her rules. Jack thought briefly about taking his car but it would stand out in Blake's neighborhood.

"Of course," he murmured, walking over to the passenger side, sitting down and pushing the seat back as far as it would go. Her car wasn't made for tall people. He placed his bag in the footwell behind Summer, where he could reach it fast.

"How long do you think it will take to get to Casterly Blake?" The Delvaux kids' term for the Glades, Blake's over the top mansion, given to it the summer everyone read *A Game of Thrones*. Blake would have made a great Lannister. He'd been all about money and power.

"About an hour. What?" This with a sidelong glance at him.

He couldn't hide the wince. It would have taken him maybe half an hour. "Nothing."

"Don't you 'nothing' me, Mr. Secret Agent man. I'm not about to get pulled over for speeding. Blake is dead. Nothing is going to change that. Speeding will get us nowhere."

Except it would get them to Casterly Blake fast. Jack hated slow driving. He was all about speed. And there was something tingling in his system, some kind of sixth sense that something was happening and he needed to move fast.

Or it could be the woman at the steering wheel, carefully taking corners, beautiful face very serious.

Maybe it was a different kind of tingle he was feeling. Not that operational tingle but one farther down.

Long time since he'd felt that tingle.

Think of something else.

"So," he said. *"Area 8."*

"Yep." She took a neat turn, an excellent driver. He relaxed a little. He didn't trust too many people behind the wheel. But she clearly knew what she was doing.

He wanted to know more about her. The extraordinarily pretty, nerdy girl had grown into a gorgeous and fascinating woman who wasn't giving him jack shit about herself.

"Where'd you get the name? *Area 8?* Is that like Area 51?"

That coaxed a faint smile out of her. "Nope, not at all. Area 8 is a part of the brain discovered by a scientist called Korbinian Brodmann. It processes uncertainty and, interestingly, it processes hope, or rather expectation in conjunction with uncertainty. We live in an uncertain world that holds out some hope."

"Hence, *Area 8.*"

"Yep."

"And the blog? You didn't study journalism." He frowned. "Or did you?" He hadn't been too concerned with the majors of the women he bedded in those days.

She shot him an ironic glance, perfectly aware of what he paid attention to in college. "I studied political science. My parents dragged me to some very unsavory parts of the world. I saw exactly what chaos and disorder could do. It wrecked lives, stunted lives. I wanted to figure out what made some societies stable and prosperous and what made some societies brutal and volatile. The ruling class is the obvious answer but there's more there. A lot of it has to do with what people expect from their society and that's what I wanted to dedicate my life to. I expect a lot and say so."

"You must get disappointed a lot, too." The unexpectedly bitter response was impossible to repress. Jack hadn't had too many kumbayah moments lately. More or less everyone he knew was venal and power hungry and the few who weren't had the bad habit of falling dead.

Her hands tightened on the wheel. "I think I had lower expectations than you, Jack."

That shut him up. Because, yeah, she'd had a lot of crap in her life at a very young age. Her parents had both come from rich families but they were druggies and had died young, but not before dragging Summer all over. She'd had no stability and God knows what she'd seen when she was a kid.

Jack, on the other hand, had grown up in a great family. Stable and loving. He'd been in his twenties before he'd had anything bad happen to him. And it hadn't even happened to him. They'd found the body of an Iraqi informer he'd recruited floating in the Tigris River, sans a lot of body parts. Body parts that had been cut out of him while still alive.

He'd seen a lot of bad shit in his NCS years, really bad shit. But he'd had a bedrock of love and stability in his early life that had acted as a shield. Summer hadn't had that at all.

So Summer was right to call him on his bullshit. "I read *Area 8* all the time," he said quietly. "It's great. Looks like you've got a wide range of correspondents."

"And informants," she answered. "Lot of wrongdoing going on. I didn't mean for *Area 8* to be a whistleblowing site. I wanted to pursue deep policy issues in an accessible fashion. I wanted to talk about the unsung heroes who work hard on our behalf. I wanted to be a sounding board for new ideas that would make our lives better. But I ended up being swamped by reports of politicians out of control and financial types openly stealing and smiling while they do it." She shook her head. "That wasn't what I wanted but it's what I got."

Jack was burningly and inappropriately curious about her personal life. Was she married? She wasn't wearing a ring but then she wasn't wearing any jewelry at all. So maybe she was allergic to jewelry but there was a guy handy to cook her soup and rub her feet.

Fucker. Jack hated him already. Summer was a catch for any man. She was gorgeous and smart and kind and she'd been really funny when they were going out, though they hadn't had a chance to talk about funny things this evening, what with trying to smoke out a traitor and murderer.

Of course, there was the eight hundred pound gorilla in the room—the way he'd treated her. He'd fucked her blind for a week and then...well, and then he moved on. He remembered clearly showing up at her dorm room door and seeing her delighted face and then—

Jack pinched the bridge of his nose.

—then her devastated face as she realized he was there to take her dorm roommate out. Because Summer had been pretty and fun but her roommate was hot too and—why not?

Jack could barely remember how he'd thought in those days, those college days before everything changed. It was like childhood memories—vague and tenuous. And just like a child he'd reached out for what he wanted, the newest shiny thing, without any thought to the consequences. He had a vague memory of Summer's roommate. She'd turned out to be a bitch, but by the time he realized that, he'd gone on to another girl on Summer's floor.

What a slut he'd been.

He might even have slowly made his way back to Summer—because she'd definitely been the very best—but then life had intervened, the CIA had come calling and his previous life was over.

And it was probably a good thing that he'd had so much sex in college because his CIA days hadn't exactly been drenched in it. Sex had been hard to find and to arrange and more or less every available female around had been off-limits. Either because she was a colleague, or a potential enemy or a potential target for recruitment or that pretty chick in the bar needed to be vetted before he could ask her out...

And he'd been undercover which meant lying all the time. It's one thing to lie for your country to a potential enemy. It's quite another to lie to someone who might be a perfectly nice woman. But who might also be a secret agent for a foreign intelligence service.

But in the days before he dedicated his head and heart and—with hindsight—his dick to his country, he had slept around on an industrial level.

And probably broken Summer's heart.

Fuck.

He sneaked another look at her, in profile.

Jesus she was beautiful. Was she so beautiful because he hadn't been near a woman in six months? Was it because he was starved for female company? Hell, he was starved for any kind of company. Except for the few days in Portland, reunited with Isabel and her fiancé and the cool group of friends they had, he'd been utterly alone for six months.

So maybe a bit of it was that but…nah. Summer really was beautiful, even more so than when she'd been eighteen. She had those bones that would still be beautiful at eighty. His mom had had looks like that and he knew his father had found her still beautiful at fifty.

His father, his mother, his brothers… God how he missed them.

Jack swiveled his head to look out the passenger side window so Summer couldn't see his thoughts on his face. She'd always been preternaturally sensitive. Maybe because of the way she'd been brought up, always a foreigner, unprotected by her parents. The eternal outsider, observing.

He, on the other hand, had had the best family in the world and he'd barely seen them during his time in the Clandestine Service. Every time he saw the twins it seemed they'd grown a foot. He hadn't been a good brother. He'd skipped the last Christmas home because he'd been debriefing a CI and two years ago he'd stayed with the family only on Christmas Eve and Christmas day. Then he'd spent two days with Hugh in his office, and then he'd flown back to Singapore. The twins had been pleasant, but distant, involved in their own lives, uninterested in his because he had to make his life sound as bland and boring as possible. Jack had been more like an uncle, not a brother.

And for what? Why had he sacrificed all that time with his family? He was protecting them, yes, but he'd been lost to them, too. On one brief trip home he found out that his mother had had a breast cancer scare and no one had told him. Teddy broke his arm when he was ten and Jack only found out when he saw his little brother in a cast walking by when he was Skyping his Dad. No one had thought to tell the brother who was far away that his little brother had broken his arm.

And these past six months he had been in complete isolation. So being in a car with another person was nice. Being in a car with a woman was nicer still. Being in a car with Summer was…great. Even if she didn't trust him, even if she was still pissed at him.

He studied her profile, strong and clean. She drove well, paying attention to the road like good little girls should. She didn't even glance his way. Jack himself drove very well, too, only really fast and he was able to multitask. He could have driven at twice the speed and still kept an eye on her.

He drank her in, in greedy little gulps that she wouldn't notice. Each time he looked at her he added to his image of her. The color and texture of her skin, the glossy dark red of her hair, that long, pale neck, the graceful fingers on the wheel…

"You can stop staring at any time." Summer was looking straight ahead.

Jesus. Fifteen years a secret agent and he couldn't surreptitiously study a woman anymore. Out of the habit of being with people. "Busted. It's been a long time."

"Yes," she said softly without looking at him. "It has."

"You've changed a lot."

She didn't answer.

"For the better," he said just in case she thought he was saying she'd aged. Fuck, he'd entirely lost his touch

with women. Could a guy fall out of practice dealing
with women? Who knew? He thought he'd been born
with that talent but apparently not, it had withered right
alongside his social life.

"You've changed a lot, too," she said. "Not for the
better."

He didn't wince. It was true. He looked old and bat-
tered and beaten. It was hard to remember what he'd
looked like that golden time fifteen years ago. It felt
like a lifetime ago. It *was* a lifetime ago.

A pretty bell-like ring came from his feet.

"That's my message tone. Can you read the message
for me? The cell's in the outside pocket."

"Sure." Jack pulled out her cell and checked the last
message. "You've got a bunch of unopened messages."

"I know. I also know what they are. Who is the last
one from?"

It was from someone called Zac. Jack thumbed the
screen.

Where the fuck R U? We need to go to bed. Zac

"What's it say?" she asked.

Jack pondered. "Zac wants to know where the fuck
you are because you two need to go to bed." He glanced
over at her, hating this Zac, whoever he was. Where did
he get off thinking he could talk to Summer like that?
Soon as he saw this Zac he was going to punch him.
Nobody treated Summer like that. "He said the f bomb
to you. Do you want me to go punch him in the face?"

"You've said the f word to me, too, and I didn't send
anyone to punch you in the face."

True. He had. Jack's jaws clenched. "What's this about going to bed?"

This time Summer did look at him, for so long he was about to tell her to pay attention to the road when she finally looked away. "You lost the right to ask me anything about my private life a long time ago. But I'll give you this one for free. Zac's one of my editors. We refresh our articles every four hours. He has a geeky love of old timey newspaper talk. Newspapers used to be put to 'bed,' that is sent to print. So he's saying we need to renew about a quarter of our articles and he wants to know if I'm going to be able to oversee that. But I am hunting down info on Hector Blake with you."

"You have editors?" Jack had only the vaguest notion of how a blog was run and it didn't include editors. He imagined Summer keying in articles during the night.

Summer sighed. "*Area 8* publishes roughly a million words a year, Jack. Of course I have editors. I have two of them, on staff. And I have twenty freelance reporters, four IT guys and over two hundred contributors on a regular basis."

Wow. "Okay." Jack scratched at his stubble. He'd done as much damage as he could in one car ride. "That put me in my place. Sorry."

"Apology accepted," she said crisply. "And don't ever—whoa."

Jack's head whipped to look forward. Whoa was right. Red glow up ahead, painting the night sky. Suddenly, a warbling fire alarm started up, far away, coming closer. Then a second one.

"I have a bad feeling about this," Jack muttered.

"They wouldn't dare," Summer said, shooting him a glance. "Would they?"

"They don't hesitate to kill. Burning down a house would be nothing to them. They probably held off until after the service, so people wouldn't connect the two. And they'll make it look like natural causes."

They were coming closer to the fire. A fire truck, doing seventy, raced past. They were coming up on the corner that would feed into Blake's street, a wide avenue lined with ancient elm trees and stately homes. Not McMansions. The real kind, at least two generations old.

"Stop the car!" Jack said and Summer immediately braked and pulled to the side. Jack reached behind him and homelessed up, not bothering with the pissed on jacket. The smell of smoke would cover it up anyway.

Summer was undoing her seat belt.

"What do you think you're doing?" Jack asked.

Her fingers froze. "Ah, coming with you. You're clearly going to the scene of the crime, because we both know that's Blake's house that's burning."

Jack's mind raced. He did not want Summer with him. Not in any capacity. It was a *fire* for fuck's sake. Set by really bad guys—either traitorous Americans or foreign terrorists. It was going to be dark and smoky and confused and he didn't think he could protect her while looking for clues. Besides which—he didn't want her near the place. Period.

However, he couldn't say that.

He was an operator, she wasn't. All she'd think of was gathering info, not understanding the kind of people who were involved. There was no way she was walking into that. Nope.

The thing was, though, that Summer was smart and capable and powerful in her own right. He couldn't treat her like a dog. Tell her "stay" and hope she'd stay. She wouldn't. So he had to wrap this all up in a reasonable, logical sequence of facts, all this while sweaty at the thought of Summer getting hurt.

Years of thinking on his feet undercover saved him. He talked fast, convincingly, as he suited up. He pulled on the wig, tugged it into place, hating the feeling of the rough under net against his skull.

"I'm going out to do a recon," he said as he then fitted the itchy smelly beard. "They won't still be there, they'll have gone and there won't be much to see, so I'll be quick. I just want to get a feel for the blaze, see if maybe the fire trucks manage to salvage something. They'll have killed cameras, but people might be out with their cells on and recording and you're a very well-known face around town, so stay here. I'll be right back."

He grabbed a small backpack from his duffel and slid out of the car before she could even respond.

Most of what he'd said was bullshit. It was entirely possible that whoever had set the fire was still there to make sure enough of the house burned down. That was the point of him going there—he was going to see if he could catch someone, force intel out of them. Break their necks if he had to, certainly a few kneecaps and fingers, he didn't care. This was war.

It was war but it should be fought by soldiers, not civilians caught in the crosshairs. He'd already lost most of his family to these fuckheads, he wasn't going to lose Summer.

Not going to happen.

He moved silently, keeping to the shadows. He knew how to move without attracting attention and it was dark and there was a fire, so people's attention would be riveted on the flames anyway.

He knew the neighborhood fairly well. His family had often dined at The Glades. He hadn't been here in fifteen years, true, but it wasn't the kind of neighborhood that changed much. It was the kind of neighborhood where families managed their affairs in such a way as to hand down estates intact, generation after generation.

He cut across two lawns, wondering whether fences had been built in the intervening years, but nope. Everything was more or less exactly as he remembered it, except the trees were bigger.

Better to hide behind.

He was coming up to the back entrance. Moving quietly, he skirted the edge of the Waterstone estate, making sure he didn't disturb any vegetation. He was behind a row of hedges and it was very dark, though the fire was catching in the back of the Blake house. He'd brought along night vision gear but it wouldn't work with fire in his line of sight. It would blind him.

Would also blind anyone else wearing night vision gear, so that was good. Quietly rounding a corner, he carefully parted the branches of a laurel hedge, the sharp scent of bay leaves overwhelming the smell of smoke for a second.

Jack stood stock-still, unfocusing his eyes, letting them run a pattern-recognition program, slowing his heart rate, breathing slowly. He had acute hearing and had been taught to use that while undercover.

The smell of smoke was now overwhelming. A few

flames licked at the walls, as the fire spread to the back. The sirens were loud, as were the voices of the firefighters out front, quickly setting up their gear. These homes were worth millions. Local firefighters would be good and fast.

The noise and smells and crackling flames were excellent cover. Anyone lingering to see how the fire was going would be lulled into complacence, thinking they'd be invisible.

And…there it was. First a noise, then a flash of light. A low murmur of a voice, head turning and Jack could see the glow of a cellphone pressed against an ear. Idiot. Who went into the field with a bright cell screen?

But clearly the fucker thought he was invulnerable, invisible. And he was, to the neighbors and firefighters out front. The guy didn't have 360 degree situational awareness. Didn't even think of checking his six.

Fire exerted a fascination to humans, most people were mesmerized by flames. Certainly this guy was. Jack imagined him—watching the effects of his arson, giving himself a little congratulatory pat on the back for a job well done. Because it was well done. The flames were now engulfing the entire house. Flashovers had been carefully planned and carried out. Investigators might or might not find arson evidence, depending on how carefully they looked, but the fire was doing its job of eating the house, fast.

Who knew how hard they would look? Hector Blake was dead. Not currently married, no issue. Insurance would take the brunt of the cost, the estate to be divided up among Blake's ex-wives, presumably, depending on his will. Knowing Blake's nastiness, he very well could have left his estate to his cats. But there would be no one to press for the investigation, no one who cared.

The Glades had essentially become an abandoned house.

The man closed the call, put his cell in a pocket of his combat vest. Now that there was more light as the fire spread out back, Jack could see he was dressed for an op. Combat vest, combat trousers and a weapon in a thigh holster. He couldn't see the type, the angle was wrong. But he didn't have an assault rifle. It wasn't that kind of op.

Didn't make any difference. He could have been armed with a nuke and Jack was going to punch his lights out. This man had a direct contact with the men who'd killed his family, who'd attacked his country, who were working for a foreign power. Traitors, in every sense of the term.

Jack moved quietly, but steadily. He wasn't making any noise but if he were, a steady background noise was better than random sounds that came from stopping and starting. Crouched low, walking toe to heel. He had the advantage of surprise and he knew the terrain well.

And he was motivated. Oh yeah. Every cell in his body was swollen with rage. He'd carried out ops dispassionately, out of duty. This wasn't duty, this was as personal as it gets.

The man was watching the fire still. Not a minute had passed—nothing to the man, everything to Jack. A minute was enough to cross the space to where the man was.

He caught the man by total surprise, snaking an arm around his neck, grabbing his right fist with his left hand to increase pressure. It was a hold that put immense pressure on the carotid arteries. The man fought, hands scratching at Jack's arms, feet kicking. But Jack was wearing a jacket threaded through with Kevlar and he couldn't even feel the scrabbling fingers, and the man's kicks against his boots were useless. But even if the guy drew blood and broke bones, Jack's hold wouldn't loosen.

The man writhed and fought from an awkward position—off the ground, head forced back—while Jack stood solid and unmoving, tightening the choke hold.

The man suddenly slumped in his arms after a minute and a half. He was lean but it was all dense muscle, probably 180. Jack held him up for another half minute then eased the man down to the grass.

He looked up and around very carefully, but they were alone.

He stared down at the man, seeing his face for the first time. The fire was roaring now and there was plenty of light. The man had a hard face, lean and drawn. Weather-beaten skin, definitely not a metrosexual. A knife scar along his right jawbone.

Jack had never seen him before.

He took out his cell and took four photos—two from the front, two profiles, left and right. Never taking his own gloves off, he removed the gloves from the man's right hand and pressed each digit to the screen of his cell and took photos.

There were no identifying documents in his pockets, but then Jack wasn't expecting any. You don't go on an op with passport and driver's license in your pocket. But the gear was really interesting, and there was a tiny tablet connected via Bluetooth to an ear bud.

The gun turned out to be a Glock 20. Which didn't mean much. There were an estimated three hundred million handguns in the US and the Glock was one of the most popular. It was probably the guy's regular piece—he hadn't been outfitted with anything special, because no one was expecting trouble.

Though trouble had found him.

Jack took the cellphone, the Glock, the three magazines in special pouches on the combat vest, together with a small knife in an ankle holder. In the last pocket he searched was a flash drive. Felicity—the computer genius back in Portland who had become a good friend of Isabel's—would go to town on the contents of the phone, tablet and flash drive.

Time to go. But Jack stood for a few seconds longer, staring at the unconscious man on the ground, hands opening and closing. He needed to dissipate tension because the urge to kill the unconscious man was very, very strong. He was a bad guy, undoubtedly part of the team that was planning another huge attack like the one that had taken his family's lives.

He didn't deserve to live, not one second more. He was already out. Jack could argue that he miscalculated the chokehold.

Sorry. Shit happens.

But a dead body made waves. There would be an investigation. Jack had been very careful but you could never be one hundred percent sure you hadn't left a few cells of DNA behind. The last thing he needed was a murder investigation while he was still underground. Law enforcement needed to focus on the coming attack, not on the murder of one more scumbag.

No. Much as Jack wanted to whack the scumbag, he

left him there on the grass, unconscious and stripped of everything.

Let him explain that to his bosses, how he was overcome without warning by an unknown enemy and that intel had fallen into the wrong hands.

Maybe his bosses would whack the guy for Jack. That would be a good outcome, oh, yeah.

Jack sent the photographs and prints to Nick along with a terse message:

Have cell, thumb drive and weapons. ID the fucker.

Between Felicity and the resources of the FBI, they'd find out who this guy was and with any luck who he was working for.

Jack checked his watch by the light of the roaring fire. He'd been gone almost half an hour. Summer would be worried. He turned and started loping back to her.

MARCUS SPRINGER WATCHED the TV monitor, liking what he saw. It was actually quite cinematic—a beautiful old mansion up in flames in the night, the bright orange contrasting nicely with the antique bricks of the façade. Hmm. Yes.

A pretty reporter showed up on the screen. Very pretty. It was chilly outside but she had on a short sleeved dress showing a great deal of cleavage. Ah, the metabolism of youth. She was probably blue with cold but who could tell under the pancake makeup? Dark, almond-shaped eyes, big luscious mouth shiny with red lipstick, matching fingernail polish. A little excited, a little cold. A hint of nipple.

"This is Lucia Almeida reporting to you from Prince George County where one of the area's famous homes is going up in flames." She turned, showing a pert profile. "As you can see behind me, fire has broken out in The Glades, the home of Hector Blake, whose funeral was held just today in the National Cathedral."

Cut to the funeral and oh my! There Marcus was, up on the podium, reciting falsehoods about Blake in a perfectly convincing way. Yes, he did cut a good figure up there. Just a touch of *avoirdupois*, alas. He'd have to tell Dorothy to tell the cook to cut down on the sauces.

The screen cut back to the pretty Latina and the blazing house. She was positioned right in front of the fire so that it looked like she was that pretty actress whose name he could never remember in *The Hunger Games*. The Girl on Fire.

"Firefighters say that the blaze has spread to the entire house and that there is very little likelihood of salvaging the structure. The house itself dates back to 1814 and was acquired by Hector Blake's great-grandfather at the turn of the last century. The house has been featured in several decorating magazines. Hector Blake has several ex-wives and no descendants. I managed to speak with a member of the police force, and he said it is too early to say whether this is an accidental fire or arson, though he did point out that these old homes have timbered sections made of very old and dry wood." She stepped slightly to the side so that a part of her pretty face was lit up, the rest in relative shadow. "So far it seems as if the fire started accidentally, with no suspicion of arson, but we expect a statement will be made tomorrow morning from the Sheriff's office. This is Lucia Almeida for *Newsweb.com*."

Springer checked the other news websites, then the various news channels but no one had anything to report. The fire was still alive and would burn until the house was gone. Then they would have to wait for the embers to cool before arson experts sifted through the ashes.

He was certain that his man, Kearns, had found someone to do a good job and if worse came to worst, and the authorities ruled it arson—well, no one could ever connect it back to him. He was safe, he was—

His cell rang, Kearns's tone. "Hello," Springer said genially. "I'm watching the fire on my monitor. Excellent." He sipped his whiskey and frowned when Kearns didn't answer immediately. The smile dropped from his face and he leaned forward to put the cut crystal glass on the coffee table. Then, sighing, put a silver coaster under it. Dorothy gave him hell if she found rings on the table. "What?" he barked. "Talk to me."

"Ah, sir, as you can see the fire is burning Blake's house down. My operator assured me that there would be no overt signs of arson. Maybe if a highly specialized forensic scientist came, but you said that there would be no one to push for an investigation and—"

"Yes, yes," Springer said testily, pressing the satphone closer to his ear. The conversation was encrypted, the sound waves bouncing from a satellite twenty thousand miles up in space. There was a slight delay and a faint echo, minor issues when all was well, but now annoying. "Come to the point."

Silence.

"The point, sir," Kearns said, reluctance in every syllable, "is that my man was found unconscious at the back of the property."

A jolt of electricity shot through Springer. He was always careful, never betrayed emotions, but this was bad news. He remained silent. There was undoubtedly more bad news and sure enough—

"Someone placed him in a chokehold, almost killed him. Firefighters found him. Unfortunately, he was in combat dress, covered in Tyvek, so as to be sure not to leave any trace behind, but any law enforcement officer would recognize that as a sign of criminal activity. His night vision gear, his weapon, his tablet and his cell were taken. He is now in custody."

A huff of breath escaped Springer, an involuntary stress reaction. Kearns heard it.

"He won't talk, sir. Guaranteed." A moment's silence. "Because he knows we'll get him out."

It was an implicit question. Would Springer work to get Kearns's idiot operator out of custody? No, a thousand times no. The man was a moron, getting caught like that. Getting caught by an unknown entity. Someone good enough to get at the man unseen, someone strong enough to knock a battle-hardened soldier out with a chokehold. That took knowledge and brute strength, yes, but Kearns's man was an *operator*. Not a newbie.

But letting Kearns's operator languish in the hands of law enforcement, satisfying as it would be, would be counterproductive. Kearns worked hard for Springer. He showed loyalty and, distasteful though it might be, Springer had to show loyalty back. And it was a measure of his power. Kearns was a good soldier, but crude. He would see it as a dick-measuring exercise. *My guy's dick is bigger than yours.*

So Springer had to figure out a way to get this

moron out of custody. He was Deputy Director of the CIA, true, and he could always cite that tried and true excuse, national security. They'd let Kearns's man go, no question.

But it would definitely raise red flags, big billowing ones. There would be written records. Kearns's man would be fingerprinted and since all his private army of operators were ex-military, the man would be in the system. He'd be identified. And even if he didn't talk, there'd be questions as big as the Washington Monument asked.

Springer was mulling these factors over in his head when Kearns spoke again. "There's something else, sir." That electric shock again. Something *else?* Besides one of Kearns's operators being found unconscious and his cell and tablet in the hands of someone unknown? What could that something else be?

"Yes." This time Springer didn't hide the coldness in his voice and he could practically hear Kearns wincing. Quite right. Springer affected an attitude of *bonhomie*, a civilized man who could be counted on to behave in a civilized manner. But they were playing with fire here and though he was certain of the ultimate triumph of The Plan, nothing was absolutely certain in this world.

World-altering events were in play, events as momentous as World War II. The world would look entirely different once The Plan came to fruition. Only instead of a four year war costing two hundred million lives with a combined military force of seven hundred million troops that left the civilized world in rubble, it would be using cyberwarfare with minimal damage.

No, this was going to be a thoroughly modern operation with very few soldiers, leveraging data instead of bullets. No atom bomb leaving ruins lasting generations. Oh, no. As a matter of fact, it was entirely possible that by the end of The Plan, many Americans wouldn't even realize that they'd fought in a war and lost. Much would go on exactly as before except the ruling class would change.

They were midway through The Plan, so any unforeseen events were borderline dangerous, possibly catastrophic.

He waited for Kearns to explain.

Instead of explaining, a photo appeared on the screen of his cell. At first, Springer couldn't figure it out. The photo was dark and most of the light came from the sky, the fire which appeared to be about a block away. A human figure, standing outside a vehicle. One of those small hybrid vehicles that looked quite out of place among the manicured grounds of the area. The photos were on a carousel and as they flicked across the screen, a feeling of deep unease, akin to fear except Marcus Springer didn't do fear, pooled in his guts.

The figure was female. In increments, she closed the door of the vehicle, moved to the front of the car. Moved to an intersection. Shaded her eyes with her hand, as if from that position she could see straight to the fire that was too bright to look at directly. Then she turned and Springer got a clear look at her, full face, and gasped.

Summer Redding.

Summer Redding who owned and ran *Area 8*, a famous—and in his circles notorious—political blog. What was she doing at the blazing fire destroying Hector Blake's home? It had just hit the news services, and the time tag on the photo was half an hour ago, so she wasn't ambulance chasing. Did she have prior knowledge? She must have had, to be there so early. But how?

She had to be connected to whoever had taken down Kearns's operator. Clearly she was investigating Hector Blake and clearly she had some inside knowledge.

She was a liability. She had to be stopped right now, before anything she learned appeared in *Area 8*. Whatever she knew, it was too much. If who she was with identified Kearns's operator, there was a path that led straight to Springer. And it would be published in *Area 8*.

This had to be stopped. Right now.

"That is Summer Redding," he told Kearns. "Find out where she lives and eliminate her. Immediately."

And he heard his two favorite words. "Yes, sir," Kearns replied.

FOUR

SUMMER WAITED AND waited and waited. And waited
some more. It felt like hours went by, though her
watch—which must be broken—showed that only
twenty minutes had passed since Jack slipped out of
the car and disappeared into the night.

Amazing. He was a huge man, took up a lot of space.
He'd been there on the sidewalk and then suddenly he
wasn't. Gone in an instant.

So he'd been a good Clandestine Service agent. Had
to be if he'd spent these past fifteen years undercover,
and if he'd managed to disable her security.

So if he was so good, what was taking him so long?

The fire was brighter in the sky, she could hear the
crackling sounds of Hector's house burning.

There were no happy memories for her in his house,
but she had lived there for two months, two traumatic
months. Her first two months in the United States,
having lived abroad all her life. The two months after
the death of her parents. Aunt Vanessa and Hector
hadn't been warm and welcoming and they'd been in
the middle of a vicious divorce, but she'd had a nice
room, new clothes—hand me downs from Aunt Vanessa that looked ridiculous on a twelve-year-old, but
better than anything she'd had before—and suddenly
the Delvauxes had been around a lot.

She spent more time at their estate than at Hector's

and her memories of them were all happy. Particularly when she could see Jack. Just seeing him had been enough to make her happy.

But she remembered the Blake house clearly. The heavy antique furniture, the thick drapes, the plush carpeting. The huge kitchen and astonishing bathrooms. She couldn't figure out how the shower fixtures worked and washed with a sponge until a maid showed her how to turn the multiple showerheads on. Her first shower in Casa Hector had lasted an hour.

Everything in the house had been expensive, even her inexpert eyes could see that, and now fire was eating it all up.

There wasn't anywhere to put the emotions she felt. There was no a-fire-is-burning-down-the-home-of-my-aunt-who-was-never-kind-to-me shaped place in her head. All she knew was she felt unsettled and sad. And she also wished that Jack's presence didn't unnerve her. And while she was at it she wished she didn't have hot flashes whenever he came near her.

Damn! All these things springing up from her past, when she'd done such a good job of pushing them all down to the bottom of her brain. Now they were simply popping up and messing with her.

What was Jack doing? Suppose he didn't come back? Not coming back was a very Jack thing to do. He'd done it before, to her and to innumerable girls. Maybe he was investigating and after that he'd find his way back to wherever it was he was staying and he'd forget that she was here, waiting for him.

In an exact replica of that terrible night when he'd forgotten he had a date with her and she waited and waited.

God, this was so unlike her. This was a *story.* Maybe the story of a lifetime. She had endless patience on the job. One story—which had won her an award—had taken weeks of going through the Snowden files, day after day after day of close study of files and she'd found a thread and pulled it and patiently pieced together a fantastic story of misappropriated funds and quite a lot of cocaine consumption by an American ambassador.

She hadn't been impatient, not for one second.

Now she felt like leaping out of her skin.

What was taking him so long?

The whole sky was bright now and she could actually see flames over the tree tops. Just like in the movies. Bright reds and oranges and yellows, and dark clots flying up in the air that were the house eating itself alive.

She checked her watch again. Jack was definitely not coming back. It felt like her entire body was one long line of stress and tension. She grabbed the steering wheel and pushed back against the seat in a vain attempt to dissipate some of the tension and it didn't work.

It was hot. She couldn't possibly be feeling the heat of the fire from a block away. It was the tension that was making her hot.

This was ridiculous. Summer opened the door and stood up and immediately felt better, even though the rancid smell of smoke burning its way through the house filled the air. She stood in the open door of her car, sniffing the air, as if she could get information through her nose.

But that's not how a reporter got news. A reporter

got news through her eyes and her brain. She slammed the car door, walked to the intersection and looked down the street. It was exactly as she remembered it from nearly twenty years ago. The houses were the same—prosperous, with well tended gardens. Many of the inhabitants of the beautiful homes of Exeter Street were out on the sidewalks, some already in pajamas. The average age of the householders was surely eighty by now. It had been a place of fussy elderly rich people twenty years ago, now they would be doddering.

Two blocks down was a riot of movement and noise as firefighters were doing their valiant best to beat the fire back. They moved fast and precisely, shouting out orders above the roaring of the fire, moving in practiced coordination, like ballet dancers, only braver.

As she watched the firefighters, faces lit by the reflection of the fire, a deep boom sounded that stopped everyone on the street in his and her tracks. The fire raged upward, reaching high up as if to touch the stars. The neighbors, huddled inward, stepped farther away from Hector's home. The firefighters moved faster.

The gas mains had blown. The house would be unsalvageable.

Suddenly, Summer felt sad and old. As if Hector's house disappearing in smoke and ruins had eaten up her past, too. A bit of her girlhood was tied up in the house, not happy memories but her memories nonetheless, and now everything was gone.

She walked back to her car and slid back behind the wheel and checked her watch again.

The door opened and closed and suddenly there he was, Jack, filling the car's interior with the smell of smoke. Summer blinked. How did such a big man move so fast and so quietly?

"Took you long enough," she said.

He looked at her curiously, then brought out an odd-looking cell. He punched in a number. "Yo, Nick," he said when a deep voice came online. "You got my text? Yeah. Well, someone definitely torched the place. I, ah, got him." He frowned heavily. "Yeah, he's still breathing, but not conscious. Christ, what do you think I am—okay, okay. I sent you fingerprints, full frontal and side views of the face, and I have his cell, we'll do an infodump of everything on it. Or rather, Felicity will. The firefighters will have this guy and will bring him in for questioning. So have someone from the Bureau scoop him up, okay, before the CIA gets to him. Because if they do, the guy will be in the wind and we'll have lost a promising lead. Get me intel on this guy ASAP." He listened carefully to something this Nick was saying. Summer couldn't make it out, all she heard was the deep voice at the other end of the line but she couldn't make out the words. Jack shot her a glance and she straightened, surprised. "Yeah, I'm with Summer. Summer Redding. Of *Area 8*. She's promised to hold off on publishing until we get more facts and she's going to help me investigate. I'll get back to you. Go get this guy and interrogate him. Pull out all the stops. Yeah. Later."

As he talked, he was tearing off the wig and beard.

"So." He turned to Summer and curled up his big hand. "Give it to me."

Oh, God. Another comment that wasn't suggestive at all, but her body read it as pure invitation, and heat flashed over her skin, head to toe. She would love to give him what she had. Her body would, anyway. Her head? Not so much. But since Jack had reappeared in her life, her body seemed to be calling the shots.

She clutched the steering wheel hard and stared straight ahead. "Hector's second apartment, you mean. He called it his *garconnière*."

"Bachelor's pad," Jack said with a shake of his head.

She looked at him in surprise. "I'm glad all those French lessons your mom insisted on proved useful."

"Those French lessons never penetrated my head," Jack said. "But I picked up street French in Cote d'Ivoire. Was undercover there for two years."

And there it was, the difference between the two Jacks, now a world of time apart. Jack's sullenness at taking French lessons the summer she stayed with Hector and Aunt Vanessa was legendary. He hated his French teacher who had chin hairs. He erected a force field around him and French just bounced off it. His passions that year were archery, shooting insane music videos and a succession of girls. Not French.

And here was the Jack at the other end of that time leap. Hard and focused and she had no doubt his French was excellent. She'd read somewhere that a facility for languages was essential in the National Clandestine Service.

Jack was still fiddling with the odd looking cell in his hand. "What are you thinking?" he asked suddenly, without looking at her.

"What?"

"I can hear your head whirring. What's going on in there?"

"I was thinking about the summer your mom insisted you take those French lessons."

His mouth tightened. "From Madame Bettancourt. Nasty woman. She had chin hairs."

"So you said, repeatedly."

"And she was cruel."

"What?"

He nodded, as if to himself. "A group of underprivileged kids had received a grant from a French immigrant who'd made a fortune in software design. The grant was for French lessons and he hired Madame to oversee the course. Some of the kids were really good, were studying hard, but Madame constantly belittled them. They could do nothing right. Whereas I sucked rocks at French, wasn't making any effort at all, but she was understanding to me. Because my father was Alex Delvaux. I hated her."

Well. Some things shifted around in her head, big heavy immutable objects were pushed aside and new ideas filled that space.

"So where's your lead?"

She was still working on the new image of Young Jack. "Huh?"

He stopped fiddling and turned to look at her. "That lead? You were talking about Blake's *garconnière*. You found out about it through your aunt?"

"Oh." She shook her head as if to clear it. "Yes. So, um. I found out about it that summer. The summer I… came home."

Jack put his hand over hers on the wheel and squeezed. "The summer you lost your parents," he said gently.

The summer she lost her parents.

She was suddenly blindsided by emotion. Something—something inside her cracked, some hard carapace that split open and roiling emotions just tumbled out.

Summer prided herself on her emotional stability. She was perfectly aware that she'd been badly parented. Her parents had been drug addicts, wayward, hapless children who'd dragged her around with them on their unending quest for highs. But she was also perfectly aware that she'd had immense help since her return as a young girl. She'd gone to boarding school and had been taken under the wing of the headmistress who had spent hours talking gently to her, which she recognized with hindsight had been excellent psychotherapy. She'd excelled and everyone had helped her. In college she'd had three mentors who took care of her, passed her on from one opportunity to the next. Fantastic internships, good bosses, she was highly recommended wherever she went.

Her life had been split into two and she'd left the unhappy, abandoned Summer behind many years ago.

Apparently not, though, because she had a flash of herself at twelve, channeling herself as a youngster who'd spent her entire life up to that point as an outsider, looking in. Lost and lonely and afraid.

She felt all those things now, keenly, piercing her with sharp shards of memories that had been repressed, but came welling up now, slicing her along the way into a million pieces. To her horror, tears came, as unstoppable as rain, and tracked down her cheeks. Oh God!

There was no controlling this, no way at all. Images blasted her brain, things she hadn't thought of for years, for *decades*. Sitting alone in a hut outside a hamlet in Costa Rica, with no food in the house and her parents gone, she had no idea where. There was no electricity and she'd sat in the house, unmoving, for three days and three nights, not knowing if they were dead. And then her parents came tripping in, high and laughing, casually said hi and went into the only bedroom to crash.

The time in Katmandu when her mother started bleeding heavily from down there and Summer had no idea where her father was. Years later, she understood her mother had had a miscarriage but at nine she had no idea what was wrong. All she knew was that her mother was turning icy white and between her legs was so much blood... Summer ran out to call a neighbor and she would never forget the kindly neighbor's face—*those crazy Americans, what now?*

The time her parents completely forgot her birthday. Her tenth. And she'd cooked herself a pancake and stuck a candle in it and sang happy birthday to herself.

The time they'd crossed to a Greek island in an ancient ferry and fire had broken out and her parents rushed to the top deck and forgot her. She found them on the pier, wrapped in blankets from the Red Cross.

Summer clenched her teeth against a sob. She'd rather crack a tooth than let it out. That summer she'd come home, she'd watched fiercely for any signs of pity from anyone and rejected them hotly, batting them away before they could be spoken. She never wanted pity, ever.

Certainly not now.

She was fine. *Fine.*

So why was she so choked up?

Two more tears tracked down her face and she widened her eyes to forestall any more. Crap! What was this about?

Staring straight ahead, she could still see Jack from the corner of her eye. He was frowning, concentrated on a tablet he held in his lap, tapping from screen to screen.

Thank God he wasn't looking at her, at her crazy, humiliating mini-breakdown. Summer stared to her left for a second, fighting fiercely for control. It slipped from her grasp, but she didn't give up and finally she wrestled herself to the ground.

The tears dried up, her throat loosened a little and she could breathe. She wasn't bombarded by memories. Her breath came in normally, she was okay.

Still mesmerized, Jack reached out a big hand, squeezed her shoulder.

Oh, God, that was going to set her off again!

She froze, expecting another flash of horrible memories, uncontrollable, unstoppable, but no. Her skin felt chilled, as if she'd been in an accident. Cold everywhere except where Jack touched her. Warmth concentrated in that one spot, spread throughout her body like a honeyed balm.

Neither of them spoke. Summer because she couldn't, Jack because he was seemingly immersed in his tablet, swiping one-handed.

But she knew he'd seen—he'd seen her sudden, inexplicable distress, her sudden frightening tears.

His hand had healing powers. All those sharp, jangled feelings smoothed out and she had herself under control. Jack somehow understood and removed his hand, behaving as if nothing had happened.

Without a word, Summer put the car in motion and started driving. Driving calmed her, made her feel in control. Jack was frowning at the tablet and she could sink into her thoughts as she made her way into the city center.

He was following their route via a GPS map. "So, where we going? Where's Hector's pad? Are we far?"

The streets became more urban, not leafy suburbia but sharp urban chic. Trendy building after trendy building went by. "Two blocks, now," she said quietly. "I haven't been to this part of town since I went with my aunt all those years ago. I'm not even absolutely certain he still has it. He was fifty-six, what was he going to do with a bachelor's pad?"

"You'd be surprised," was all Jack said. He finally lifted his head to look at her. Thank God he didn't make the mistake of asking if she was all right. She was, but just barely. "If you remember the exact address, I can look up the ownership records."

"Now?" she asked, startled. She gave him the address. "You can do that now?"

"It would be nice if I said yes, because then you'd admire me," he confessed with a wry smile. "But the truth is that I'll have someone else do it."

"Nick?"

"No. He's in the office now and the Bureau tracks all intel requests and we want to keep this close. Right now it's me, Nick and the Director."

Wow. "The Director is taking a personal interest?"

Jack frowned. "We might have US government agents responsible for one of the greatest terrorist attacks on US soil. Yeah, he's taking it seriously. And personally. And to tell you the truth, after Hugh's death, I don't trust anyone in the CIA. So handing the official investigation over to Nick and Director Corning makes a lot of sense to me."

"The CIA's strong suit was never trustworthiness," Summer said wryly.

Jack looked up at that. "Not true. There are some true patriots in the Agency, men and women who have dedicated their lives to defending their country. There are stars on the wall of the Old Building to commemorate those who lost their lives doing it."

Summer ducked her head. "Sorry."

"No, it's okay. And it's true that whoever is behind this also has people inside the Company. All it takes is a couple. And since we don't know who they are, and since they are more than willing to kill, we're keeping the circle small."

"So who's doing the checking of ownership records?"

Jack looked at her and smiled. So strange to see that old, charming smile on that now-rough face. "A friend of Isabel's, Felicity. Back in Portland. She's sort of a genius."

"Yeah? That's handy."

"She's amazing. I hope you get to meet her. There's not much she can't do with a computer. Her father won the Nobel Prize for Physics."

"Oh." A tiny little thread of jealousy—really small, hardly there at all—snaked through her. Jack sounded almost proud of this Felicity and there was affection in his voice. Well, no way could Summer compete with a computer genius and a Nobel Prize winning father. She was good but not great with computers and her dad had been…well.

So really this tiny spurt of jealousy—hardly worth noting—was stupid, because—

"Her boyfriend's pretty cool, too," Jack said casually. "Former SEAL and medic. Real good guy. The whole team over in Portland is pretty cool, actually. Oh good, Felicity, you're the best."

Something appeared on the tablet propped on his knees. "So, here's the dope. The building is owned by a company" —he swiped his way through several screens—"a holding company. A DAC, actually."

"A dack? Is that like a Dr. Who thing?"

He smiled, not looking up and, oh God. A dimple appeared. An honest to God dimple that looked totally out of place on that harsh face. Enough looking at him. It distracted her.

"No, darling," he said lazily. "That would be a Dalek. This is a Distributed Autonomous Company. Essentially, a company without people."

"That's a thing? A company without people?"

He nodded, the dimple disappearing. "They are supposed to operate under strict regulation, but essentially they operate via software that makes them autonomous and fast. But that is only the first layer. Bless her, Felicity never stops at the obvious." He tapped another screen. "I'll spare you the links, but Felicity hunted down the ultimate owner, and it's—"

"Some corporation so he doesn't have to pay taxes." Summer started remembering some of the buildings along the street. There were two new ones she didn't recognize, built after she'd been to the apartment with her aunt. "Which means he was dirty long before now."

"Bingo. So…my GPS says we should be parking right…about…now."

Summer swerved and parked.

Jack was still studying the screen, pinching to expand the scope of what he was seeing, then opening the screen up with three fingers. She cocked her head, trying to understand what he was looking at. She saw cones and lines that looked like streets.

Jack reached behind him to pull a small backpack out of his sports bag. He extracted what looked like a pencil-thin flashlight, the coating a dull matte black. "Let's go." He looked at her. "What?"

Summer waved vaguely at his face. "You're not going to—you know. Homeless up?"

"Told you the damned things itch." He rummaged in his backpack and came up with a beanie hat and a baseball cap. "Particularly when I wear this. Put yours on." He handed her the beanie and slid the baseball cap on. "They have LED lights and will blind any cameras. I checked all the vidcams in the area, I know where they are, and this will take care of them."

"Is that what you used at my place?"

Jack just smiled then climbed out of her car. It should have been awkward for him. It was a small car and he was a big man. But he seemed to have no problems at all. He simply unfurled himself, stood straight, shouldered his backpack, came around to the driver's side. He held out a big hand to her and she got out. It had been a long time since a man had helped her out of a car.

He kept her hand in his.

The area was more trendy than the neighborhood of The Glades, not an area of stately homes but more luxury service apartments. She imagined diplomats and visiting businessmen stayed. She remembered the building—expensively appointed and absolutely bland and unmemorable, like a hotel. Better than a hotel if you had things to hide. No nosy neighbors and all the privacy you wanted.

"You think someone might be watching us?" Summer looked around but didn't see a living soul.

"I doubt it, but we're keeping our guard up." He met her eyes. "I looked at sat photos. All of the buildings here seemed to be zoned for privacy. I mapped out a pathway to Hector's building where there are the fewest security cams. If make a wrong turn, let me know."

Summer stared. "Felicity can hack into satellites?"

A corner of his mouth lifted. "She can, easily. But as it happens, so can I."

"When this is over, can I hire you?" Summer blurted. "You probably won't be going back to the CIA anyway, right?"

He froze and waited so long she thought he wouldn't answer. "No. Whatever happens, I won't be going back to the CIA. If Nick and the Director and I can stop this—whatever it is—then cleaning house at the CIA will take a generation. I don't want to be part of that."

Too painful. He didn't have to say the words for her to understand. She understood that the agency he had dedicated his life to was broken beyond repair. In the space of six months he has lost most of his family and he'd lost his life's mission.

Jack lifted his hand, ran the back of his forefinger down her cheek. "If writing were part of my skillset, I'd come work for you in a heartbeat." He dropped his hand. "But breaking and entering is part of my skillset, so let's go. Do you mind if I take point?"

"Take point?"

"Lead the way."

"Oh, of course. So, yeah, take point. If I remember

correctly, the building is in the center of the block. You can't even see the street from it."

"So you can't see it from the street, either. Neat."

It was neat. Her younger self hadn't appreciated how hidden away this building was. She had been dragged there many times by her furious Aunt Vanessa, as a witness, she now realized, in the divorce proceedings. As it happened, Hector had settled a very generous sum on Vanessa and the divorce went smoothly.

She also remembered wondering why Vanessa was angry and not sad when they uncovered clear evidence that Hector was cheating on her. And again, with hindsight, she realized it was all about the money and Vanessa's upcoming loss of status as wife to Hector Blake that burned her.

Not the end of her marriage.

Summer hadn't seen too many decent marriages in her life up to that point. The Delvaux's marriage had been the first happy marriage she'd ever seen up close. Alex and Mary Delvaux had been devoted to each other, and it was clear in every word they spoke. They also liked each other. That, too had been clear.

She hadn't even thought to be jealous of Isabel and Jack. What she saw in the Delvaux family was so rare it was like being jealous of unicorns or fairies.

The greenery had grown out, matured. A groundskeeper kept everything in shape and clean but now you walked through a maze of head-high shrubbery. Anyone living on this block, particularly in the internal buildings, really liked their privacy.

The night wasn't warm but there was a slight breath of coming spring in the air. Faint, unmistakable. And

like all springs it brought with it ancient emotions—
the tribe has survived another winter! Let's celebrate.

The shrubbery was dense with leaves, a few fruit
trees had tightly furled blossoms that would soon burst.
It was chilly but somehow the scent of the coming
spring was in the air. Spring was her favorite season.

She brushed by a thick magnolia bush and a sweet
scent exploded and filled her head.

Up ahead Jack came to a halt and she stopped immediately behind him. He held up a big hand, palm up
like a traffic cop.

"Shouldn't you hold up your fist?" she whispered.

Jack turned his head and looked at her, eyebrows
raised.

"That's what military guys on patrol in the jungle
do, at least in the movies. Raise their fists, and everyone stops."

"Not quite the jungle here," Jack murmured, voice
low. She'd read somewhere that whispers carried farther than low voices. "And you're not a soldier. So if
I read the map correctly, Blake's place is around this
corner to the right. That feel right?"

She consulted her inner map and nodded. "There's
a main entrance but there is also a side entrance that
isn't used much. If they haven't changed it, I remember that code, too."

Jack nodded, flipped up his jacket collar so it disguised his jawline. He took off his scarf, wrapped it
around her neck, covering her mouth. Basically only
her eyes were visible.

Jack took her hand. He tugged and she stumbled
forward. Oh, man. Her hand actually tingled where he
touched it, which was insane. Jack was not connected

to a source of electricity, the tingling was entirely in her own head and if he had any idea what effect *holding hands* with him had on her, she would die of embarrassment.

His hand was huge, warm, hard as wood. And it made her feel safe.

She wasn't even aware of fear until Jack's hand touched hers. It was just a touch creepy out here in the dark, in this maze of shrubbery, intent on breaking into the house of a dead man. A dead man who might have been behind the greatest terrorist attack of the last fifteen years and who might have been connected to who knew what else.

Those feelings of dread that she wasn't even aware of vanished completely the instant Jack took her hand. Poof! Gone. In its place warmth and an immense feeling of safety. Which was crazy, of course. Safe didn't exist in the world. Her entire childhood had been all about never lulling herself into feeling safe, because she wasn't. And her work as a political journalist taught her that we all live on a knife's edge. So any sense of safety was illusory.

But nice.

Walking beside Jack made her feel completely safe. Like taking a stroll through a park on a sunny day. Because no matter what else he was, he was visibly strong and he was incredibly vigilant, eyes darting everywhere, from the sky to the ground and everywhere in between. He walked like he was expecting an attack at any moment, muscles tense and ready. Jack glanced quickly behind him and she saw a vague outline of something under his jacket. A gun, maybe. Was he armed? When did that happen? But she'd seen quite enough military attachés in civilian clothes to recognize a shoulder holster.

It was probably no coincidence that he was holding her right hand with his left, leaving his gun hand free.

Though she'd taken self-defense courses and didn't consider herself a shrinking flower in any way, if they were attacked Jack would have to fight them off. She wasn't going to fight anyone off. She could take notes.

The walkway was made of aged brick, which every once in a while became loose gravel. She sounded like an elephant walking across the gravel. Jack wasn't making a sound. Summer glanced at their feet and noticed that Jack was walking toe to heel. She did the same and made much less noise. Still more than he was, though.

"There!" Summer kept her voice low, pointed straight ahead. "That's the main entrance. The side entrance is to the right."

Ahead of them was the building she remembered— ten stories tall, still sleek and modern though it was over twenty years old. If it was designed for rich men who cheated on their wives, it was very well done, discreet, tasteful, secluded right in the center of the nation's capital. Maybe there was an architecture studio somewhere out there that specialized in that sort of thing. Chic and glamorous second homes for the unfaithful.

They walked around to the side and again, Summer marveled at how hidden it was. All the shrubbery was designed to provide privacy. Maybe in the summer everyone had trysts on the hidden lawns?

The door was large, smoked glass which barely gave

a glimpse inside. The doorbells had no names, only numbers.

Summer reached out to see if the code she remembered still worked, but Jack caught her hand, engulfing it in his and again, that amazingly annoying flush of heat hit her. "Use a knuckle. Don't leave prints."

She nodded. Yes, she'd seen that in the movies and hadn't even thought of it.

Summer punched the numbers with the second knuckle of her index finger. 4151947.

"You remember that after all those years?" Jack shook his head. "Sometimes I don't remember yesterday."

"My aunt said it was set by the supervisor and it was Jackie Robinson's first day of playing baseball. April 15, 1947." Her aunt had said it with poison, as if she couldn't fathom celebrating a positive event like breaking the color barrier.

They both stood waiting while nothing happened.

"Too good to be true," Summer said. "Probably they have a new administrator who likes tennis. So now what do we do—"

She stopped. Jack had attached some kind of electronic lead to the keypad and was holding a small display. Numbers were rolling on the display, stopping one by one. When the last number stopped, the door clicked open.

"Well, that was impressive," she said.

Jack held the door open above her head, using the back of his hand, and looked around carefully. "They switched from a seven digit code to an eleven digit code. A million times harder to crack."

"Took you about three seconds," Summer observed.

He flashed her a brief smile, the Jack of old. The charmer and the seducer. "It's what I do, darling. Crack things open."

Like you cracked my heart.

She shook herself and followed him into the building.

The lobby was elegant and deserted. No porter. Not if it was a place for shady people to tryst. Clean, gleaming, elegant and impersonal. Jack called the elevator and it was already on the ground floor. Inside it was just as she remembered—wood and polished brass. Jack looked at her, knuckle poised over the elevator button panel.

"Third floor."

On the third floor Jack held her back with an arm as he exited the elevator then gestured for her to come out. She turned right, then right again and stopped outside the door she remembered. Apartment 317.

There was a keypad and she punched in the number her aunt had impressed on her. 72735, using her knuckle. To her surprise, it worked. Hector had been so sure of the privacy of the apartment he hadn't changed the entrance code.

The door clicked and Jack reached behind him and pulled out a gun. Summer looked up in surprise at his face, that he'd feel it necessary to go in armed, but he wasn't looking at her, he was staring grimly ahead.

They walked in, Jack in front, leading with his weapon. Summer followed. There was no light other than that coming from the corridor through the still-open door. "Stay here," Jack murmured and she stopped. This was his area of expertise.

He disappeared around a corridor and she heard

nothing. Absolutely nothing. If he was checking the apartment, he was doing it in complete silence. No sounds at all until he suddenly appeared in front of her. The gun had disappeared from his hand. "Here." He pulled two sets of latex gloves from that magical backpack. "Put these on while I pull the curtains."

Summer put on the gloves and though she didn't hear Jack moving, she did hear the whirr as the curtains in the living room and bedroom pulled shut. There were blinds in the kitchen. She was about to call out to Jack when she heard the light clatter of plastic as they were shut, too.

Jack returned, shut the door and turned on the lights. "Okay. We're going to search this place and we can leave nothing behind. That includes hairs and any kind of DNA, is that clear?"

Summer nodded. Absolutely. Hector was dead and as far as she knew, he had no relatives other than ex-wives who would have been written out of his will. But just in case the bad guys he'd been working with knew about this place and came to check…she gave an involuntary shudder. No way did she want to get into the crosshairs of the people who'd planned and executed the Washington Massacre. They were merciless.

"Very clear."

Jack put his hand on her shoulder. "So, first thing, walk around and see if it's the way you remember it. Maybe he redecorated or something. Then we'll do a systematic search, okay?"

Summer nodded again and stepped from the corridor into the living room. Memories rushed at her, blasting at her like a cold winter wind. Her Aunt Vanessa had had bitterness and rage coming off her in waves as she found clear evidence of a mistress, maybe even two. Then, too, they'd been careful not to leave any evidence behind of their passing but her aunt had been taking snapshots of everything, which she handed over to her lawyers.

"Talk to me, Summer," Jack said.

Focus, she told herself. He wouldn't be interested in her emotional reactions. He needed info. What he called "intel". Not the memories of a twelve year old girl. She looked around carefully.

"The furniture has changed. Originally the sofa and armchairs were off-white and had curved backs. He's replaced them but the look is basically the same. The coffee table had been glass, now it's bamboo and wood. But it's almost exactly the same size and it's in exactly the same position as the old one was."

Summer walked around carefully. She sniffed the air. It was cold and smelled stale. When she'd come with Vanessa those couple of times, it had been lived in and there had been a definite feminine touch. Potpourri, scented candles.

"From what I can tell, a decorator has been in but hasn't changed the look much, just updated it and kept the same kind of furniture more or less in the same position."

"Pictures on the walls?" Jack asked.

"The same," Summer answered promptly. She didn't even need to think about it. The view in her head was the view she was looking at. "Except for this." She touched a watercolor of a seascape.

"Looks like a Winslow Homer," Jack said.

"It does. Maybe Hector had been investing." Though she didn't remember Hector showing any interest in art whatsoever. He had enjoyed money, though. She remembered that.

Jack looked around. "There's plenty of undisturbed dust here and in the bedroom. I don't think anyone's been here, either to stay or to clean, in weeks. So we should be okay."

He was right. A thick patina of dust covered everything, strange to see in such an expensively appointed place. Maybe Hector had a cleaning service come only when he'd been here, not on a regular basis.

A thump at her back and Summer turned to see Jack overturning an armchair. He examined it thoroughly, running his latex-covered fingers over the seams carefully. Then he studied the next armchair.

"Will you need help with the sofa?" she asked. The new sofa had a wooden structure and looked bulky and heavy.

"Nah." He was taking the three cushions off and studying them carefully. "Can you check the bedroom please? See if anything catches your eye?"

"Sure." Though, frankly, she'd rather stay in the same room as Jack. This whole place creeped her out. She'd had a friend in Lhasa, a little girl her age. The family next door shunned the crazy drug-addled Americans but Summer and the little girl became friends without anyone noticing. Very pretty, with a nut-brown face. Badi. Badi had had visions, mostly of places. She'd had this fey sense of place and would shiver when they went by certain buildings. Once she'd dragged Summer away, white-faced, from a building at the edge of town. Later Summer learned that the Chinese had gathered up all the men in town and killed them all in that building in 1954.

Bada kismata Badi murmured whenever she didn't like a place. Bad juju.

Badi would have paled in this apartment. It was definitely *bada kismata*. The stale, dull, lifeless air, the ostensibly luxurious furniture without one personal touch.

The bedroom was more of the same. The air smelled dead. Summer lingered at the threshold, reluctant to walk in.

Nonsense, she told herself briskly. She was a reporter and reporters faced danger daily in their quest for truth. An empty bedroom didn't even qualify on the danger scale.

She entered. It was a big room, sort of oddly shaped, with an L corner on the back left hand wall. There was a little nook there, with an armchair made of plexiglass, visibly not hiding anything. On the wall facing the door was a built in bookshelf with only a few books on it.

Summer examined the dust covered shelves and the spines of the books. Law tomes, mostly about international law. Hector had been a lawyer specializing in international law. Apparently a renowned expert. Many of the books were separated by objects. A glass ball, a silver bowl, a bronze sculpture.

She heard another thump from the living room.

There was something about the arrangement of books and objects that looked off. There was nothing personal in the entire apartment but by the same token there was nothing ugly. A designer had come, designed a five star hotel type accommodation, then left. Everything was covered in dust, but perfect.

Tasteful decorations, tastefully arranged. She would have expected the decorator to take the books and arrange them in aesthetically pleasing ways. God knows Hector hadn't been a reader. The books were heavy and expensive looking, there were even a few antique books, with attractive leather spines with gold lettering. Clearly there for show.

She checked the tops of the books and sure enough they were covered with dust.

She cocked her head to one side. The only way the arrangement made any sense was if Hector had been reading the books and put them back out of order. But no one had touched the books in a long while.

Another thump. Jack was sure doing his best to be thorough. So she should, too. She should check every single drawer, check the mattress. And there was a laptop on a plexiglass desk, too. Check that out.

But she stood rooted to the spot.

Summer had an innate sense of symmetry, of balance. The group of books to the right on the fourth shelf down from the top needed to be broken up. Given the airiness of the rest of the bookshelf, it was like seeing a clot of books.

Without thinking, she slid the clot of the books to the left and right there on the inside of the upright was a small keypad. No wonder things looked asymmetrical. Hector had probably had the keypad put in after the decorator left and hid it with a grouping of books.

Well, this was interesting and explained the odd L shape of the wall. The walls had been reconfigured to create an internal room.

Would the same code as the door work? Only one way to find out. She punched in the code and nothing happened. Well, of course. Who would—

A loud *click* and the entire wall cracked open. She tried to look inside but there was only darkness.

"Uh, Jack?"

Summer tried to keep her voice level but Jack appeared immediately, big black gun in hand. She pointed at the crack.

"Don't open it," he said sharply and she withdrew her hand.

Jack placed the gun on a shelf where he could grab it in a second and pulled something out of his magic backpack. It was like a long, slender microphone, bigger at one end, connected to a small tablet. The stalk was extendible. He pulled it out until it was a foot long, then inserted the end into the crack, watching the tablet carefully.

He spared her having to ask what he was doing. "It could be booby-trapped," he said, tapping on the tablet. "This scans for electronic devices, explosives or bioweapons."

Summer's eyes widened. "Bioweapons? You mean something like smallpox could be in there?"

"Or ricin or anthrax." Jack nodded, then tapped sharply on the tablet. "But it looks like the space is clean. Nothing more dangerous than stale air."

"Should we open the door then?" she asked. "Look inside?"

"Yeah." Jack carefully stowed the sensor in his backpack and stuck his gun back in the waistband of his jeans. He pushed the entire library open and lights came on automatically.

Summer stepped into the room and her mouth dropped open. "Oh my God," she whispered.

FIVE

KEARNS WAITED OUTSIDE Summer Redding's apartment in Alexandria. He'd checked the security cameras but they all seemed to be disabled, which was odd for a relatively upscale place.

Kearns didn't like odd. Anything out of place was a potential source of danger. But since there was no way to know why the security cameras were out of order, he dismissed it. If this had been a regular op and he'd had time to research the mission, he'd have hacked into the building supervisor's office to see if regularly scheduled maintenance was going on, or whether there'd been a malfunction at the central level, just to eliminate uncertainties, but that wasn't possible.

Springer had been quite clear that the threat had to be eliminated *now*.

The cam issue stuck in the back of his head, though, because one possible explanation was that another operator had been here before him and had disabled the security cameras. That would be a complication and complications were always bad.

Kearns had never failed a mission yet. The mission that got him cashiered from the Clandestine Service hadn't been a failure, but that fucker Hugh Lownie didn't like the way he'd carried it out and had given him a dishonorable discharge. With no pension rights. Twenty years he'd busted his hump for the CIA and for a little collateral damage he was tossed away like garbage.

The day of his discharge he'd gone on a three day bender. The morning of the third day, Marcus Springer had knocked on his door, made a proposition and changed his life.

Who the fuck cared about a DD now? Kearns was making ten times the money he'd made in the CS with no limits on what he could do as long as he got the job done. Springer was a great boss, generous and with no rules of engagement. Just—get the job done.

Which he fully intended to do.

He understood very well that this Redding woman was a pain in the ass. Maybe she was about to write something bad for Springer on that blog of hers. Kearns understood the principle of eliminating problems before they festered.

Well, no security cameras sure made this easy.

He crouched outside her door with an IR gun in front of him and waited. The IR would capture signs of anyone inside, even through walls. He moved the sensor around carefully, watching the tablet until he was satisfied that there was nothing living in the apartment. Not even a cat.

The door security was good but not hard. The clandestine service trained well and his new employer hired black hat hackers on a regular basis to give refresher courses to his troops. Unless it was a bank vault, Kearns could crack normal security pretty quickly. A bank vault would take some time.

Inside of four minutes he was opening the target's door, closing it quickly behind him. He had two options here. Either wait for the target to come home or leave a booby trap. It was late. The target was either out to a late dinner, at the movies or the theater or she was with a boyfriend. If a boyfriend, it was possible she wouldn't come back for the night.

Kearns was a believer in not wasting manpower. He had been working on security for the next op and he didn't want to waste his time lying in wait for a journalist chick.

There were other ways.

He dug out a special kit from his backpack, treating the items very, very carefully. He wasn't afraid of bullets and he wasn't afraid of knives and he could take most men down fast in hand to hand. But this stuff—this stuff terrified him. Invisible enemies that he couldn't fight scared the shit out of him.

Kearns hoped she'd come. A clean kill, made to look like a fall that broke her neck. He could do that, no problem. This stuff—

Fuck.

His hands had almost trembled. You could not have shaky hands with this shit, because it would kill you deader than dirt. Worse than a bullet. A bullet was fast. This shit was not fast but deadly and painful.

He waited another five minutes for Redding to show up, so he could do this the old fashioned way, but the bitch wasn't coming. Probably out fucking someone.

Okay. He looked inside his pack. Everything he needed for this was in a neat little kit. He pulled it out, gingerly. He knew from the briefing that nothing would go off until he set it off, but nonetheless, he treated it like the most fragile crystal.

It opened at a touch and he lifted out ten strips of adhesive material, two of which had a small bubble.

Sarin. Twenty six times more lethal than cyanide. Kearns had been around death a lot in his career. You could even say his career was dedicated to death and he was fine with that. But this scared him. It was a horrible death, unstoppable unless someone had a massive dose of atropine on hand, to be administered within ten minutes of exposure.

Kearns put an adhesive to the doorknob. The instant it stuck, the adhesive starting changing color until it became transparent. He put adhesives on every doorknob, on the refrigerator handle, on the intercom receiver, on the landline cordless handset. Two were placed inside the kitchen faucet and the bathroom faucet. At the first stream of water, the gas would release. All of that was redundant because she was going to be hit the instant she entered her apartment. Everything in the apartment was just overkill.

Kearns opened the front door, put the bubble adhesive to the frame of the front door, at the height of the face of a five foot five woman, placed a tiny trip wire that would disappear the instant the door was pulled open. When it was, a puff of sarin would blow right into her face.

Problem solved.

Kearns got out of there as fast as he could.

JACK KEPT SUMMER back with an arm as he pushed open the secret door. When the light came on, he saw instantly what this was and put his weapon away. Interesting, but not dangerous.

Well, dangerous maybe if it came out while Blake was alive. Summer was a journalist and Blake might have cared if people knew how he liked to fuck, but the fucker was dead and no one cared about his sex life.

Even if that sex life was…something else.

He heard Summer take in a shocked breath and turned to see her face. Those beautiful, silvery-gray eyes were wide, lovely mouth an O. She tried to come across as a tough-guy journalist but Jack had known her as a girl and she'd shown every emotion very clearly when she was young. When she'd first arrived, she didn't even need to talk, everything was right there on her face.

She'd grown tougher, of course. And he was certain that political corruption and wrongdoing wouldn't put that look on her face.

Whips and nipple clamps and butt plugs, though—those did.

Jack stepped farther into the room.

"It's…huge," Summer said, whispering.

"Yeah. I think it's the entire next door apartment. He probably bought both at the same time." They walked into a large room which would have been a big open space living room/dining room if people lived there instead of fucked there.

Everything was top of the line, looked brand new. There had to be half a million dollars in equipment there.

"Good God," she breathed and Jack had to admit it was impressive. There was more than enough space and equipment to accommodate a good fifty people.

Summer stood in the middle of the room and made a complete circle. "I have no idea what half this stuff is for. This, for example." She pointed to an intricately woven cylinder hanging from the ceiling.

"A bondage cage. Whoever is inside can't move, is suspended in air."

Summer wrinkled her nose. "God, I wouldn't like that. And these?" She pointed to the glass top of a long beautifully crafted walnut case made out of an antique pool table. She leaned over to peer in, brow furrowed.

Jack leaned over with her, pointing to various items. "Okay, these are butt plugs, of various shapes and sizes and made of various materials."

She turned her head so quickly her auburn hair whipped across his face. "But some of them look like they are made of glass!"

"They are made of glass, darling."

"Isn't that dangerous? What happens if it breaks... inside?"

Jack had never thought of that. "I doubt they break but if they did...ouch."

She was so amazingly pretty when she concentrated. It was as if she'd been handed this puzzle she had to solve. "And these?"

He knew what they were for, too. "Butt plugs with horse hair attachments."

"Whatever for?"

"When the plug is in, the horsehair pony tail sweeps down to the floor. For playing horsie."

He guessed. It had never been his scene.

She looked sideways at him, frowning. "How come you know so much about this? Are you into kink?"

Jack kept a straight face but it was hard. "No, darling, I'm not into kink. If you haven't forgotten, I am into pleasure. The old-fashioned way."

They were looking into each other's eyes, noses an inch away from each other. Summer blushed a fiery red, a teenager's blush. Something unusual to see in a grown woman.

No, she hadn't forgotten.

Summer ignored the blush completely and was still frowning. "Then how come you know so much about—" She swept her hand around the large room positively bristling with bondage toys, and paddles and whips and clamps. "This."

"I had a CI—a confidential informant—in Bangkok. We used to meet in an S & M club. Those places define discretion. We asked for a private room and were guaranteed privacy. But I picked up a lot of... the lore. Saw some interesting things on the way to the private room."

"I'll just bet," she said tartly.

Neither of them had shifted, they were still nose to nose.

Jack watched her eyes as he moved a tiny bit closer. She didn't move. Didn't blink. Didn't even breathe.

"But the thing is," he said softly, looking around at all the sex toys lined up and arranged like well-organized and very expensive props backstage for a production directed by the Marquis de Sade, then looking back at her, "the sex is staged more than felt. It's all carefully scripted. Nothing spontaneous about it at all. They are enacting something they see in their heads and it has nothing to do with the partner. Often they don't even look at each other. They're not looking at what's..." he moved his head closer, "...right..." closer yet, "...in front of them."

He closed his mouth over hers. Just their lips touching. He kept his hands to himself though what he wanted was to grab her head, hold her still for his kiss and just dive into her.

He wasn't into kink, none of that bondage garbage moved him, but seeing some of the equipment, the sex toys, a whole room dedicated to sex—well, he'd flashed on having sex with Summer. He'd have to be dead not to. That week they'd been together fifteen years ago was imprinted on him.

Once Jack realized he was her first he'd been super careful with her. Gentle touches, soft sighs, lots of fore-play, making sure she was ready, was more than ready. He'd pulled out every thing he knew about sex to make it good for her. She'd been so shy and timid, everything had been so new to her.

But this was a grown-up Summer, a strong woman, one who'd meet him halfway. Not shy and passive, no. Strong, confident, sure. And he desired her. Was nearly crazy from wanting her.

Walking around this place dedicated to pure sex, he'd flashed on fucking her hard, moving in her as fast and as hard as he could and he'd gone stiff as iron. Thank God for long winter jackets.

Her mouth was warm and soft, but unmoving.

Damn. He'd miscalculated. The stab of lust he'd felt for this Summer—the smart, grown woman—wasn't reciprocated.

Well, what did he expect? He'd fucked her and run all those years ago.

He moved his mouth gently over hers, barely touch-ing her. He should open his eyes to see what was going on with her but he couldn't. This was way too pleasur-able and if he opened his eyes to see her indifferent or even disgusted...

He'd pull away.

Sure he would.

Jack didn't go where he wasn't wanted, never had, never would. But if his eyes were closed and he was drinking in the smell of her skin so close to his nose, the softness of her mouth, he didn't have to stop right now. Did he?

Maybe he did.

He was just about to move his head away when— there! She sighed into his mouth and moved closer to him.

Yes! Jack all but shouted. He wasn't alone in this. Or at least maybe she was only feeling one hundredth of what he was feeling, but she was feeling something. He moved closer, slowly brought up his gloved hand.

Something felt not quite right with that hand. He remembered how soft and warm her red hair felt, and he wasn't quite getting the stimulus input he was expecting but there was no room in his head to examine this phenomenon because she was kissing him back. Her mouth opened and he slid inside and it was soft and warm in there, so fuck the hair. Jack's hand covered the back of her head as he tilted his own to get a better taste of her and oh God, she was delicious.

When was the last time he kissed a woman? The memory was lost. When was the last time he'd kissed soft lips, felt another's breath against his face, could lose himself in a woman? How could he have forgotten the magic of a woman, the soft scented fragrance of a woman's skin?

And this wasn't just any woman. This was Summer. Summer who'd been so sweet all those years ago. Summer, whose articles he read faithfully so he felt like he knew how her mind worked, felt like he'd walked around inside her head.

And Summer, with the glossy auburn hair and the pale gray eyes and the slim curvy figure who made men's heads turn. Summer, whose mouth tasted like heaven, like some impossible heaven made just for him, after so many years spent in hell.

Jack lived his life in a state of Defcon IV which had been bumped up to Defcon II these past six months. He was ready for an attack on his life 24/7, all his senses open to the outside world and its dangers. Danger could come from any corner and he'd lived the last six months waking up each morning accepting that it might be his last day on earth. Walking around, he'd felt a constant prickle up and down his spine, all senses projected outward.

Yet in here, surrounded by whips and things designed to hurt and degrade, right here he could feel his senses spiral inward until the only thing in the world was his mouth on hers.

And all the sexual desire he'd repressed in these past six months—sex being the very last thing on his mind, too dangerous to even contemplate—came rushing back in one hot liquid flow, right here, in a den of pain of all places. Well, he was feeling pain, that was for sure. His dick was about to explode out of its skin. Splat—Jack-dick everywhere.

He'd been in hiding so long, trying to be invisible, completely on his own, out on the farthest tip of the branch, that he'd forgotten he was a man. Forgotten about other people, about women. But he remembered now. God yes, he remembered.

They were standing now, pressed against each other,

Summer's soft, small hands clutching his shoulders as if she needed help staying upright. Fuck yeah. He needed some help, too. He moved slightly so that Summer's back was to the table and he was pressing against her, first because it felt so good to have his dick pressing tightly against her belly, easing just a little of the pain and second, because his knees felt weak, like they couldn't support his weight. But leaning against Summer, dick against her belly, chest against her soft breasts, mouth to her mouth—yeah. He could do that.

The kiss grew harder and she was into it. He slanted his mouth over hers again and didn't have to open her mouth with his. No, she was right there, tongue stroking his. The first time she did that he felt his dick swell. Even though every drop of blood in his body was now in his dick, even though he was sure he couldn't get any harder, he did.

Jack settled more heavily against her, feeling all that warmth and softness after so long in the cold, hard world. He drew in a deep breath, breathing her in too, and oh, God, the sheer delight.

Delight warred with pure lust. They were two entirely different things. Delight was lazy, willing to cling to the moment for hours, kissing on the lawn on a sun-dappled afternoon. Losing yourself in the kiss, no time element at all, no driving toward any goal, just a long meandering path amid the flowers.

Lust no. That was entirely different. Lust was harder-edged, more driven. More single-minded. Lust knew exactly where it wanted to go. His lust did anyway. It wanted to dive straight into Summer, slide into her, feel her all around him. As it was, he could feel his heartbeat in his dick, pumping hard, faster than normal.

Lust was winning out. Jack held the back of Summer's head still, latex or not, and dove deeper into her mouth, licking her, pulling back for an instant to nip at her lips with his teeth, then back in.

His other hand went around her back, slid down her coat to cup her ass, press her hard against him. Through the layers of their clothes, she felt him. There was a tiny little jerk when she felt how hard he was. Maybe she could feel the heat, too, through all those clothes, because he could feel it. His dick was on fire, about to spontaneously combust.

He hitched her up, ready to lay her across the display table of butt plugs—and Christ, that idea excited him even more, even if he didn't even like the idea of them—when she stiffened and pulled her face away.

Jack's eyes opened and he saw her, mouth wet and swollen from his kisses, cheeks a deep rose that was the most gorgeous color he'd ever seen, her normally smooth hair a wild, dark red tangle around her face.

If there was one thing Jack knew—besides recruiting and running agents and infiltrating bad places—it was female arousal and he was looking right at it. Dilated pupils, vein hammering in her throat, mouth slack to pull in oxygen. She was ready and by God, so was he.

He bent his head to kiss her again and she jerked away and when he looked at her again, it was all over.

She'd closed up completely, face as expressionless as a porcelain doll's. He looked down at her and read absolutely nothing there.

She was gone. That beautiful woman kissing him like there was no tomorrow—she'd left the building and left a beautiful mannequin in her stead.

Summer pushed against his chest lightly, but no matter how light the touch the message was clear— *get off me.*

Jack stepped back, but it was hard. Was it all those months—years really—of abstinence? Because he didn't remember it being this hard. Not many women had said no to him, but there'd been a few. He'd never had a problem with stepping back but right now his body wasn't obeying.

His knees were weak, his hands didn't want to leave her, above all his dick didn't want to be left out in the cold like this, all revved up with nowhere to go. If it couldn't be inside her, at least it could be pressed against her.

But Summer was slipping out sideways and was no longer between him and the table. She was standing a foot away from him, smoothing out her hair, expression cool.

"God." She gave a harsh laugh but laughter didn't reach her eyes. "Nothing has changed, has it? Still the same old Jack."

Everything has changed, he wanted to answer. *And I'm not the same old Jack. I'm someone else entirely.*

But what good would it do to protest? From Summer's point of view, she'd last seen him when he'd left her for no good reason and now, after fifteen years, he was trying to seduce her again.

No use explaining that the Jack who'd left her was a boy long dead. And the Jack who desired her was another man, who was turned on by the woman she'd become. He wasn't any longer the young man who could be turned on by any woman who didn't make dogs whine in the streets and had the right plumbing.

So he shut up and tried to beat down his hard-on.

He ran a shaking hand down his face, hoping she didn't notice the trembling. Luckily, she was looking elsewhere, so she wouldn't have to look at him.

If she thought he'd apologize she was wrong.

"Let's shoot the place."

Her head turned sharply to him, hair belling around her face. "Let's what?"

"Shoot." Jack pulled his cell out. "Take photographs. And videos of the place."

She studied his face for a moment and he hoped that fifteen years in the Clandestine Service were enough to hide everything he was feeling at the moment. Massive loneliness. A desperate yearning to connect with this woman. And a lust that was barely in his control.

Training won out because she didn't say anything, just pulled her own cell out and studied the room. "I'll take these two walls." She pointed to the north and west walls. "And you take the other two. Then we'll shoot the rest of the apartment."

Jack nodded and swallowed a lot of things he wanted to say.

It went fast. The place had no hidden compartments. Why should it? The whole damned room was hidden from view, from outside eyes. Jack filmed, not just shot. On a grid, as if the entire wall were a crime scene.

Blake had been really thorough—he had every toy on earth and some Jack had never heard of. Better Homes & Dungeons.

It was interesting in a freakish sort of way, but there was nothing there from an intel point of view.

Jack and Summer finished more or less at the same time and exited Blake's House of Pain into the bedroom. Jack gently pushed the bookcase until he heard the click of the lock.

"Now." He looked at Summer who looked back, perfectly calm, as if he were the postman or her banker. Nothing to do with her.

For an instant, Jack rebelled. There had been an undeniable connection when they'd kissed. He'd kissed enough lady frogs to understand that. And goddamn it, Summer had felt it, too. Pretending indifference wasn't going to work, he'd break down that wall, whatever it took. Now was not the right time, but the right time was coming up real soon.

He walked into the living room and Summer followed. "He'll have a safe somewhere. This was his hideaway and he'd want cash and other stuff. I'm hoping he'd also keep some intel in the safe. Where do you think he'd keep it?"

Summer frowned, thinking. She turned and walked slowly around the perimeter of the apartment, observing carefully. Jack let her do it. Something was going to trigger a memory or she'd find something out of place. Summer was smart. Just let her do her job.

"There's another bedroom." She disappeared into the second bedroom as Jack turned slowly in a circle. He thought he knew Blake. He'd grown up with him. All the Delvaux kids had called him "uncle."

And he'd had the Delvaux family massacred.

Rage rose up, uncontrollable, a hot heavy mass like magma from the earth, too hot to handle. He'd been mourning his family for six months but only recently his suspicions that Blake had been responsible were confirmed. And Blake had had Hugh killed, too. Though the fucker was dead, the Delvauxes and Hugh cried out for justice. One day they'd have it. One day, the truth would—

"Jack," Summer called from the bedroom. "Come here."

He shot into the bedroom, alarmed, looked around. No obvious threats. No obvious leads, either.

"What do you see?" Summer asked.

"What do I see?" Jack focused. "We already know about the Den of Pain. So okay, super big bed because clearly Hector liked playing around. Two bedside tables with nothing on them but brass lamps. Big chest of drawers—I'm assuming you checked inside?"

Summer nodded.

"Okay. So big chest of drawers with nothing interesting inside. Walk in closet." Jack opened the closet door and blinked at the *Fifty Shades of Grey* style array of suits running the gamut from dark gray to light gray, at least thirty identical white shirts, several sports jackets and colored sports shirts. To the left were open shelves with sweaters arranged by color—Jesus! Who *did* that?—and to the right a shoe shelf with maybe fifty pairs of shoes.

Jack spent a few minutes tapping the walls, systematically and thoroughly, and got sore knuckles for his pains.

He walked out, dusting his hands. "Nothing in the closet."

"I didn't find anything, either."

Jack bit back the obvious response. *Then why the fuck did you make me knock on those fucking walls?*

"What else do you see?" Summer asked.

Was this a trick question?

"Okay. No bookshelves in this room. Presumably

he didn't need to impress his bed partners with his erudition. Turkish carpet. Looks antique. Expensive."

"And on the walls?"

Jack glanced around. "Couple of lithographs. Probably brought in by the decorator. Glory wall. Hector with three presidents. Hector and the president of Harvard. Hector with the Director of the FBI and the CIA. Hector with two Nobel Prize winners."

"And?"

"And a big oil painting. A portrait."

"A portrait of—"

"Of Aunt Vanessa." Light was beginning to dawn as Summer looked at him steadily.

"Aunt Vanessa whom he—"

"Hated." Jack sprang to the wall and lifted the big heavily-framed oil portrait from the wall. Tried to anyway. It wasn't moving.

"Try running your hand along the bottom of the frame."

Jack did and felt something. A tiny lever. He shifted it from left to right and felt a mechanism disengage. A pull and the frame came away from the wall, on hidden hinges, opening right to left.

And there it was—a keypad.

"There we have it," Summer said. "Keypads don't scare us. You have your magic doodad, right?"

Jack didn't answer. He brought his backpack into the bedroom, set it on the floor, and took out some equipment. "I've got two things here. Let's try this one first. Hit the lights, will you?"

Summer dimmed the ceiling light to dark and Jack lifted his UV light flashlight and shone it on the keypad. So, it was going to be the easy way.

"Wow." Summer peered closer. "Even I can tell that the code is some combination of 2, 4, 6 and 7."

"Most likely 4627," Jack said absently, punching the numbers in. Blake definitely did not take his security seriously in this flat. It was clearly not set up for him by pros. He obviously thought the place would never be searched. "DNA samples show up in different concentrations. Usually when keying in a code, you hit the first number hardest and the last number lightly."

With a click, the safe door opened.

"If that hadn't worked, I have the electronic keypad cracker we used to get in the side door. Can crack most anything in under four seconds."

"Is that what you used on my apartment?"

Jack felt inside the safe and started hauling things out. "Bingo."

"I need better security."

"Told you."

"So, what do we have here?"

"First of all, money." Jack pulled out bricks of $100 bills and started filling his backpack. He peered into the safe and made a rough calculation. "I figure there's upward of one hundred thousand dollars in cash here."

"Whoa." Summer watched him then placed her hand over his. "What are you doing?"

Jack straightened. "First, Hector had no heirs and his ex-wives are total bitches who are doing just fine. Second, Hector was party to wiping my family and over seven hundred souls out and this money is going to help find his backers and maybe stop another attack. Why? Do you want it?"

Summer's gray eyes went wide and she put her hands behind her back. "God no! That's tainted money."

"Yeah. It's tainted and it's going to be put to good use." He finished stacking the bricks and unzipped the sides of the backpack, making it more capacious. "And even better than the money, we have some flash drives. Three, to be exact. Felicity is going to have a field day. And, last—" Jack pulled out four US passports, two French and British passports in EU burgundy, an Australian passport with a silver crown, a New Zealand passport with a silver royal coat of arms, New Zealand in Maori and a leafy plant along the right hand side. A light blue Republic of the Fiji Islands passport and most interesting of all, a burgundy Chinese passport.

Jack showed it to Summer, opened it to the passport photo. A definitely recognizable Hector Blake.

"Treason," Summer breathed. "Was he going to run to China? What could he possibly want with a fake Chinese passport?"

"Maybe absconding to China. Or anywhere in the Commonwealth. Or the Fiji Islands. He has—had—over a billion dollars squirrelled away."

Summer huffed out a breath. Her face was pale, set in angry lines. Anger came off her in waves. She was stiff with it.

Yeah. Hector Blake had been a terrorist and a traitor. If it was the last thing Jack did, he was going to unearth and expose everything Blake had done.

"I want him," Summer said crisply. "I want this story. I want to take down everyone who has ever worked with Hector, I want to unmask what he's done, how he has betrayed his country. I want to expose every step of this. With details. I'm going to kick ass and name names."

Jack's neck hairs rose. He knew Summer was smart

and dedicated. She'd attended Harvard on full scholarships even though her education had been sketchy because of her hippie parents dragging her around the world. *Area 8* was one of the best known political blogs around and she'd built it from the ground up. So. Smart, dedicated and tenacious. If she said she wanted to expose all this shit to the public, she was deathly serious, and he had no doubt she would do just that. She was like a dog with a bone.

The other thing he knew was that the people involved in this conspiracy were vicious and ruthless. They had not stopped at assassinating his father, the next President of the United States, together with over seven hundred people, they hadn't stopped at murdering the head of the CIA's National Clandestine Service. They sure wouldn't stop at killing Summer.

Whatever was going on was very big, run by powerful, ruthless people. The idea of Summer in their crosshairs made fear skitter along his skin, made his heart give a huge painful thump in his chest, made him break out in a sweat.

Because they would swat her away like a fly, without thought or remorse. Bullets were cheap and triggermen who would shoot a woman were cheap, too. The bullet would come flying to her head from a sniper's nest and by the time the medics came, the sniper would be far away, the fatal weapon disassembled and placed neatly into its foam packing. The gun and the bullet would be clean of any markers and any DNA. Summer would be a broken doll on the sidewalk, another tragic victim of senseless violence in a year that had seen so many.

That beautiful woman, dead on the ground, brains and blood and bone spattered everywhere.

He couldn't even go there. Now that he'd found her again, he realized suddenly, he wasn't letting go.

He'd dedicated his adult life to his country, his family had been decimated, he'd lived in hiding for six months, putting himself in a dark deep hole, isolated and alone—and then he'd found Summer again.

She made him feel alive after a long time feeling like he'd been buried in the stone cold ground. She made his heart beat again.

No one was going to touch her.

However, saying *no, no way are you coming near this fucking story* was not going to cut it. He had no say over her life, though he'd like to. He'd like to have the right to tell her to do whatever she wanted as long as she stayed far away from Blake and whatever fuckheads he'd been conspiring with.

If he had a staple, he'd have stapled his mouth shut because that was what it was going to take.

"Um, we'll see. Ah, I'll make sure Nick feeds you intel as soon as we've verified it. So don't worry that you'll, ah, miss out on this story. It's, um—" He licked suddenly dry lips. Fifteen years lying for a living, lying for his country, and he sounded like a moron whose hand had been caught in the cookie jar and was lying his way out of it. "It's a big story, I know—"

Summer's eyes widened with every stuttering word. She crossed her arms and tightened her lips and everything in her body language told him she was rejecting him and what he was saying.

"Jack Delvaux." Her nostrils flared. Damn, she was pretty when she was angry. Color high in that pale rose skin, light gray eyes flashing like lightning. He shouldn't be thinking this. He should be marshaling his facts, preparing a counter argument, preparing to convince her that this story was like grasping a third rail. Instant death.

Instead, like a crazy fuck, he savored the feel of the air around her heating up, watched her eyes flash and thought about her mouth that very recently had been touching his.

Focus, you fuck! he told himself. But he was AWOL.

He tried on a smile. "That's my name, don't use it up." The old childhood response when his mom reprimanded him for something he'd done.

"That's not funny. This is serious."

He nodded. Yes, it was. And she seriously was not going after this story until it was over and all the bad guys were in jail. And even then...

"You have that look."

"That look?" He feigned innocence, though it was hard. He looked every minute of his thirty-four years and then some. And on his face it was clear that he hadn't spent all that time reading in the library and helping little old ladies cross the street.

"That look of someone who wants to keep information secret. I encounter that look every single day of my working life, and let me tell you I make my living—a very good living at that—by getting past people who don't want me to know anything."

Shit. She thought this was about keeping secrets? Fuck no. This was about keeping her *safe*.

Jack no longer had a smile lurking in his voice. "These are very dangerous people, Summer. You know that. I'm just trying to keep you alive."

Summer stepped closer to him, until she was almost touching him. Which was fine, fine. Except she hadn't stepped closer to him because she wanted to give him another one of those amazing kisses. No, this was pure aggression, stepping into his personal space, up in his face.

Her expression was all business, sober and serious. "I have never run away from a story I felt to be in the public interest. Ever. And I have no intention of running away now. So you can take your fake concern and stick it—"

Jack kissed her. He couldn't help himself. It was wrong wrong wrong. He told himself that even as he reached out to pull her toward him and crushed his mouth on hers. And yes, it was just as magical as the last time, and he was expecting the magic so it was real. It wasn't just him being starved for a woman, any woman. He was starved for *this* woman, who felt so perfect in his arms. Mouth so soft, skin so warm...

Summer wrenched herself out of his arms and slapped him, hard, across the face. It was a real slap, too. Not a slap for form's sake. His skin tingled.

He'd been tortured once. For eight hours before Hugh sent backup. It had been totally dispassionate and he'd survived.

This...*hurt*. Seeing Summer so angry at him hurt. She was absolutely right of course. You don't shut a woman up by kissing her. Even Jack knew that. He'd been out of touch with women for a while, and over the past six months women had been like an alien species to him, but he knew that.

The thing was, he had absolutely not been able to resist her. Even now he was looking for a way to do it

LISA MARIE RICE   149

again. How could he say he was sorry when he wasn't? Saying he was sorry for kissing her was absurd. It was the best thing to happen to him since the Massacre.

But—he had to take a stab at making amends because he saw coldness beyond the anger in Summer's eyes and that scared him more than the anger.

He hadn't thought it through. Jack Delvaux, ace super secret agent for fifteen years, hadn't thought it through.

It was entirely possible that a lot of men had tried to get her to shut up by trying to kiss her. That just now occurred to him. She lived in a man's world and men were pricks. Jack should know—he was one of them.

So he opened his mouth to give an apology when he didn't feel in the least apologetic and he was saved by the bell. Or at least a ring tone. *Sinnerman*, Nick's ringtone. Nick had programmed it in himself.

Jack held up a finger and watched as her jaws flexed. *Just a minute*, he mouthed then answered with the fervor of a man who'd been saved from annihilation.

"Nick. My man. Wassup?"

"Where are you?" Nick usually started off with *howzzit hangin'?* so his deep sober tone made Jack stand straighter and shoot a glance at Summer. Whatever this was about it wasn't about Summer because she was standing right in front of him, glaring.

Except it was about Summer.

"I set up—or rather Felicity set up—a surveillance bot for Summer. Felicity's a big fan of the blog and she wants to keep Summer safe. So she checked the cameras across the street from Summer's place and got this—"

"What?" Summer asked Jack. "What is it?"

Grimly, Jack angled his screen so she could see and put it on speakerphone.

Summer cocked her head as she stared at the screen. A night view of a suburban street, greenery, an old jalopy parked on the street. His.

"I don't see what—"

And then she could see what it was because it was a view of her apartment building. It was static, from a security camera. Not much appeared to be happening.

"There!" Jack said, and checked the timeline. Half an hour ago. He moved the slider from right to left and pointed to a spot on the screen.

Summer frowned, leaned closer. "What is it?"

Jack watched it again. "The head of someone, moving against the blinds. While we were here." He met her eyes. "Someone's been in your place, Summer."

Blood drained from her face. "An intruder?" she breathed.

"An intruder." Jack nodded. "Not me. So he didn't mean you any good." He addressed the screen. "Tell Felicity good catch." She'd done superb work.

"That isn't all that we caught tonight," Nick's voice was grim. "There's more. Two agents I trust were nearby and I asked them to go into Summer's place, see if we could get fingerprints, DNA, something. Summer's triggered some kind of trip wire and if we can get the identity of the intruder we'll have a trail to follow. Or we thought we'd have a trail to follow."

This wasn't sounding good. "And?"

"These two guys are good, and discreet. Don't worry about any leaks. One of them had the presence of mind to take out a sniffer and wand the door."

Fear pumped a sudden icy jet in Jack's veins. His voice turned hoarse. "There was a bomb?"

"No," Nick said and Jack's shoulders slumped in relief. "Something worse."

Summer's face was icy white. Her hands were clenched, knuckles pale. "Worse than a bomb?" she whispered. "What's worse than a bomb?"

The screen changed and Jack could see Nick's face, narrow-eyed and tense. "It was a new type of sensor we're testing and it picks up about twenty types of explosives and four major bioweapons. Sarin, ricin, anthrax and botulinum."

Summer swallowed, that long white neck bobbing. "And—and which was it?"

"Sarin," Nick said. "They left a booby trap. The next time you opened your door, you'd have received a blast of sarin in your face. You'd have been dead inside the hour, Summer, and a sarin death is not pretty. They're evacuating the building now."

"That's it," Jack said, decisively. That was it for him. He couldn't continue investigating in DC, not with Summer. And he wasn't willing to leave her for a second. So he was done. "I'm taking Summer to my safe house and tomorrow we're flying to Portland. Tell ASI to send a plane."

San Francisco

THE HOUSE WAS PERFECT. In the Mission, but enough on the edge of the fast growing and gentrifying tech sector to make it plausible for four young tech slackers to share the rent.

Drunks and addicts to the left of them, Google to the

right, they set up shop. It was an old building, practically with a sell by date on its façade. It would fall to the tech giants soon. If not this year, then the next. As inevitable as looking at an old dog and knowing that it would die sooner or later.

Ostensibly the four young men were renting but actually the building and the two neighboring buildings were owned by a shell company that, if you wanted to spend about six months digging, was ultimately owned by the PLA. No one was interested enough to spend those six months and if they were, by the time the six months were up, the PLA would own most of California anyway.

The four young men operated very discreetly. They had a satellite uplink disguised as an HVAC on the roof, which was a weak spot. It was the only HVAC on the block, but the rooflines were changing monthly. No one would notice.

They had reinforced internet connections via a thick cable that snaked out of the building.

That was for the primary mission.

They were ready for the post-mission period, too. The basements of their building and the two adjacent buildings contained brand new powerful generators that could keep electricity running in their buildings for months. Special films had been put over all the windows. They were invisible from the outside but they acted as light filters. The time would come when there were no lights in the city and their building would be a beacon.

Thanks to the film, no light would escape. No one would know they were the only ones with power.

The three buildings were four stories tall. The team

operated out of the first floor of the central building. That was where they worked, ate and slept. The other rooms on the other floors were filled floor to ceiling with supplies. Food, water, arms. They could live twenty years on what was in the buildings.

Twenty years wouldn't be necessary, of course, but it was good to be prepared.

The generators and supplies had been brought in by stealth, at night, unloading vans from the alleyway in back. Supplies had been purchased from valid credit cards in fake names within a radius of a hundred miles, no purchase so big it would raise eyebrows.

Two of them had studied in the US and could easily pass for American. They made a point of hanging out in the local coffee shops and noodle shops, until they became a familiar sight. There were plenty of twenty-something slackers dressed in torn jeans and tees. One of them had a favorite tee with KEEP CALM AND CODE on it. That got him knowing smiles from the baristas.

Finally, the preparations were over. They were fully stocked. Their use of power from the grid was perfectly normal—no billing anomalies would be noted. They used the grid for light and for the monitor they used for entertainment. The rest came from the monster generators in the basement.

The leader—lean and handsome, straight black hair down to his shoulders, wearing a Daft Punk T-shirt—was about to send an encrypted message in the secure uplink, directly to the overhead satellite and it was then bounced down to a secure receiver in Pudong. It was a message that could not be intercepted by the NSA.

The leader could just see the general receiving the

message. General Chen Yi's office was on the twelfth floor of an anonymous-looking building in the Pudong District of Shanghai. The General had come up with the plan, a brilliant one, for taking over the most powerful country on earth without firing a shot. Funded by the billions and billions of dollars siphoned off the American economy after the Massacre. An audacious plan, using America's strength against it.

General Chen Yi knew that a fighting war was unthinkable. America had a million and a half active military personnel, eight thousand tanks, fourteen thousand military aircraft, twenty aircraft carriers and seventy submarines, backed by a military budget of six hundred billion dollars.

A huge, powerful dragon standing guard over the hoard of treasure that was the United States of America.

An enormous fortress, sky high and incredibly wide, almost invincible.

And the back door was wide open.

They were ready.

The leader, who blended right in with the other slackers in the coffee shops of the Mission, was actually a lieutenant in the PLA and hand-picked by Chen Li to lead the mission. In San Francisco he was known as Jason Lee, his private joke, as a huge fan of vintage Bruce Lee films. He passed as a third generation Chinese-American, fully blended in.

In truth he was Zhang Wei, handpicked by Chen Yi when he was twelve and a computer prodigy.

Zhang Wei was very aware of what he was doing and of the upheaval to come, orchestrated by him and his team. The plan was excellent. And necessary.

He sat in his chair and opened up the satellite link for the first time.

Mission-ready, he keyed in, sending his message to General Chen Yi in person.

Excellent. Everything on schedule, the reply came immediately.

SIX

SUMMER WAS FROZEN, incapable of moving, even of breathing.

Someone had booby trapped her home. If not for Jack, she'd be dead by now, or dying. *Area 8* had done a special series on bioweapons and she knew enough about sarin to know that she'd have had a horrific death.

Sarin turned the body against itself. Within seconds there was an acetylcholine buildup that made the system go haywire. Sarin gas had no smell and no taste. Summer would have no idea what was happening.

Within seconds, her body would start to go crazy, nose running, eyes leaking tears, suddenly vomiting, bowels and bladder loosening. She'd be on the floor, panicking because her body was out of control. She wouldn't have the energy to call 911. Not that 911 could arrive in time.

She'd be dead by the time they came pounding at her door. Dead in a pool of tears, feces and urine.

Summer had seen photographs from a secret file of people who'd died of sarin poisoning and the world tuned out as she saw those photographs in her mind's eye. Superimposed her face on those contorted bodies who'd died wracked with pain.

"Summer!"

Someone shook her, hard.

She jolted, came back to herself. Jack had her by the shoulders and was shaking her.

"Summer, snap out of it!" He bent, put his face next to hers until all she saw was him. He was frowning, concerned. "You okay?"

She looked at him, chilled to the bone. Her mouth opened to say she was okay but she wasn't. Not in this universe or any other could she be okay knowing someone had tried to poison her with sarin.

"We're getting out of here." Jack's words barely penetrated. He disappeared and Summer felt even more chilled. Having that big body next to hers had given her some heat but now she felt frozen, bereft.

Dimly, as if from a great distance, she heard him rummaging around, with no idea what he could be doing. She couldn't move, couldn't even turn her head to follow what he was doing, she was nailed to the floor, trying to contain the wild trembling, trying to focus through the spots dancing before her eyes.

Something heavy and warm fell on her shoulders and her hands reached reflexively to hold it around her. The trembling eased.

Jack was back, some of that amazing warmth was back. He lifted her chin so she was forced to look him in the face. His eyes were narrowed, skin tight over the cheekbones. He had a big black hat on. A Fedora. "You're in shock, sweetheart, and you have every right to be. But we can't stay here, we've got to go. I have the flash drives and Hector's computer. You can't go back to your apartment so you're coming with me."

Nothing penetrated except the words—*coming with me*.

God, yes. After flashing on a horrific death, writh-

ing on the floor alone, unable even to call for help—
staying close by Jack sounded like a burst of heat in
the Arctic. Because underneath the horrific image of
her body on the ground in death throes was something
else. Not an image, a truth.

She was alone.

If she'd been blasted by sarin gas, she'd have called
911 if she could. But who else would she call for help?
She didn't have any close friends she could call and
there sure wasn't a lover. A man who cared for her,
who wanted her safe and happy.

Area 8 was mainly staffed by freelancers. Her
editors—she knew them at work, had little idea of their
private lives. And they were journalists—word nerds.
No one you'd call for help in an emergency.

She'd have died alone, without anyone even in her
head to say goodbye to.

Summer shuddered.

"You can have a breakdown later," Jack said. He
lifted her arms and put them in the heavy overcoat
he'd dropped around her shoulders. Just like dressing
a child. A big soft scarf replaced the one she had on.
Jack wrapped it around her lower face and covered her
neck and jawline. Finally, Jack placed a big brown hat
on her head. Felt, with a brim. It was a little large and
settled low on her head.

She focused on him, focused on his eyes as if they
were waltzing and she had to look at him not to get
dizzy. Then she was able to focus on more than those
sky blue eyes and saw that he'd changed, too, with
another heavy dark blue overcoat, a big scarf and the
Fedora.

"I raided Hector's closet. We weren't seen coming

in, but there are no guarantees. If someone did catch us, we'll look different going out."

Summer nodded. The warmth of the overcoat and Jack's big body so close to hers were chasing away the bone-deep chill she felt. But her throat was too tight to talk.

"Sweetheart, we really have to go."

She nodded again, a jerky movement. She had no control over herself at all.

Jack bent and gave her a quick kiss, heat and light blossoming on her mouth. As if he were prince Charming—which he certainly wasn't—it brought her back to life.

"Okay," she whispered.

"Good girl."

They walked swiftly out, Jack's arm around her back. She could feel the heat of his arm through the overcoat, her coat and shirt. He bent, murmured in her ear. "Keep your head down. The brim will cover your face."

She watched her feet. He didn't even need to say it. She was feeling so shell-shocked she'd have had to watch her feet anyway. Her whole body felt as if someone had cut some strings—she had to focus to put one foot in front of another, not stumble, not walk into a wall.

Luckily, Jack was right there. He had the backpack slung over one shoulder and had his other arm around her. She wasn't going to stumble and she wasn't going to walk into a wall. Not while he was holding her so tightly.

In some dim corner of her mind Summer realized that Jack had shortened his stride for her—they were matching steps exactly—and yet they were moving fast. Through the fog in her head, she observed as they walked down the stairwell and out the side door. In the stairwell, her footfalls were the only sound. Though he was much bigger and heavier than she was, Jack managed to make not a sound going down.

Then they were out in the open air of the night and Summer gasped, taking in a huge breath of night air. She finally felt like she could *breathe*.

A big hand clasped her neck warmly and forced her head down.

"Big breaths," Jack ordered and she obeyed. One big breath, two.

"Better?"

"Yes," she gasped. "Better."

"Okay then." He took her arm, looking around carefully. "Let's get going. You can break down at my place."

Break down. Oh, God. Yes. She'd nearly had a breakdown in Hector's secret apartment. It had felt exactly like the bottom dropping out of her world, like going into shock, like extreme trauma.

"I'm so sorry," Summer whispered miserably. "Sorry to wimp out on you like that."

Jack stopped examining their surroundings and turned to her with a deep scowl. "Jesus, Summer. You just found out someone wanted to kill you with *sarin*. Do you know what sarin does to people?"

"Yes," she whispered. "I do."

"So I think you're justified in freaking out just a little, don't you?"

She nodded numbly.

"And you can freak out later all you want, but right

now we have to go." Jack's eyes seemed to glow in the dark. "Okay?"

She nodded again.

"Good girl." Jack gave a half smile and bent to give her another one of those heart-stopping kisses that seemed to heat her up from the inside. "Let's go."

In moments they were out on the street, Jack, eyes darting left and right under the brim of the Fedora. They passed her car and kept on walking fast down the street.

"Hey, Jack." Summer slowed down. "That was my car back there."

The street was full of Mercedes, Lexuses and BMWs. Hers was the only Prius. How could he have missed it?

Jack didn't answer immediately. He just gave a grunt of satisfaction next to a big luxury car Summer didn't recognize, bent and pulled something out of his backpack. A few seconds later, he had the front and back plates in his hand and as she gaped, he switched plates between a monster black SUV and the luxury sedan. He walked quickly back to her Prius and took two plates out of his backpack, and switched those with her Prius's plates.

"They'll be on the lookout for your car, but for the moment they'll be scanning traffic cams for your license plate number. They won't have the tag numbers I just put on your car." He pointed to the black SUV. "I'll take that vehicle. Follow me in your car and when I pull over, pull over behind me. We'll leave your car far away from here and proceed with the SUV."

"How can you get in the car? You don't have the

key!" Summer objected. Jack just looked at her. "Oh. Okay."

If he could break into her super secure apartment surely he could break into a vehicle.

By the time Summer got her Prius started, Jack had already broken into the huge SUV and stopped ahead of her. She pulled out and followed him. They headed south, crossed the 11th Street Bridge. Jack stopped at a suburban used car lot. Summer pulled in behind him and parked.

Half the street lights were broken. It was a bad part of town, barely clinging to a low end kind of respectability, but she knew that four blocks farther south, it became no man's land.

He got out before she did and was at the driver's side door in an instant. "Don't lock the door," he said as she was getting out.

"What?" Summer waved her hand at the grim surroundings. "It'll be boosted before dawn if I don't lock it."

"Exactly." Jack met her eyes. "I'm really sorry sweetheart but you're going to have to sacrifice your cute little car. If we leave it here unlocked, inside of twenty-four hours it will be in a chop shop or taken out for a joyride and left in a field somewhere. The best way to get rid of a car. They'll never find it."

"Oh." Instinctively, Summer reached out a hand and put it on the fender, caressed the metal. She sighed. "I just paid her off."

Jack hooked an arm around her neck, pulled her to him and kissed her forehead. "Sorry."

Not sorry enough to change the plan, though.

Her car. She loved it. It had never broken down or

abandoned her, not once. It had served her faithfully like a knight of old and she was going to abandon it to a fate worse than death. Maybe cut up for parts or left to rot and rust in some abandoned field.

"Summer." Jack cocked his head at the SUV. *Time to go.*

"Yeah, yeah." She gave the fender a last farewell pat and followed Jack to the SUV, having now lost her home and her car. Her last attachment to her old life was the broad-shouldered man in front of her, bending to open the passenger door of a stolen vehicle for her.

JACK WAS ABOUT as sure as he could be that no one could know he and Summer were in this SUV. They could track it as much as they wanted. It was anonymous and had someone else's plates on it and no one could possibly know they were inside. The windows were tinted very dark. He'd chosen it for that reason.

Behind his safe house was a covered alleyway. He'd park there, safe from overhead drones or even satellite surveillance. The safe house had no security cams around it. He'd made sure of that.

But there was another reason he wasn't taking evasive maneuvers. He wanted to get to the safe house as fast as was humanly possible. He drove at the exact speed limit. Getting pulled over would be hard to explain away so he didn't give any police officer any opportunity to do so.

He knew the route so well he was on automatic pilot. He checked all the mirrors constantly, was aware of the cars behind him at all times and knew he could pick out a tail immediately, but he did this without thinking too much.

All his attention was focused on Summer. She was way too silent and way too pale for his liking. She had the uncoordinated movements of someone who'd had a bad shock. She'd stumbled when getting out of Hector's little hideaway, something someone as naturally graceful as Summer wouldn't do.

Even in the uneven light of the street lamps he could see her skin was pale as ice, almost cadaver pale. Even her lips were white and he knew for a fact that even without makeup her lips were a full, rich rose color. She looked drawn, as if she hadn't eaten or drunk in days, as if something had sucked vital things out of her, leaving a husk.

Well, something *had* sucked vital things out of her. Her home had been invaded. That was a very basic trauma, almost as bad as being physically attacked. He hadn't told her and he wouldn't tell her for as long as he could get away with it—but her home was basically gone. That lovely flat, decorated with style and pretty personal touches, full of watercolors and fresh plants and tons of books and CDs—gone. The Chemical, Biological, Radiological and Nuclear Sciences Department of the FBI would go over it molecule by molecule but no one would guarantee that every single possible booby trap had been eliminated and Jack wouldn't let her go back in if there was the faintest possibility of contamination. Every single soft surface of the apartment—curtains, sofas, all clothes, all tablecloths and sheets, the bed mattress—would be encased in plastic and removed to an FBI laboratory and she would never get them back again.

And anyway, Nick and the Director wouldn't let

her go back in until the investigation was completed. Which might be next month, next year. Might be never.

And her car—that was over, too.

Jack reached over and squeezed her hands. She was clasping them in her lap. They were cold, dry. He held them until he felt them start to heat up. There wasn't much Jack could give her right now. He didn't even have a home to take her to. But she was welcome to as much of him as she'd take.

"I'm sorry," he said softly. He spoke quietly, as if she'd been in a bad accident.

She didn't respond. Her pretty profile was still and pale.

Jack drove on in the dark, windy night. The straight route home took them through some trafficked avenues and he kept close watch on the cars around him, but nothing pinged on his radar.

About twenty minutes from the safe house, Summer finally spoke.

"I'm really sorry I freaked on you back there."

"You're allowed, when you discover that your home has been seeded with a deadly bioweapon."

She sighed. "It's not that, it—" Her lips clamped shut.

"It's what?" Jack asked. The road was broad and almost empty. He swiveled his head to look at her directly. She seemed a little less in a state of shock now. Sad and afraid but not devastated.

Summer shook her head. "Nothing."

Jack slowed down. "This is a serious situation, Summer. You were about to say something. It wasn't nothing. Tell me."

"Or what?" She turned to give him a faint smile. It

was a sad effort but he was happy to see she made that attempt. "You'll beat it out of me?"

God.

"No, sweetheart." Jack picked up one of her hands, brought it to his mouth. It wasn't icy cold any more. He kissed the back of it, as if she were his liege lady. "I could never hurt you and you know that. But I'm trying to keep us alive here, doing my very best, and I don't like question marks, things left unsaid. They could get us killed. So I would be very, very grateful if you could finish that sentence for me."

"Not fair," she complained, and this time the smile was less strained. "You're appealing to my better nature."

"Anything that works, sweetheart."

She sighed. "It has nothing to do with" —she waved her hand "—with whatever is going on. Back there, at Hector's secret little love pad, when I heard that my house had been booby-trapped with sarin, I flashed back on something that happened in my childhood. A bed memory. That's all."

Summer's childhood had been really rough. Jack knew that. He'd heard his parents talking about her when she lived with Vanessa and Hector, who'd totally ignored Summer in their vicious fights with each other. His parents, bless them, had tried to take Summer under their wing.

"Tell me," he said gently. "If you talk about it, it'll pull the punch of the memory. I don't know what else is going to happen, probably not a whole lot of good things, so I'd like to know what could be a trigger for you. Drag up memories that make you freeze."

She sighed. Looked down at her lap. Clasped her fingers together then pulled them apart.

She was going to talk. She wanted to talk. Jack recognized the signs. He gave her the time she needed.

"Okay," Summer said finally. She stared straight ahead, not looking at him, which was not a good sign. Summer always looked people right in the eyes. This was going to be bad. "The summer I was eight my parents and I were living in Cartagena, Colombia. It wasn't a happy place. We were surrounded by cartel soldiers and pushers but I suppose that was sort of the point, for my parents. They got high a lot. Sometimes they left me alone for days. Once, they left to go somewhere—I have no idea where—and I ate something tainted. It gave me violent food poisoning. For almost two days—I think it was two days, I lost all track of time—I vomited and voided everything that could be voided.

"I spent two days and two nights curled around the toilet in blinding pain, drenched in my own waste, and I begged God to let me die. I've never been so sick before or after in my life. I thought I was going to die alone in a miserable hole in Cartagena and I didn't want to die alone." Her long lashes swept down as she looked at her hands again. They were trembling and she clenched them so hard the knuckles turned white. "That's what I was flashing on. Being violently sick, all alone. Dying alone."

Jack swallowed but didn't allow anything at all to show on his face. Nothing. Because he felt such vast pity for the little girl who'd been left alone while so sick, and a murderous rage at her careless junkie parents who hadn't taken care of her at all.

The summer Jack had been eight, he and his parents

and Isabel—the twins hadn't been born yet—had taken a long vacation in Disneyworld and it had been sheer heaven. They'd all had a fabulous time. The memory of that summer still made him smile. He'd been loved and protected when he was a little kid. He'd lived in a bubble of happiness all his childhood, looked over by loving parents.

It had never occurred to him that not everyone's life was like that and he doubted he'd have understood it at the age of eight.

He'd had no idea of what the world was like and by the time he discovered it was full of fuckheads who liked inflicting pain and chaos, he was a man, and he'd started extensive training to handle them.

Not eight years old like Summer had been, helpless and vulnerable and abandoned. Nearly dying on her own in a foreign country would have been an imprinting experience—something that colored the rest of her days.

He understood completely how she flashed on that experience.

This was a woman who'd known adversity as a little girl beyond anything he'd ever had to experience. And now someone was after her.

Whoever these fuckers were—and he suspected the DD of the CIA, among others—they weren't going to touch Summer. He was going to make sure of that. He was going to stick by her side and he was going to take her away to the safest place he could think of.

And then he and Nick and the FBI and the guys at ASI were going to go on the attack.

"I'm sorry you had to go through that," he said quietly and she nodded.

Now that he was close to the safe house, Jack made his usual rounds to check for tails. He drove three blocks in every direction, in a grid. Circled his block twice. And he was clean.

"We're here." He turned quickly into a little driveway then took a right under a canopy in the alleyway out back.

"Good thing." Summer picked up her purse from the footwell. Her movements were smoother now, hands no longer trembling. "You went around the block a couple of times. I thought maybe you were lost."

Lost. Jack *never* got lost. He was about to say so when he saw her smiling at him. A genuine smile. She was teasing him. He put on his seducer's voice, the one he hadn't used in years. "I always know where I'm going, darlin'. You can count on that. Stay here."

He rounded the big vehicle and opened her door. She'd been unsteady on her legs when she got in. She didn't seem to be unsteady now but…he wanted to help her down. He wanted that badly. He wanted his hands on her in the worst way. Layers of wanting. He wanted to make sure she wasn't trembling and was steady on her feet. He wanted to reassure her that he was there for her, in the most basic way there was—by physical touch. And he wanted his hands on her because he wanted her.

Not now, he told himself sternly. He'd learned to control his dick a long time ago. In college he'd been guided in most of his decisions by his dick, but that hadn't been him for a long time now. So this sudden lust in the middle of the most dangerous op of his life, with the greatest consequences, danger at every turn for Summer too—that was wrong.

It threw him off his stride. He'd been a top operator for Hugh because he was focused like a laser beam on the op, always. The people he loved—his family— were far away and safe and that always allowed him to be concentrated on the mission. He had no idea how his fellow Clandestine Service operators managed to focus when they had loved ones living in the same city.

Now Jack had a taste of that and he didn't like it. Didn't like being operational and looking after someone he cared about. It messed with his head, big time.

The sooner they got out of Dodge the better, because right now all he could think about was Summer's mouth and the feel of her beneath his hands. And memories of how sweet she'd been in bed filled his head so that he wasn't calculating how many traffic cams they'd passed, even in a SUV that wasn't being looked for. All he could do was keep his head low, Blake's Fedora hiding his features. Making sure Summer's face was covered, too.

This was amazingly stressful—hiding his tracks and hers while wanting her in his bed. She was a huge distraction and yet you'd have to get bolt cutters to separate him from her. She wasn't going anywhere without him right by her side.

Damn.

Jack opened the passenger side door. Man, he'd swiped a humongous SUV. He'd been able to put his boots on the ground no problem but Summer was much shorter than he was. She'd have to slide off the seat and hop down.

Well, there was an app for that.

"Lean forward," he ordered.

Jack had killed three of the four street lights at both

ends of the alleyway. It wasn't the kind of neighborhood where street lights were replaced often. Only one was working but it was enough to see the pale oval of her face inside the vehicle, light gray eyes almost glowing. She smiled faintly at him. She looked exactly like someone who was scared but was putting up a brave front.

His heart gave a huge thump in his chest.

She leaned forward until their faces were inches apart. He clasped her small waist through enough material to fashion a yurt and lifted her out and down, telling himself to let go of her once her feet hit the ground.

The entire world seemed to have stopped. The blustery wind that had shaken the tree branches had stopped, or at least here in the back alley they were sheltered from the wind. A full moon was rising above the rooftops of the buildings around them, pure silver magic.

Jack totally lost his situational awareness. He was aware of absolutely nothing but Summer as he stood there, hands still around her waist, so close he could feel her breathing. The only sound he heard was the roaring in his ears.

His eyes became heavy and hers did, too. He was bending down and she was stretching up when a loud clatter sounded behind him and he was wrenched back to where he was and why.

He was behind his safe house with Summer, who had narrowly missed dying the most atrocious death possible thanks to the fact that she was with him. He had to yank his head out of his ass, and get them inside pronto. Some very bad guys, with an agenda so huge one death among so many would mean nothing to them, were after her. And him, too. Only he'd been trained hard to win in scenarios like this. Summer hadn't. Her bulwark against danger was him.

And he was an idiot who'd actually contemplated standing outside kissing her. And fuck him if it *still* didn't seem like a really good idea.

Another clatter and he moved forward, taking her elbow.

"Stray dogs?" Summer asked. She was keeping pace with him. Good girl.

"Hmm." Knowing the neighborhood, it was more likely rats, but he didn't say that. He concentrated on getting them inside as quickly and quietly as possible. There was a flimsy gate that wasn't at all as flimsy as it looked. Actually, it was made of steel with a titanium core. It had a print-activated keypad that got them quickly into the backyard. Jack pushed the gate behind him and heard the soft snick of a well-machined lock close behind them.

The back door was much harder than it looked, too. Again, a thumbprint activated coded keypad to open the door.

The small backyard was bristling with hidden sensors including IR, motion sensors, audio sensors. Only blank brick walls surrounded the yard. At the push of a button, a covering that mimicked a dirt yard would stretch out from side to side and from the back wall to the gate. If he needed to be shielded from a drone or a satellite, all he had to do was push that button.

Hugh had chosen the safe house very well, but then he'd been a master of the game. For a second, Jack had a pang of pain in his chest. The fuckers after him had taken his family and the man who'd been like a second father to him.

Well, they weren't going to get him and *by God* they weren't going to get Summer.

Inside, Jack helped Summer shed Hector's heavy overcoat and her own coat and helped her unwind the long scarf. He took his stolen overcoat and his own coat off and hung everything in the hallway closet.

His mom had drilled neatness in him but he also couldn't stand the thought of being cooped up in a small apartment that looked like weasels nested there. He'd spent way too much time here over the past six months. If he didn't keep the space clean he'd go crazy.

Crazier.

It wasn't nice like Summer's apartment was, but it was okay. If you squinted.

"It's not that bad," Summer said, turning around. Surprise was in her voice.

"What were you expecting?" Jack asked. "Animal house?"

She sketched a smile. "Not quite. But in thrillers, safe houses are stacked high with fast food and pizza boxes and empty beer bottles and they smell like a zoo." She sniffed. "Doesn't smell like a zoo, doesn't smell of anything, really."

Jack shrugged. "Yeah. I try to keep it livable."

He tried to look at the space through her eyes. You could take the whole thing in at a glance. Living room, with round dining table near the kitchenette. Two other doors. One door open into the bedroom—thank God he'd made the bed—the other door closed. The bathroom.

It was a far cry from his family home, a sprawling

two hundred-year-old complex on two acres of land-scaped grounds. His mom had turned it into a showcase and he'd taken it entirely for granted until he'd come home for the first time from college and realized how beautiful his home was.

It had been lost after the Massacre. Yet another thing Hector Blake had taken from him.

"You hungry?" he asked.

Summer turned around, wide-eyed. "You cook?"

Jack lifted a corner of his mouth at her expression. "You don't have to make it sound like rocket science, beyond my ability. Though, to be frank, I actually *don't* cook. But there's an excellent deli around the corner. And I happen to have four big pastrami on rye sand-wiches I can nuke. And some beers in the fridge. You game?"

"God, yes," she breathed. "I'm starving."

"Danger will do that." Jack sat her down at the round dining table, grateful that he'd swiped off the crumbs from that morning's bagel. Max's pastramis on rye were a wonder to behold. He put two huge sandwiches on a platter, stuck it in the microwave, put two plates on the table, two glasses, two napkins and for Sum-mer a knife and fork if she wanted it. Personally, Jack wouldn't let a knife and fork touch Max's masterpiece.

When the microwave dinged he took the steaming platter and put one huge sandwich on Summer's plate, the other on his. He'd nuke the remaining two when they'd finished these.

"Wow." Summer lifted her eyes from the monster sandwich, filled with two inches of juicy, thinly sliced pastrami. "Looks good. Looks gargantuan."

Jack wrapped a napkin around his and brought his

pastrami to his nose and closed his eyes. It smelled as heavenly as it always did. "Dig in."

Summer used her napkin to hold the sandwich, too, and took a huge bite. Meat juice spilled down her chin and she laughed.

Jack reached out and wiped her chin. "Good, isn't it?"

Her mouth was so full she just nodded. Swallowed. "God. Fantastic."

He finished his second sandwich a little before she did, but it was close.

"Have a pickle." Jack held a dill pickle spear in front of her mouth and she took a big bite out of it.

For some crazy reason, it gave him enormous pleasure to feed her. She'd had nothing but shocks since he'd showed up in her apartment. In the time since he'd inserted himself back into her life, she'd lost her apartment and car and, for the time being, her job. Crazy danger had attached itself to the both of them. They were on the run and God only knew for how long. Jack had been investigating the Massacre for six months and so far hadn't made much headway.

It might be possible that her life would be put on hold for six months, too. Longer. Maybe forever. It was entirely possible that life as she knew it was over.

He represented nothing but pain and loss for her.

So, by God, feeding her felt really good. Just like it felt really good watching a little color return to her face, and a half smile form. She had a naturally serious face but her smile could light up a room. He wanted to see her smile. He wanted that a lot.

"More," he said and held the spear to her mouth again.

She took a big bite out of it and as he watched her luscious mouth open and close over the pickle spear, his dick gave a hard kick in his pants.

Could she feel it? Did his dick send out a disturbance in the air? Because she swallowed and stared at him, mouth a little O.

"You're aroused." It wasn't a question.

Jack stopped himself from glancing at his crotch. Christ, his crotch was under the table. How the hell could she tell? Did he have a light switching to red on his forehead?

But however she knew, she knew. It was pointless lying.

"Yeah." His voice was hoarse. "God yeah."

"You were aroused back in Hector's place."

He nodded. No use denying it. Was it vibrating?

Where was she going with this? Was it her way of showing him he was the lowest of the low? Here she was, running for her life and all he could think about was sex?

You haven't changed, she'd told him. But that was the thing. He *had*. He had changed. Getting a hard-on, thinking about sex while he was on an op, was definitely not like him. So okay, he'd felt temporarily safe in Hector's place and he knew this place was safe. He was not going to get a hard-on out on the streets or in a public place. But he had major wood now.

His dick had reverted back to adolescence, when it had a mind of its own.

Was he making her uncomfortable? Was he being a dick? Was his dick being a dick?

He opened his mouth to apologize and she said, "Okay."

His mouth closed with a snap. *Did she just say what he thought she said?*

"Okay?" he echoed. Okay what? Because it couldn't be—

Summer stood up, gestured with her head to the bedroom. "I'm incredibly tense and a little bit scared and I think sex would loosen me up. I remember sex with you and it was fun and I think I could use a little of that right now." She searched his eyes. "But here's the deal. It's sex and nothing else. I don't expect anything from you and you don't expect anything from me. We're thrown together right now and I'm hoping to get a major story from all of this. So we have a little fun together but it won't be more than that."

Jack stood absolutely still. He had no idea how to answer all that. The old Jack, his asinine adolescent self would have shouted *hell yes!* Because no-strings sex was every teenage boy's dream. Quick roll in the hay, out of bed, out of mind.

But he wasn't the old Jack and he knew absolutely that he couldn't do what she asked. He couldn't keep himself separate from his emotions. Couldn't fuck her and walk away with a wave. Couldn't do it.

It had been a long time since he liked anonymous hookups. Sex with someone you cared nothing about was fake. Like eating cardboard food when you were hungry. He wasn't a walking sack of hormones like back in the day. He was a person. Not a dick with extraneous meat around it.

He liked Summer. He more than liked Summer. He'd found, to his vast surprise, that there was a Summer-shaped hole inside him and she was filling it up just fine. She was beautiful, fascinating, brave, smart.

She was everything he could ever want in a woman. He didn't want to jeopardize a future relationship just because she had an itch he could scratch.

No sir.

He was better than that and so was she. He wanted to have sex with Summer in the worst way, but he wanted sex and other things, too.

He opened his mouth to refuse because he wasn't that kind of guy, but what came out instead was, "Great. Let's go to bed."

SEVEN

KEARNS WOKE HIM UP at 1:00 a.m., which was vastly annoying. Springer's wife, Anna, had been nursing a cold and she needed her sleep.

Marcus Springer thumbed the ring to silent before answering, not bothering to keep the note of annoyance out of his voice.

"Yes," he said coldly, searching with his feet for the Prada slippers. Ah. He stood up, pulled the silk comforter over his sleeping wife's shoulders and went out into the hallway. "Is something wrong?"

"I waited for the target and finally left some packages for her to discover."

"And?"

Kearns was silent a moment. "I left a camera outside her door, and outside the front door of her building. Camouflaged. She did not return to the building, but…"

"But?" A cold feeling settled in his gut.

"Somehow someone tipped off the FBI. Their bio team is there right now. I'm watching them going in on my tablet."

They were very close to completion of the Plan. Springer had wanted to send a message. A strong one. *Don't mess with us. We are stronger than you and we will destroy you.*

"Any sign of the Redding woman?"

"No, sir. No sign."

"She's gone to ground."

"Yessir."

Springer thought. Redding was a good journalist, but she was a woman alone. She had no partner and she ran a business that was good but fragile, like all web-based businesses. Isolate and destroy, he thought.

But first intimidate. Strike terror in her heart.

"Blow up her house. Don't even try to make it look like an accident. Wherever she's gone to ground, she should know we have a scorched earth policy."

"Sir." No hesitation.

"Then destroy her office."

"Sir. I don't think *Area 8* has an office. I think it's headquartered at the woman's personal address."

"Even better. We'll take out her office and home at the same time."

"Yessir."

"Who are her co-workers?"

Springer heard tapping, then Kearns came back. "There are two people mentioned on the masthead besides Redding. The rest are freelancers."

"Take out the two on the masthead. Where are they?"

Another pause. "In the DC area. I'll take care of those. It'll be done as fast as possible."

"Excellent. Hide the bodies. They need to seem to have disappeared. It'll keep Redding anxious, off-balance." The Redding woman should know she had no place to turn to. They would come after her and she had no place to hide. She was a journalist, used to pressing forward, not hiding. How long could she evade them? "Full out effort on the Redding woman. Check city-wide cameras, check credit card use, check her usual haunts, run her to ground and eliminate. Are we clear?"

"Yessir," Kearns replied and signed off.

His team had access to vast resources and he could run this off the books almost forever. He didn't need forever. He just needed three more days and then utter chaos would rule.

No one would remember Summer Redding even existed.

SUMMER KNEW EXACTLY what she was doing. She was going to have blow-your-mind sex with a guy she knew could provide it. Guaranteed. Unless, of course, her memory was off and it had been perfectly normal sex, only she didn't know that at the time, being so new to sex and all.

But the fact was, no other man had come close to giving her what Jack gave her.

No other man had dumped her like that, either. She'd chosen very carefully after Jack and no one dumped her. She'd never been the dumpee ever again. She was the one who dumped, as carefully and gently as she could.

Red-hot sex was what she needed right now. She needed it to wipe all this destruction from her mind. She knew precisely what she needed and the only man in the world guaranteed to give it to her was right here, ready and willing, to judge by the erection in his pants, so what were they waiting for?

One thing she knew—she didn't want an aftermath. She didn't want anything from Jack other than a good time in bed that would make her feel strong again, not a weak cold thing. She didn't want cuddles or words of devotion.

She'd had plenty of that the first time around. And then he'd disappeared in a puff of smoke and left her broken-hearted.

Not this time. She was an entirely different person now. Much less vulnerable. Not vulnerable at all, actually. She didn't want him forever, she just wanted him right now, to get rid of this tension that was humming all through her body.

She didn't want *anyone* for forever. Not doing that. The only couple she'd ever seen that wasn't sick or temporary or had an expiration date stamped on their foreheads had been the Delvauxes. Jack's parents. They'd been a *couple*. A real one. Two people who loved each other and shared their lives. But other than them, Summer hadn't seen anything that really tempted her out of her single state.

Why would she give up her life? She had a great apartment, a great job, great friends.

Of course—the apartment was gone and probably *Area 8* too, since she couldn't just surface and report things, carry on as if nothing happened. Also—it was entirely possible the shadowy forces after her would go after her friends, too, so she needed to stay off the grid.

With the only other person she knew who was off the grid. Jack.

He stood there watching her as she worked it all out in her head.

"Well?" He cocked his head, studying her.

"Well, what?" Those blue eyes, sharp as a laser... they made her feel almost too seen. Too understood.

"We're going to have sex. I'm down with that. But

there seem to be ground rules. No expectations, no happily ever after. Is kissing allowed? Or are we just going to grind genitals together?"

Summer drew herself up in outrage. "That's a terrible thing to say!"

Jack reached out a long finger, drew it slowly down her cheek. Over her jaw, down her neck, reaching under her shirt with the back of his finger. It made her shiver.

"I didn't say that, sweetheart, you did. Me? I'd be perfectly happy having sex the old-fashioned way. Kissing, face to face, cuddling afterward. You're the one who's setting boundaries."

He was putting words in her mouth. Her teeth ground. "I wasn't setting boundaries for sex itself! I was setting—" She drew in a deep breath, let it out in a long, controlled stream. Good yoga technique for stress. "I was setting emotional boundaries. Keeping our expectations in line. And I was also saying that sex does not imply a relationship. That's something you can relate to. You never seemed too keen on sticking around, if I recall."

Jack's face suddenly hardened. It was amazing to see. He dropped ten years when he teased her, clearly thinking about the sex. Returning to the younger Jack who roped women in by the handful, delighted them, then let them loose again into the wild. They staggered back out into the sun, blinded by pleasure, wishing it could have lasted longer.

This Jack was…something else. Someone else. Harder and more focused. Still sexy but in an overpowering way, not a seductive way.

"Wait," he said. He still had his finger inside her open shirt, but it was to hold her shirt, just in case she wanted to bolt. "Let's get one thing straight here. I don't care what goes on in that complicated and beautiful head of yours. Tell yourself anything you want to. But the fact is that after we have sex on that bed in there" —he jerked his head toward his bedroom—"you are not getting up and leaving. And neither am I. No way. Don't even think about it. You were in shock and didn't hear what I said back at Blake's place. You are sticking close to me and tomorrow we're going to go to the safest place I can think of, where we will have a team around us. Portland."

Her jaw dropped. "What?"

"Tomorrow we're going to Portland, Oregon. I told you my sister has fallen in love with a former Navy SEAL. He works for a company made up of former Navy SEALS. It's the coolest company on earth, made up of super competent people and if we come out of this alive, I might go to work for them, too. They're the best of the best. There are two things here you can take to the bank. Whatever happens to me, you are going to survive. These guys will keep you safe. And so will I. So you can toss me away like a used Kleenex after sex if you want, but you will still be sticking close to me. And by close I mean *close* close. Like glued together."

Summer was trying to put this together. While trying to handle in her head the idea of having hot sex with Jack and then not walking away. Having hot sex with Jack and sticking *close* close to him. She latched on to the only thing that sounded rational. "We're going to Portland? But how? Won't they be watching airports?"

"Yes. ASI, the company, will be sending a private plane. There will be no record of us crossing the country, arriving in Portland. And I'll make sure no cameras catch us."

"But—but—" Summer's head was still whirling. It was really hard to focus. The idea of sex with Jack on that shadowy bed she could see through the bedroom door was like a black hole, bending all light and reason into it so that there was no room for anything else. "But I have a business to run! People depend on me."

Jack sighed and his face took on a sad cast. He just looked at her and she could almost see the wheels spinning. He clasped the back of her neck, kissed her cheek, then leaned his forehead against hers. If she thought they were going to start having hot sex right now, she was wrong.

He was close to her, his forehead against hers as if he could transfer his thoughts into her head. This wasn't sex. This was communion.

"Sweetheart," he said, then stopped.

His eyes were fixed on hers and all she saw was sadness in their blue depths.

"What?" she whispered. What could make a man who'd seen his family slaughtered, his boss killed, who'd been on the run for the past six months look that sad? She'd have thought all the sadness had been knocked out of him.

"Summer, I don't know how to tell you this, but someone has to. *Area 8* is gone."

It was like an electric jolt to the system. She shook, stood straight, moving away from Jack. "What? *Area 8* is *gone*? What does that even mean? I mean, I know I'm not going to post anything today, maybe not this week, but…gone?"

Area 8? Her brainchild? The thing she'd dedicated

years of incredibly hard work to? It couldn't disappear overnight.

Jack pulled her in his arms. Instinctively, she turned her head so her ear was against his chest. He rested his cheek on the top of her head. "Think about it, Summer. These people have somehow latched on to you. They think that you know something that can hurt them and they are scared of you. Further, you personally have one of the biggest sounding boards in the US. Everyone who is anyone reads *Area 8* and your articles are picked up by major news services and a million bloggers. Anything you reveal would go viral in a minute and they know that. Not only that. Anything you post will be proof that you are *alive* and about and investigating. You already have a target on your back. This will make that target big and red. Right now, you have disappeared. Nobody knows what happened to you. For all that these guys know, you inhaled the sarin and got sick and died somewhere else. They don't know if you are alive or dead and that's how it's going to stay."

Jack pulled away for a second, looking down at her, his face fierce.

Very little of what he was saying penetrated. All she could think about was the death of *Area 8*. Her baby. What she'd dedicated her life to.

Jack's face changed, from fierce to something else. "Ah, honey." He embraced her again. Held her tightly, one arm around her shoulders, another around her waist, keeping her close. "I'm so sorry," he whispered.

Summer needed him. That deep cold that came from somewhere within her, not the outside temperature, was back. Inside she was freezing, even her bones felt chilled. She clung to Jack who seemed to be the only source of heat in the entire world.

The walls tilted, the ceiling moved. Jack was carrying her into the bedroom and she turned in his arms, burying her face against his neck. His entire apartment was completely quiet, a hush that seemed to extend all over the world. No sounds from outside penetrated, it was just the two of them. Their breathing—his calm, hers harsh. She was seconds from bursting into tears and tried desperately to rein herself in.

Summer didn't cry. She never cried. Tears had never served her as a child, they only alienated her parents. She'd learned never to cry at such a young age it was part of her, like her hair or eye color.

She wasn't crying now. She couldn't cry, she didn't know how. Water was leaking from her eyes, that was all. She swiped her face against Jack's tee, which looked dirty but didn't smell dirty. He reached his bedroom and gently put her on her feet. Summer kept her face averted, and he didn't try to turn it.

His bedroom looked like the rest of the house—plain, not attractive, but not dirty.

Summer shivered again. She needed heat. The closest source was Jack and the amazing sex she knew for a fact he could provide. The cold was eating her up. Though her muscles felt stiff, like she'd been out in a snowstorm, she threw her arms around his neck, lifted on her toes and kissed Jack on the mouth. She missed.

He was so freaking tall. He hadn't been quite this tall in college. She distinctly remembered having to reach up but not having to stand on tip-toe. Well, if she had to... She rose on her toes.

Her kiss landed awkwardly again, on the side of his

mouth. But that wasn't what she wanted. She wanted one of those amazing kisses you could sink into, lavish and luscious, open-mouthed, tongues touching. Oh yeah. That kind.

She opened her mouth and moved greedily toward his. He opened and yes, there it was. That kind of kiss. Pure heat bloomed in her mouth and she wanted it all, now. All that heat, against her bare skin, chest to breasts, feeling his heavy weight on hers, anchoring her, his sex in hers, moving hard, generating friction. Giving her an orgasm that would nearly knock her out.

He could do it. He'd done it before.

With a wordless sound, Summer wrapped her arms around Jack's neck and melted into the kiss which was spreading heat throughout her body.

She could feel Jack's muscles against the inside of her arms, against her breasts. He'd always been muscular but these muscles were a man's not a boy's. Hard, dense, fascinating. All that strength, all that heat—she needed it all next to her skin. She took her arms from around his neck—it felt almost painful not touching him—and with a shrug her blouse was on the floor. Then she scrabbled for the hooks at the back of her bra.

Oh *why* weren't her breasts smaller so she could go without a bra? And why hadn't she splurged on that La Perla bra that closed in front, that was all silk and frothy lace? Why had she opted for the plain cotton sports bra that closed in back?

She made a sound of disgust in her throat as the hooks stupidly refused to disentangle. Argh!

Jack lifted his head and looked down at her. He stilled her hands with his own, flattening them against her back. "Shh," he murmured. "There's no need to hurry."

"Yes," she said. "There is."

Jack made a sound that was like a laugh and it unnerved her. Angered her. Fine for him to say, to establish the pace. She was cold and hurting *now*. Needing heat *now*. Wanting sex *now*. As a matter of fact, if she could push a button and both of them could beam to the bed naked, him on top, inside her—well, she'd push that button in a heartbeat.

A slow undressing, gentle touches, foreplay. Summer didn't want any of that. She felt too shaky, out on a limb with nothing beneath her. Maybe if he took his time they'd have to…talk. She didn't want to talk, she didn't want anything but straight up sex. Right now.

Jack pulled her arms down to her sides and dipped his head to her neck. His lips and tongue moved up and down some kind of nerve there that only he had ever discovered. Goosebumps broke out all over her skin.

But his arms were not only holding her, they were holding her hands down. She couldn't move them. Summer tried, gently, to lift her arms to her back to attack the hateful hooks but she couldn't. Jack simply pressed a little harder against her arms. He wasn't using force. He didn't have to. He was so strong the weight of his arms kept hers down.

"Let go." Summer had never liked being held down. Jack knew that, damn him. "Let go of my arms."

"Shh," he said again. "I want to undo your bra. Will you let me?"

Summer shifted her weight from foot to foot. She felt…something. God only knew what. Like her body was swelling and her skin couldn't contain it. Itchy and scratchy and restless. She twitched herself away from Jack's mouth. He was kissing his way up and down her neck, and every single inch of the skin under his mouth burned.

But she didn't want seduction. She didn't want slow sighs and soft touches. She didn't want to think, she wanted only to feel and she wanted to feel him on her, in her, *right now.*

"Can I?" His teeth took just the slightest nip of her skin. Not pain, just a tiny little shock. "Can I take off your bra?"

"Only if you do it fast." Summer clenched her teeth. "And then you get naked fast."

"Tsk, tsk." Jack's voice was deep and lazy. The beast. "Such haste. Now why is that, I wonder?"

It was a miracle Summer didn't crack a tooth, she clenched her jaws so tightly. "I thought we agreed on sex. I didn't agree to spend hours standing in your bedroom."

"This *is* sex." Jack nipped her skin again and she shuddered, all through her body. Goosebumps rose on her skin. Surely, even in the penumbra, he could see them. "It's all part of one continuum."

"It is *not* part of a continuum." Summer was so frustrated she wanted to scream. His hand was hovering over her back, as if he couldn't quite figure out how to undo her bra. Jack Delvaux, who'd made bra unfastening an Olympic sport. "You know precisely what sex is and I want…"

Her voice died away as her bra fell and her naked breasts came against his chest. He had on a tee but the muscles underneath were ridged and she felt every one as he rubbed himself against her. She rubbed back, hungry for the contact, hungry for his warmth.

This wasn't the sex she wanted, but he was right— it was a form of sex. Particularly when Jack pulled off his tee and pulled her to him so tightly she could feel him breathing against her breasts. Skin to skin. What an amazing sensation. Heat skittered across the entire front of her body. His chest hair had thickened. He'd had a neat little vee of chest hair at twenty and now it covered his chest in a springy mat, from nipple to nipple right down to underneath his loose jeans waistband.

Below that was the biggest erection she'd ever felt, right there against her belly. Her nipples hardened with the abrasion against his chest hair. Her sex felt like a furnace. He thrust his hips against her, hard, and her womb clenched.

The prelude to an orgasm. Just from holding him bare-chested. They still had their pants on and she was about to come.

It was crazy, it was wonderful.

Every single problem seemed so far away, outside the miraculous things that were happening under her skin. The world was a few dark clouds on the horizon of an amazingly blue and bright sky. Hardly worth noticing while her body was singing with joy.

Why oh why didn't she have sex more often? What was wrong with her? Why had she forgotten how incredible it felt to have every single nerve ending on fire? Why did she deprive herself of this?

Jack was still working on her neck, every touch of teeth and tongue shooting sparks through her. Her neck muscles felt lax, unable to hold her head up. Her knees were about to go. She opened her mouth to say that they should get to the bed because she couldn't stand any longer, when Jack unzipped her pants, swiped his big hands over her hips and carried pants and panties down with them.

Awkward moment. Yeah, this was one of those awkward moments and maybe one of the reasons she didn't have much sex. All these fiddly things—getting undressed in an attractive way, not fumbling with your clothes, getting shoes or boots off while standing—that was why not many dates ended up in bed.

Awkward, embarrassing moments.

But it turned out not to be awkward or embarrassing at all. Somehow Jack had some magic wand, probably connected to his magic penis, that did everything for him. His mouth left her neck for about two seconds as he kneeled and then voilà! Like magic. There she was, naked, in his arms. He was somehow naked, too. Nothing awkward or embarrassing about it.

Everything about him was so exciting. Impossibly broad shoulders, smooth skin over hard muscle...

Not so smooth skin.

Her fingertips wandered over his back and oh, God. He was covered in scars. Raised keloid tissue over his rib cage, two round puckered scars that could only be—

She pulled away, looked up into his face.

His expression was harsh, closed. "They bother you?"

"The scars? No. Well, actually yes. There must have been a lot of pain attached to these." There was distance now between them and even in the semi darkness, Summer could see more scars on his chest. Two that must be the entry wounds to the puckered round scars she felt along his back. And another long, raised scar with staple stitches along it. She hadn't seen scars like that since her childhood in third world countries. Nowadays no scars left stitch marks like that.

It must have been a field dressing.

For a second she mourned the old Jack, who'd been scarless, inside and out. Such a happy golden boy, to whom nothing bad had ever happened, and nothing ever would. The Jack that had been blessed by fate.

This Jack was scarred, darker, tougher. He'd been to war.

Jack shrugged one massive shoulder. He gave a small smile. "If the scars don't bother you, then can we get back to what we were doing before?"

Oh God. Just like that, her body simply lit up. Her spirit had darkened feeling Jack's scars, knowing how much pain each one represented. But he was revved and whoa, so was she. Sorrow and darkness and the past simply vanished, like the mist at morning. What was left was fierce heat and electric currents running over her skin. What was left was hard, aching breasts and wet heat between her thighs.

"That's my girl," Jack murmured and bent to her neck again, licking behind her ear. Even Summer could hear her breath coming more harshly.

"I didn't say a word," she protested, but her voice came out weak and thready.

"You don't need to say anything, darlin'. Your body talks for you. It's tellin' me what ah need to know."

She sighed heavily. In bed, Jack slipped naturally into a soft southern accent and it had excited her enormously. She assumed that it came from his mother, Mary, who'd been from South Carolina and had spoken with a honeyed southern accent. Jack obviously equated affection with that accent and it simply spilled out of him. It had turned her on like a light bulb.

Still did, apparently, because her sex clenched again. Just from his tone.

"What's my body telling you?" Summer tilted her head so he could kiss that special spot where her neck met her shoulder. *Yes*, she thought. *That one.*

"It's telling me exactly where you like to be kissed." Jack's mouth moved up to just under her jawline and nipped again. She jumped as an electric current shot through her body.

"It's telling me exactly where you like to be touched." Jack's mouth settled over hers, tongue licking her lips until she opened for him. One big hand smoothed its way over her back, down over her buttocks, down, down…

With his hand he silently told her to widen her stance and she opened her legs and oh my God! His fingers found her slick heat and she shuddered. He touched her just so. A Goldilocks touch. Not too hard and not too soft and oh! A probing finger rubbed over her clitoris then dipped inside her heat and she clenched. She clenched with her entire lower body, it was so intense.

She opened her mouth under his and gasped.

"That's my girl," Jack murmured.

"Jack," she whispered.

"Darlin'," he whispered back.

Something came from her throat and though it was impossible, it actually sounded like a growl. Jack chuckled.

He was *chuckling*! It meant he was in control while she was losing hers. That was wrong. They had to be on equal footing here.

She brought his head down to hers for a fierce, aggressive kiss, tongue licking into his mouth, teeth nipping at his lower lip. She rolled her hips against him and felt his penis swell.

Jack made a noise in the back of his throat, stepped to the bed. Three steps. Her legs followed his, as if they were dancing. The backs of her knees hit the bed, then her back and Jack covered her. He was amazingly heavy but it didn't bother her, all that heat and power felt so delicious. His mouth hadn't left hers, her arms hadn't left his shoulders.

"Open your legs," he whispered hoarsely.

Oh yeah. Her legs slid apart quickly, because she needed him like she needed air. A big hand reached down to her sex and, like before, circled her, rubbing her at the top of her sex, exactly at the pleasure point.

She'd had clumsy lovers who pressed too hard there, until it became almost painful. They didn't understand women's bodies, that a touch had to be just right. The perfect amount of pressure, but never too much.

Jack understood a woman's body. Though his hand was huge, strong and had become rough with calluses, his touch was as delicate as could be. He circled her slowly and her thighs began to tremble, the prelude to orgasm. Just from his touch.

She could feel him, hot, heavy, swollen, against her thigh. When she contracted around his finger, his penis moved against her thigh, swelling even further.

The last time she'd been this excited had been with Jack. That Jack had filled her with joy. This Jack filled her with heat, heat that prickled up and down her spine, pooled between her legs.

She pressed upward with her hips and Jack understood. He could read a woman's body like other men read books. He lifted his head and looked down at her. They were so close she could feel his breath wash over her face.

Jack had always looked so happy when making love, big grin on that beautiful face. Right now he wasn't grinning, he looked serious, eyes narrowed as they watched hers. He shifted his hips until they were in alignment with hers and held her open for him with two fingers. She felt the big head of his penis against her and he was as hot as molten steel. Maybe they would blow up where they were touching, it felt that explosive.

Summer placed her open hand on his hard buttock and pressed. She didn't have the words to say it. There was no breath in her lungs, her throat was too tight for words. But the pressure of her hand was enough. She could feel his buttocks tighten as he filled her slowly, watching her face so carefully.

His look was intense as his body filled hers. She closed her eyes because the ferocity of his gaze was simply too much, and because she had to concentrate on him inside her, at last.

So hot, so hard, so…right. It was like a homecoming, something she'd wanted, missed for so long. Her legs rose, wrapped around him as tightly as her arms around his shoulders as she savored a connection that was a missing piece of her. As if she'd been half dead and was coming back to life.

Jack withdrew slowly, pushed back in, and it was sheer bliss, her body had missed this, she'd missed *him* so very much. To her horror, tears sprang to her eyes but her body saved her in the nick of time. She tipped over into orgasm and tears were perfectly normal while climaxing.

And she could pretend it was just sex instead of her heart opening to Jack Delvaux once more.

EIGHT

JACK MOVED HIS hand under the covers, expecting to feel warm woman and felt cool sheet instead. Moment of cognitive dissonance here because he knew for a fact that he should be finding a warm woman.

An amazing warm woman.

A woman he'd spent the night loving.

Last night he had come alive in her arms. The memory of his lost family, the last painfully lonely six months with everyone thinking he was dead—that had faded into the background instead of being the fabric of his days.

There wasn't even a lingering warmth, so Summer had gotten out of bed some time ago. There was a slight noise from the kitchen. Aha.

Smart CIA agent, highly trained, lots of field experience. He could guess where she was.

Jack rolled out of bed and was so eager to see her, hold her, he was halfway across the bedroom before he realized he was naked and his eagerness to see her was stiffly waving from his groin.

Better cover up. He didn't want to. He wanted to walk in, grab her—if he could grab a cup of coffee too that wouldn't be too shabby—and carry her right back to bed. He could get her aroused fast because he'd made a study of Summer last night. Pilots had check lists and now he had a Summer check list before take off.

Neck. Mouth. Neck again. Breasts. Both of them. Not at the same time. Hands caressing her between her legs.

That did it. If only they could go back to bed, spend the day in bed together. God.

It had been so fucking *long* since Jack had had a woman in his bed. And even longer where the woman was so sweet and soft and giving. So long ago he couldn't even remember. Maybe never.

Maybe he'd never had a woman like Summer in his bed before.

That exquisite sense of closeness when he'd been so freaking lonely. Lost and alone with his grief over the loss of his family. Night after night alone in this barren place, knowing he was alive only by the dull beat of his heart. Mourning his losses, trying to find the strength to go out the next day in search of clues, risking discovery, and finding very little. Doing that over and over again.

He'd had to let his little sister, Isabel, think he was dead. That was the hardest thing of all, but it had had to be done. Isabel wore her heart on her sleeve. She would have been totally incapable of pretending her brother was dead if she knew he was alive.

Such a horrible, heartbreaking six months.

Last night he had come alive. He wanted more of what he'd just tasted last night. More of it right now, more of it in the future. A lot more of it in the future. Oh yeah.

They were a little stretched for time, he thought, as he pulled a pair of pajama bottoms from the single chair in the room. He sniffed the crotch because, well, he did his laundry, but he'd been a bit lax lately. But yeah, it passed the sniff test.

At some point, the ASI jet would arrive and they'd have to be there on the tarmac, unrecognizable, operational. There wasn't that much time. But if they could grab a little quickie...hmm.

Ordinarily Jack didn't like quickies. He liked to take his time, enjoy the journey. They would have plenty of time in the future, because Summer was definitely going to stick around—or rather he was going to stick around her—so there'd be lots of opportunities to fool around.

But he'd tasted her and he wanted more, right now, a little joy after a long, sad barren stretch, so if he could get her to agree to a fast little roll in the hay...

"Hey." Jack stopped on the bedroom threshold and watched as Summer rinsed a cup in the sink. The smell of his crappy coffee filled the air. Another steaming cup stood on the counter. She was fully dressed. "Thanks for making coffee." *Let me drink my cup and let's go back to bed and do some more of those amazing things.* It was on the tip of his tongue and he was just about to say it when Summer turned slowly around and *uh-oh*.

His dick deflated almost instantly.

That was not a look conducive to sex he was seeing on her beautiful face. She was cool, completely unreadable, pale-gray eyes as expressionless as marbles.

Jack hadn't really thought much beyond wanting her back in his bed. "Hi, uh." His mind whirred uselessly. "Sorry there isn't much for breakfast." He scratched the back of his neck.

"There isn't anything for breakfast," Summer answered coolly. "Except this terrible coffee. I made you a cup, though." She gestured to the counter. Jack knew for a fact that it was gray and unappetizing.

She was standing straight, very stiff, nearly every line in her body a big back-off sign.

There were all sorts of things Jack could do or say. He could offer to suit up in his homeless kit and go get some bagels at the corner deli, which wasn't really around the corner but four blocks away. He could run it fast, get back here in ten minutes.

He could talk logistics, using his low and gentle voice. Outline their day, the trip to Portland, touching her, smiling, getting her used to his touch again.

He didn't do any of that. Seeing her so stiff and cold terrified him. His feet carried him across the room before he could stop them and he gathered her in his arms and held on tightly, as if they were in a storm.

He couldn't stand that look on her face, simply couldn't go there. He wanted his Summer back, the Summer who'd smiled up at him as he was inside her, the one who kissed him so fiercely, the one who held him so tightly, the one who didn't make him feel so alone in the world.

She stood stiffly in his embrace but he wasn't backing away. No. He was going to hold her forever, if he had to. Certainly until he could feel the coldness melt, the stiffness soften.

Jack buried his face in her neck. He needed her to embrace him, smile at him. Together with Isabel, Summer was the only person on earth he cared about. He couldn't lose her.

He kissed her neck. "Don't pull away from me," he

said, his voice muffled against her skin. "I couldn't bear it."

Summer's arms came up slowly, clutched his back. *Yes, darlin', cling to me because I sure as hell am clinging to you.*

They stood there, swaying in the dim morning light. "Last night was amazing," he said. Just in case she hadn't gotten the memo. He waited for her to say something, but she didn't. It hurt his pride, but he finally said the words. "Was it amazing for you?"

He felt more than saw her smile. "Really, Jack? You're really asking me this?"

Jack nodded against her neck. Kissed it. He was going to ruthlessly use every trick in the book. "I have to know."

Summer sighed. She sounded exasperated, but her body language had changed. Jack spoke woman very well. He understood the body language of women. Back in the day he'd been a master. He was no longer fluent but he was still okay. Summer's back was no longer stiff and her tense muscles had relaxed.

"It was fine." He could practically hear her eyes roll in her head.

"More than fine," he said, nudging her with his shoulder.

Another big sigh. "Fine. More than fine. Are you happy now?"

"Sort of." Jack straightened, looked down at her lovely face. Some color was back in her cheeks and though she looked annoyed, annoyed was much better than that blank, cold façade. "I'd give anything to get back in that bed again but I think we're going to have to get going."

She gave a faint smile. "You always were insatiable."

He clenched his jaws. "Is that what you think this is about?" He waved a finger between them. "Me getting as much fucking as possible?" He was deliberately crude to hide the fact that he was genuinely hurt.

Horribly, she looked blank. Now, *that* hurt. "Well, yeah. I mean you'd use any possibility to go to bed. And my roommate said—"

She broke off, looked to the side.

Oh God. Jack barely remembered her roommate. Some chick with long brown hair. He couldn't even remember her name. He did remember Summer's blank look when he showed up at the dorm room to take the roommate out and not her.

Jack looked her straight in the eyes. "I'm sorry I hurt you. More sorry than I can say. All I can tell you is that the Jack who was such a dick is gone. Dead and buried. I don't know what he was thinking. Not much, apparently. He sure wasn't thinking with his big head. But this Jack—" He thumped himself in the chest hard enough to hurt. He welcomed the little bite of pain. "This Jack thinks with his big head and with his heart. This Jack hasn't had sex in more time than I care to think about. These past six months were sexless for security reasons. But I hadn't had sex in a long time before that because there wasn't anyone I cared about. I had sex last night because I cared about you. Care about you. What I feel is real and what we had last night was real and I'm not letting it go. Not letting you go."

She stared at him while he babbled, utterly astonished. Jack shook her a little by the shoulders.

"Are we clear on this?"

Summer nodded shakily.

This broke every single one of the relationship rules. Jack was showing his hand early, laying down his cards, each and every one. You don't do that. You showed your cards one by one, and only after your partner showed hers.

He didn't give a fuck for the rules.

Jack had spent the past fifteen years masking who he was. Showing a bland fake façade to the world, never ever revealing his true self. He'd been trained, and trained hard, to do it. It was the essence of his job, and he'd been really good at it.

At times, over the course of his career in the NCS, he'd wondered whether he could ever show his true self, ever again.

The answer was yes.

Jack opened himself up completely to Summer. He put a little distance between them so she could see him. Really see him. Every inch, from his face to his toes, including his slightly inflated ever-hopeful dick.

Everything he felt was right there. He'd been hopelessly lonely. Not just these past six nightmare months, but before, too. Lonely and dispirited and a little bit lost. When he'd seen Summer again, something had clicked for him. Just lit up something inside him and he recognized that he'd never forgotten her. He'd thrown something good away but he'd been young then. Hadn't understood what he'd had.

He understood it now.

"Look at me," he said. "Really look at me. See what I am now and not what I was then."

Summer understood exactly what he meant. And he realized she had always understood him. He could talk to her and not have to explain the subtext because she got it. Maybe because she was a journalist and sensitive to nuance, maybe because her horrible childhood had forced her to develop antennae, maybe they just vibrated on the same wavelength, but Summer got him.

"I'm looking," she said, gazing straight into his eyes.

"This is not like before. I'm not leaving you. As a matter of fact I'm going to stick to you like glue. You're going to be sick of me."

"Because I'm in danger." Her voice was flat.

"That, too. But I've been on protection detail before and this is different. You're in danger and I'm here to protect you, I'm here to make sure you come out of this intact. And you will, because anyone gunning for you will have to go through me. But most of all, when all of this is over and everyone who has to be dead is dead and everyone who has to be in jail is in jail, after that—I'm still going to stick to you like glue. We bonded last night."

"We had sex last night, sure," Summer said evenly.

"That wasn't sex."

She smiled for the first time. "Sure felt like sex."

"I mean, yes, it was sex, of course it was, but—" Jack's tongue got all tangled. He knew what he wanted to say but he didn't know the order. Or he didn't have the right words. Something was wrong. The things he wanted to say were…big. And let's face it—a little scary.

He opened his mouth again, hoping to not put his foot in it, when his cell pinged. Joe. Joe Harris. His sister's lover and the reason he could be across the country from Isabel. Isabel was safe. Joe was in love with his sister and he would protect her with his life. Had saved Isabel's life not long ago.

"Yo," Jack said, stepping slightly away from Summer.

They were in the middle of something really important, but he didn't mind the interruption. Gave him some time to work things out in his head before saying them to Summer.

"So the ASI plane should land in about an hour at Reagan. Can you and Summer get there unobserved?"

"Absolutely." Jack was already walking back into the bedroom. "We'll be there."

"Get to the general aviation section, I'll text you the plane tail number and the pilot's cell. Don't let anyone see you."

"Dude."

"Okay, okay. I've got Isabel on my back about this. Big time. I swear to God, Delvaux, if anything happens to you and Summer, my life won't be worth living, so make sure nothing does."

"Hen pecked," Jack said. "How does that feel?"

"Great. Love it. Food's definitely worth it. So we'll call while you're in the air. I've never met Summer but tell her she's got a lot of fans around here. Lots of admirers. And that we're all sorry about her place."

"Yeah." Jack scrabbled for his jeans. "Sarin's no joke."

"No. I mean the bombing."

"Wait." Jack froze. His eyes met Summer's, she'd followed him into the bedroom. She sensed something. "What is this about Summer's apartment?"

"Shit," Joe swore. "Don't tell me you don't know. That Nick didn't call you."

"Fuck." Jack had done the unthinkable last night. He'd toned down his cell ring so that if someone called in the middle of the night it wouldn't wake Summer. And then he'd fallen into a sex-induced coma and had missed a call. This was unforgiveable. "I didn't get the call. I'll ping Nick right now. So what happened?"

Summer was close by him, a hand on his arm. He put his hand over hers, watched her eyes.

"Her apartment was blown up around 4:00 a.m. Nick will tell you about it. Right now the best guess is a grenade launcher. The place looks like Beirut, man. Nick showed me pictures."

"Fuck." Summer was clutching his arm, staring up at him wide-eyed. "Talk to you from the plane then," he told Joe and thumbed off.

Fuck yes. He was getting Summer onto that plane as fast as humanly possible and he was keeping her in Portland, surrounded by the toughest guys he'd ever met, and their super friendly women, until every possible danger was over.

"What?" she whispered. "What about my apartment?"

"Gone. Bombed." Jack delivered the stark news and watched the blood drain from her face. "I'm so sorry, honey." He grabbed her hands, holding them tightly. She was shivering with shock. The intrusion, the discovery of sarin, dredging up horrible memories of being so sick in Cartagena, had been bad enough. This was much worse. "They're looking into it but the truth is—your place is gone."

"Gone," she whispered through stiff lips. Fuck. That lost, disoriented look was back. How many blows was one person supposed to handle? "Everything. Gone.

All my records, too. Luckily I keep everything in the cloud but now—"

"Now we're going to Portland," Jack said firmly. "Where you'll be safe."

"*Area 8*. What about *Area 8*? It just dies?"

"You're going to have to close up shop. I know what that means, believe me. I know how hard you must have worked to create it. But like I said, you have to stay off the grid for now. Whoever is orchestrating this has to think you're dead. We already talked about this."

"I am dead." Her voice was low and flat. "Or close to it."

"God no." Jack wrapped his arms around her and rocked her. They had to get going right now but he needed to comfort her. "Don't say that. Don't even think it. You're going to go underground and when you emerge, you'll be stronger than ever. And you're going to write articles that will make Woodward and Bernstein look like pikers. You're going to win the Pulitzer. Guaranteed. I promise you."

"The Pulitzer." He pulled back and saw that she was trying to smile. It was an awful effort and wasn't convincing but he was grateful she was trying.

"The Pulitzer," he nodded. "But for now we have to get going."

"Wait."

Jack felt urgency thrum through his veins. He was nearly vibrating with it. But he obediently stopped.

She was frowning. "Is there anyone who can check up on my staff? Find out if they're okay? Without letting them know that I'm alive?"

"Who are they? I'll get Nick on it as soon as we're airborne."

"Zac Burroughs and Marcie Thompson, they're based here in DC. Write the names down so you don't forget."

"I won't forget," Jack promised. He was used to memorizing eighteen digit codes. Two names were nothing. "Now let's get going."

Summer put on her coat and Hector's coat over it and started wrapping the scarf around her lower face.

"Forget that." Jack pulled out two full face helmets. "I've got something better."

Summer stared. "How are you going to drive with that thing on?"

Jack pulled his helmet on, pulled down the visor. His voice came out muffled as he fitted hers on. "We're not taking the SUV, we're taking something faster."

KEARNS PUT DOWN his newspaper for a second and watched the young man sitting next to the coffee shop's windows. Zac Burroughs. Young, trendy haircut. Shaved on one side, long on the other. Completely oblivious to the outside world, head totally inside his laptop. This was going to be easy.

Kearns was sitting on a bench across the street from the coffee shop. He'd been careful not to leave any prints and he'd take the newspaper with him. He hauled out his cell and pretended to be engaged in it. People read books on their cells, he knew. It wasn't hard to fake absorption. Kearns could see into the coffee shop and it was filled with people who were absorbed in their own stuff, no one was looking round.

There were also no security cams, which to Kearns meant the place didn't earn enough money to warrant being robbed.

Great.

Burroughs finally closed his laptop and got up. He didn't seem to be the kind to move fast, so Kearns gave him a big head start. When he got up, he put on his baseball cap with IR lights along the brim. Any security cams on the street would simply see a big blurred white dot instead of a face.

The target was walking along his street, with old growth trees whose roots were cracking the sidewalk. One building in three was abandoned. Zac lived in an old building six blocks down, at the end of the street— he was headed home. Home was the basement apartment. Kearns had checked.

Civilians were just clueless. It never failed to astonish Kearns. There was no way someone could follow him for six blocks without him being aware of it. He would be able to just clue in. Did soldiers develop some kind of sixth sense with all that intense training? Maybe subconsciously notice patterns that civilians didn't? Whatever it was, it sometimes seemed to him that civilians walked around with PREY tattooed on their foreheads.

There was no need to hurry. Kearns kept back several hundred feet until Burroughs got to his block, then he started catching up with him. Countersurveillance training had taught him how to go fast without appearing to hurry. A lengthened stride, keeping the torso straight, not pumping his arms—anyone watching him would have to be an operator to notice that he had increased his speed by fifty per cent.

He caught up with Burroughs ten feet from the front gate. Keeping his head down, Kearns took the kid's arm in a friendly grip. Two old friends meeting up.

"Hey, Zac," he said with an easy smile.

The kid looked up at him, frowning, but not concerned yet. If Kearns had been his own age, the kid wouldn't even be frowning. He'd just assume that Kearns was part of that vast world of young people who congregated by the hundreds in bars and conventions. As it was, Kearns was visibly not of Burroughs' generation and warranted a frown.

"Hey," Burroughs answered cautiously, surreptitiously trying to pull away. Moron. The guy's arm was so thin, Kearns's hand fit around it. And as for pulling away—what Kearns felt beneath his fingers was soft, untoned muscle. Kearns's grip had been measured at almost two hundred pounds. Thompson had about as much chance of tearing himself away from Kearns as he had of flying to the moon.

"How you doing, man?" Kearns asked genially. He was gripping Burroughs' right arm with his left hand, while his right hand brought the jet syringe to the biceps and pressed the end, shooting five hundred milligrams of ketamine into his system, enough to induce what in clubs was called a k-hole, a ketamine high, strong enough to give the user an out of body experience.

The kid's stride broke, but Kearns shifted his hold, putting his left arm around Burroughs' shoulders and guiding him with his right. Kearns easily held Burroughs' entire weight up. An outsider would see only a friendly bro-embrace. Two old buddies meeting up. Conveniently, Burroughs had a set of keys in his front right pocket. Really fast, but with no jerky movements at all, Kearns had him through the gate, down the shallow concrete steps to the basement apartment and inside.

The apartment was small, messy. The military beat messiness out of you. Burroughs would have earned an extra 150 pushups for keeping his personal space like this. Not that he could have done them, not with that muscle tone.

Kearns dropped Burroughs immediately inside the door, pulled out a pair of latex gloves and went hunting for the right place to dump the body. He found it immediately. A small closet just off the kitchen. Perfect.

He'd come prepared. In his backpack was a small spray bottle of bleach and a folded body bag taken from a small town morgue.

Back at the entrance, he held one gloved hand over Burroughs' mouth and with the other he pinched the kid's nostrils shut. The kid was so deeply under, his autonomous nervous system didn't even kick in. In three minutes he was dead without having moved a muscle. Even better, his bowels and bladder didn't void. That was always messy.

Burroughs was so light it was easy to fit him into the body bag. Kearns sprayed bleach on Burroughs' upper body, zipped up the bag and shoved it into the closet. He took a tube out of his backpack—a new molecular binding agent that hardened into a glue stronger than concrete. He spread it around the jamb of the door, closed the door and squirted the binding agent into the keyhole.

Someone would have to take an axe to the door to get it open.

The underground apartment had a back door that gave out onto steps leading up to an alley. He walked out into the alley and would begin the long, slow series of evasive maneuvers to shake any possible tails.

One down, one to go.

d see her face. Then he placed h
er so it hung gondolier-style.
wo rules. Hang onto me tightly
I'm leaning. You got that?"
ght and lean when you lean,"
t mirrored visor nodded.
e bike from its resting place

NINE

SUMMER BLINKED AT the huge black monster of a motor-cycle then up at a Jack. Or at least at what she knew was behind that visor. The visor was tinted and not a trace of face was visible. Jack could just as well have been the headless horseman of Sleepy Hollow for all anyone could see. "We're going to ride that to the airport?"

He nodded. "You ever ridden a bike before?"

"Not like that. When I was eleven we lived in a village above Bangalore. Someone gave us an old scooter and I used to ride down to the city to do the shopping."

She didn't have to tell him why she was the one who had to ride the scooter. He knew. Her parents would have killed themselves riding a scooter when high. Which by the time she was eleven was basically all the time.

It was one of her few happy memories—putt-putting down the hillside into the cheerful chaos of the city then back with bags full of produce hanging perilously off the handlebars. After the first few trips, farmers along the way recognized her and waved. She'd felt free on that trip, free and unfettered.

This monstrous thing didn't smile at her and promise freedom. It snarled and promised broken bones.

Jack handed her the helmet and helped her fit it over her head. She saw out surprisingly well and knew for a fact no one could see her face. Then he placed her purse over her shoulder so it hung gondolier-style.

"There are two rules. Hang onto me tightly and lean in the direction I'm leaning. You got that?"

"Hang on tight and lean when you lean," she repeated and that mirrored visor nodded.

He rolled the bike from its resting place against a backyard wooden wall where it had been covered with a tarpaulin.

"Hop on." Jack's head was turned to her, that alien visage a little creepy. He held out a big hand and she lifted her leg and mounted the bike. Her legs didn't reach the ground but his did. She put her feet onto the footrests and put her arms around his lean waist. They sat there for a moment, as her arms expanded and contracted with each breath he took. He switched on the engine and she felt a powerful surge of energy between her thighs, a low thrumming almost sexual in its intensity. That insectoid head turned. "Hold on!"

She held on as Jack rolled them out of the asphalt square and onto the road. He kept it slow in the city and opened up on the Parkway, weaving in and out of traffic. He was going really fast. When she could open her eyes, Summer peeked at the speedometer and saw 110 mph. After which, she closed her eyes, lay her head against his back and simply hung on, matching his every move by feel and not by sight.

She opened her eyes when they crossed the Potomac on the Woodrow Wilson Bridge. He slowed down a little because there were gusty winds halfway across, but they crossed the bridge without incident and picked up speed again. They turned east but if they had continued, the road would have led straight to her apartment.

The apartment that was no longer there. Summer lifted her head from Jack's back and looked behind her, where her home would have been if she still had a home. Everything she owned had been in there. She actually hadn't owned that much. Summer had learned to travel light at such a young age it was ingrained now. But still. A Shaker chest of drawers she'd restored herself. A pretty Limoges tea set she'd given to herself at the first 100,000 views. Two watercolors by a college friend that hadn't been worth much on the open market but which she found incredibly pretty. Her clothes.

Most everything could be replaced and her most important possessions—her files—were in the cloud.

It made her sad to think that it had been so easy to wipe all her material possessions out. The past was gone and the future...the future seemed so dim, impenetrable.

Since she'd landed in the US and started attending Darby's School for Girls, she'd been very goal oriented. The next class, the next course—she'd followed her own internal plan and it had been crystal clear to her every step of the way. Now the future wasn't clear, it was murky and muddied.

The past gone and the future dim, what was left?

Jack lifted his hand from the handlebars and placed it over her hands clasped around his waist. He was wearing thick rider's gloves so of course she couldn't feel the touch of his skin, but crazily, she felt a little better.

Wherever she was going, she wasn't going alone. She had company for this part of the ride, anyway.

The turnoff to the airport was ahead of them and Jack banked sharply into the feed road. Instead of going to departures however, he took a side road that eventually took them to a section of the airport she'd never seen before. Jack drove right out onto the tarmac, past a couple of planes, until he stopped at the foot of a set of stairs leading up into the cabin of a small jet.

Jack cut the engine and the world went silent. She slid off the back and swayed for a second, her legs weak. It felt like she was still riding that monster bike. Jack held her hand tightly as he dismounted, providing stability. Summer started taking her helmet off when he stopped her hands, shook his head and motioned to the stairs.

It wasn't until they were in the actual airplane cabin, away from the door, that Jack took his helmet off, and lifted hers away. All the shades were down in the cabin, which was lit with soft lighting.

Two very serious-looking men emerged from the cockpit, dressed in short sleeved white shirts with wings on their collars. The older pilot shook Jack's hand. "Delvaux. Nice to hear the rumors of your death were wrong."

The other pilot shook Jack's hand, too, then shook hers. "Ma'am," they said in unison. At no point did they introduce themselves or call her by name.

The senior pilot turned to Jack. "We are here to pick up a Mr. and Mrs. Whitmore of Reston, Virginia. No trace of your presence is anywhere in writing. Nick said someone will pick the bike up and store it somewhere safe. Flying time will be six hours, we'll land at 2:00 p.m. local time. There's coffee and soft drinks, sandwiches and a cheese platter in the galley. Felicity assured us that inflight communications will be encrypted so feel free to contact anyone at ASI. If you get settled, we're scheduled for takeoff in ten minutes. Have a nice flight." He touched two fingers to his forehead and turned to her. "Ma'am."

She nodded. They disappeared into the cockpit as Jack took her elbow. "The plane has a small office, through that bulkhead door. Please sit down and prepare for takeoff."

Through the door was indeed an office. It looked expensive but not luxurious. A working office, not a sop to a rich businessman's ego. There were eight business class-sized seats in two rows of two side by side. The rest of the area was taken up by a miniature office setup—a round table with four seats around it, an array of laptops and tablets secured against the wall and plenty of wall sockets.

A bell sounded, the senior pilot's voice came on the air. "Prepare for takeoff."

Jack waved his hand at the seats. "Here. Aisle or window?"

"Window." Might as well watch as she flew away from her life. They sat down and Jack buckled her seat belt for her, as if she were ten years old. Summer didn't say anything because Jack seemed to derive some kind of pleasure from taking care of her, seeing to her comfort. She had no idea why, but hell, might as well roll with it. She wasn't often pampered.

He handed her a glass of sparkling water and sat down himself. "It could be champagne if you wanted. There's a bottle in the fridge."

She shook her head. "It's sort of a rule of mine. No champagne before noon." Summer smiled, drank the water and handed him back the empty glass. "Thanks."

The plane taxied for a few minutes, then rolled to a

stop at the head of the runway, waiting for permission for takeoff. When the plane started accelerating, Jack reached for her hand and held it tightly.

She stared out the window at the scenery streaking by and smiled. "Please tell me you're not afraid of flying."

"Nope. I've flown in a billion third world rustbuckets, with pilots who were either drunk or high or both. I'm not afraid of a Gulfstream and two former Air Force pilots. Just wanted to hold your hand."

He held it as they accelerated and leaped into the sky.

Summer enjoyed flying, being above the earth, away from its cares. Lately, she'd spent all her flights working, as she was always under deadline. She was going to do some work on this flight too, later, when the jumble in her head settled. There were three laptops available and she'd start putting order in her thoughts, start doing some research. There was no deadline. There were no deadlines at all, if *Area 8* was down.

Summer looked down as the plane banked over green suburban Virginia and lifted its way west. Below, at the very edge of visibility, was DC, with its monuments and power structures.

There was a very real possibility that people down there, Americans who were part of that power structure, were plotting to bring the country down. Undoubtedly they'd plotted the Washington Massacre. They were more dangerous, more insidious than the foreigners who hated America.

This was the most hated sin of all—treason. The enemy within. She had no concept of why they would do it. Maybe those most potent of temptations—money and power. It was inconceivable to her, but there it was. In her job she'd seen what a lot of people would do for money and power.

So many lives had been lost in the Washington Massacre—swept away in violence, like swatting flies. Her life had been lost, too, though her heart kept beating. As she watched DC fade into the distance, she realized she was flying away from her own life, left behind in dust and ashes, like her apartment. Her home, gone. *Area 8*, gone.

Zac and Marcie would be worried about her. The news of her apartment blowing up would break soon. When Zac and Marcie heard that, they'd try to contact her via the cellphone Jack had thrown into the Potomac as they crossed the Woodrow Wilson Bridge.

They'd be frantic, but she couldn't call them and reassure them.

Her life was unraveling so quickly, she couldn't hold the threads together.

Her old life was lost, tossed away by evil forces. What would the new life be like, standing in the rubble of her old one?

"Hey." Jack reached over with the hand not holding hers and turned her head away from the window and toward him. "It'll be okay."

"No," she smiled sadly. "It won't. But thanks for the thought."

His face was sober, serious. "We'll get them, Summer. Whatever it is that is happening, we'll stop it and catch the people behind it. These are *Americans*. Plotting against our country. They are going to be caught and tried for treason. The Director of the FBI has set up a secret task force, and we've got the guys of ASI. None better."

She tightened her hand around his. "Who are these people, anyway? ASI. I assume we're in their plane?"

"Yeah." His face lightened slightly. Clearly thinking about this ASI made him happy. "It's a security company set up and staffed mainly by former SEALs. We joked a lot about the snake-eaters in the Clandestine Service and we liked to think we were better, certainly sneakier, definitely better-looking and better-dressed, but the truth is, SEALs are the best of the best. The company was founded by former Commander John Huntington and former Senior Chief Douglas Kowalski. They were famous for getting the job done, back in the day. And their company is quietly famous. They get the job done but keep a low profile, just like when they were in the military. They don't advertise their services, but they have work pouring in because they are really good. They also recruited a super genius to head their IT section, Felicity Ward, the one I told you about. She used to work with the FBI."

"Sounds like a good company," Summer said. She tried to keep the wistfulness out of her voice. *Area 8*, in its own way, had been a good company, too. And it, too, got the job done. *Area 8* worked with the top people in the field and she'd always tried to create a collaborative atmosphere.

Summer had worked so hard and had had such high hopes for the future. And now everything had been blown apart.

"It is." Jack had shifted in his seat so his whole body was facing hers. Wide shoulders blocked her view of the rest of the plane. The wall behind her, his broad body on the other side—she should have felt hemmed in, but she didn't. He'd managed to create a sort of cocoon with his own body and she felt oddly protected. It was like they were in a small space together, sharing confidences. "My sister's fiancé is their newest employee. Joe Harris. You heard him on the phone. Got shot up badly but he put himself back together and just started working for them."

Summer smiled. "I'm so happy for Isabel. I hope he's a good guy. She deserves someone nice." Like Jack, Isabel had lost everything in the Massacre. Her entire family except for Jack, the family home, the family fortune--everything.

"Joe? He's the best. Not only does he make Isabel happy, he's guaranteed to keep her safe or die trying. And SEALs are really hard to kill. He saved her life when Hector kidnapped her. It's an incredible story. I'll tell you about it."

"You will, very definitely. Remember you promised me this story. I'll publish the articles in *Area 8*, when I can go online again."

"A book," Jack said. "You need to publish a book and it'll win a Pulitzer."

"Unless we're all dead."

Jack kissed her hand. "We won't die. You sure won't. Not as long as I'm alive."

He took her breath away. Summer blinked back tears, changed the subject. "Well, Joe Harris is getting a good deal, and eating really well, too." Isabel was a superb cook—chef level, though she didn't do it professionally. She'd had her own blog, *Foodways*, that Summer had been addicted to. It stopped right after the Washington Massacre.

"Yeah." Jack was watching her carefully. "What I'm trying to say is that there are some good people working on this. You've been caught up in something horrible and it must seem like your life has stopped, but it'll get straightened out. I won't—"

He stopped abruptly, jaw snapping shut.

"You won't what?" she asked.

His jaw clenched.

"You won't what, Jack?"

He curled his fingers through hers, brought their conjoined hands to his mouth, kissed the back of hers. Then looked straight into her eyes.

"I told you and I meant every word. I won't let anyone hurt you. I won't leave your side. I won't let you go."

Summer just stared back, wide-eyed. She had no snappy answer, no facile answer, no answer at all. That wasn't a player's kind of comment. It wasn't flirtation and it wasn't an attempt at seduction, it was stated as bald fact, by a very serious man.

Searching his face, Summer saw no sign of the beautiful golden boy. All she saw was the tough, determined man, who had just made a hell of a declaration.

He'd turned into a warrior, so stating that he would protect her was part of who he was now. But that he wouldn't leave her side? That he wouldn't let her go?

"I don't know how to answer that," she said softly. Somehow their faces had become closer, noses an inch apart. She could feel his breath on her cheek. Feel his body heat, feel the strength in that tough callused hand holding hers.

"No answer needed," Jack said. "I'm not looking for an answer. I'm just telling you how it is." A slight bump of turbulence jolted them closer together. Jack didn't move away and finally his mouth closed over hers and she sighed into it. The world faded. The horror, the danger, the threat—it was reduced to background noise, like the sound of the plane's engines. Of no importance, certainly not compared to the infusion of white hot heat from Jack's mouth.

The outside world was gone.

She remembered that. Kissing Jack, having sex with Jack—it had been like inhabiting some magical kingdom with waterfalls and frolicking animals and butterflies and unicorns. A land of eternal sunshine and incredible bliss.

Last night had been about overwhelming heat, and it too had made the entire outside world go away.

Jack moved closer, lifted her arms around his neck, moved over her, pressed her against the chair back. This kiss wasn't fun and distracting, this kiss was like a nuclear explosion—pure heat and power.

The kiss was endless. He'd lift his mouth only to get a better position and every once in a while to breathe. She didn't need to breathe—she breathed through him. He kissed with his lips and tongue and teeth. He kissed with his whole body pressing against her, a heavy hot weight holding her down.

How did that happen?

The seats were lie-flat and he'd turned both of them into beds and eliminated the arm rest. In between sharp biting kisses, he said, "Tell me no if you don't want this." A deep kiss, her mouth taken over by his. He was lying on top of her now. He lifted his head and stared down into her eyes, face drawn, a nerve ticking in one cheek. "If you don't want it, I'll stop. But I need you,

Summer. I need to lose myself in you. I need your arms around me and I need to be deep inside you. I need to feel you coming around me. I need that like air."

He didn't even have to say the words. Desire, *need*, came off him in waves. It was in the steely penis against her belly, in the drawn, almost painful lines of his face. This wasn't happy happy sex, a friendly roll in the hay. It felt important, serious, necessary.

No man had ever looked at her that way—like he needed her, like she was a vital part of him. Her few lovers had looked at sex the way she did. A nice ending to a day, fun but not as important as work.

This wasn't like that at all.

Jack was waiting, poised above her, one hand cradling her head, the other over her left breast where no doubt he could feel her pounding heart.

Because this wasn't like anything she'd ever felt before for anyone. She hadn't even felt like this for the young Jack—as if she'd die if they didn't make love. As if his body was necessary for her to breathe, for her heart to beat.

She didn't answer him. It was almost too big for words, words wouldn't do it. She lifted her head slightly and kissed him, holding his head still for her kiss with both hands, as if he'd run away from her

No, he wasn't running away. He pressed down on her again, the entire weight of his big body like a heavy mantle over her. There was nothing besides this, besides Jack overwhelming her every sense. His taste, his smell, the feel of him—that was her entire world.

His hands moved slowly, giving her every possibility to resist. To say no.

God no. Why on earth would she say no when she had a whole universe of pleasure right there in her arms?

"Yes," she whispered and it was like letting a race-horse out of the gate. It happened so fast. He slid her pants and panties down and off. As if he couldn't wait for one second more, not even to undress, Jack un-zipped and unbuttoned just enough for him to slide into her, with no foreplay.

Turned out she didn't need foreplay. He seemed to have understood this with his Jack-radar. His thrust was hard but she was ready, could feel herself slick and warm, closing around him tightly. He groaned and started thrusting heavily, thudding into her so hard it would have hurt if she hadn't been so turned on.

There was something exciting about being half dressed, having to keep quiet, some whiff of the forbid-den. He was thrusting hard. He reached down, opened her up even further with his fingers so that his penis rubbed right...there.

She went up in flames. She clenched heavily once, twice and came with a huge electric rush, wanting to cry out but Jack covered her mouth with his. She couldn't move and couldn't cry out and it was as if her body turned in on itself, exploding.

Blinding pleasure came in hot waves that couldn't die down because Jack was still moving so deeply in her, on and on and on. Her hands were clinging to his shoulders, nails dug into the heavy muscles, feeling them moving as he worked her mercilessly.

His face was buried in her neck, panting breath hot against her skin. Summer was barely aware of the rest of her body, unable to control it. Her head fell back against the cushion, her hands opened, no longer strong enough to cling to him. Everything she was was concentrated between her thighs as another climax started building. As if his body felt it—and maybe it did—Jack increased the rhythm of his thrusts. They became deeper, harder, as he rode her through another climax.

Summer was done, she went lax. Her sex was soft and open to him, slick with her juices. Jack's movements became less rhythmic, jerky, moving in short hard thrusts so fast she was surprised she didn't burn up from the friction. He gasped, thrust hard one last time and started coming in hot spurts inside her that, impossibly, gave her another climax.

Her head tilted even further back, eyes closed, drinking in the moment. She could smell them—a hot salty smell, like the ocean. Amazing and elemental. They were sticky where Jack was still inside her, sticky with his semen, her juices, their sweat.

None of it was distasteful, it smelled and felt like life itself.

Jack sprawled on her, panting, face buried in her neck.

Summer slowly came back into herself, bit by bit. Arms, legs, her head. Jack was still inside her, softened from his climax but still hard enough to stay inside.

Completely without her control, her vagina contracted one last time, like a little aftershock from an earthquake, and he responded immediately, growing thicker and lengthening.

She laughed and he smiled against her neck. He kissed her right under the ear and whispered, "Welcome to the Mile High Club."

TEN

Washington DC

MARCIE THOMPSON WAS amazingly easy to track down. Her cell was on the masthead.

Sometimes Kearns thought people were too stupid to live.

Her cell showed she was in a bookstore. He checked it online, The Political Reader, on Connecticut Avenue. The internet kindly gave him a view of the façade—broad book-filled windows, purple awning with the name of the bookstore in white font—and a view of the shops nearby. A dry cleaner to the left, an organic produce shop to the right.

There was a talk going on about Freedom and Information. Or Information and Privacy. Some kind of nonsense with a talking head whose name he recognized, but knew to be a blowhard who made a very good living writing idiot books and appearing on TV as an expert on everything.

So she was attending a cultural event.

Well, he had ways.

And some docs and an accent, too. In an instant he became Liam Nelson—the name close enough to that of the actor to reassure people subconsciously—a Dublin-based writer for the Irish Times. Everyone loved the Irish and Kearns did a really good accent.

Marcie Thompson had given a TED talk—whatever that was—and he listened to about a quarter of an hour of it before he closed the screen. Political responsibility and freedom of the press and the right to privacy, yada yada.

Anyone who led a life online had no business talking about privacy. Kearns could know her menstrual cycle if he really studied the FB feed hard enough.

That wouldn't be necessary. He didn't want to fuck her, he wanted to kill her.

He put on his journalism duds. Thick, heavy fake beard shot with gray. Porkpie hat with IR lights along the brim. Linen collarless shirt with a photographer's vest over it. Cargo pants and sockless loafers. He hesitated at that last touch because, Christ, what if he had to run? He was used to his combat boots and could run miles in them. The loafers would slip off in the first five hundred yards.

But onscreen Marcie Thompson was pretty, earnest, thin. No match for him. He wasn't going to need to run. He needed to convince. But it stung because no warrior in the history of the world wore loafers on an op.

The bookstore was huge, larger than it seemed from the outside, stretching almost a block in depth. Kearns could hear a droning voice from another room, rounded a corner and saw about sixty people on folding chairs listening to the talking head. Some former something or other. Considered an expert on Africa.

You want expertise on Africa? Go fight in Sierra Leone, with two rebel armies and a rag tag government military force trying their best to kill each other and kill you, every minute of every day.

This weenie had probably never ventured outside

the air conditioned confines of his hotels when visiting Africa. There were no chairs left so Kearns leaned his shoulder against the corner of a bookcase and listened to crap for about two minutes then tuned the guy out.

There she was, at the end of the third row, taking notes on a tablet connected to a tiny wireless keyboard. God knows what she was noting down, the speaker wasn't saying one smart thing.

She was a little less pretty than her photo on the masthead. Or maybe she'd had a tiring day. Well, it was a day that was going to end very badly for her. She seemed to be sitting alone, unconnected to the old lady sitting next to her.

Good. It was always hard having to cull out a victim from a crowd.

Without moving his head, Kearns studied the terrain. There had been a security cam at the door, right over the shoplifting detector, and a few in the front room but none in this meeting room, designed for author talks. None of the staff were paying them any attention at all. He debated going back outside and waiting for her on the street but if he approached her here, harmless Irish journalist, in a bookstore, she'd be lulled. Easy to fool.

Finally the writer stopped his interminable pitch for his new book and sat down with a pile of copies to sign. People shuffled toward the author and toward the door. Marcie Thompson walked past him and Kearns made sure she heard his intake of breath.

He let her get five yards, ten yards away, then walked up to her, tapped her on the shoulder. When she turned he smiled and stepped back, hands down.

Very clearly not invading her personal space. The very picture of enlightened manhood.

He pretended to peer as if she were a mile away. "Ms.—Ms. Thompson? I'm sorry but are you Marcie Thompson of *Area 8*?"

She gave a tentative smile, body language closed, clutching her satchel as if it could defend her. "Ahm, yes. Yes I am."

"Wow. This is a stroke of luck," he said, a half smile on his face, Ireland in his voice.

He'd deliberately put on loose clothing to hide his soldier's physique, and he rounded his shoulders and ducked his head—body language for a non-threatening male. He smiled shyly, held the smile for a couple of seconds too long.

"Oh!" Shaking his head ruefully. "Sorry." He dug in his backpack, which he'd been holding by a strap. He handed her a laminated card with a fuzzy photograph of his bearded face and *IRISH TIMES* across the bottom. "Name's Liam Nelson, I'm a journalist for the *Irish Times*. I'm over here for a series of articles on issues of privacy and the new media. And, well, you're one of the top people on my list to contact. I would have called from Dublin, but my editor assigned this to me at the very last minute and I had to rush to make the flight. I was going to call you later today, but I saw this really interesting talk advertised, he's a well-known expert and I read his book last week and thought I'd treat myself to his speech before starting to contact people—"

Kearns broke off, smiling sheepishly, showing her the sheet of paper with a list of digital media people, a thumbnail photo, contact info. Marcie Thompson's name was top of the list.

"Sorry. I tend to babble when I'm nervous. Anyway, I was going to go back to my hotel and start making appointments for tomorrow and—here you are! One of the editors of *Area 8*. Everyone back home reads it, it's brilliant. Do you think I could buy you a cup of tea— or coffee if that's your tipple—and interview you?"

He cocked his head, eyebrows raised, looking at that thin neck and thinking—*I could snap that with my left hand.*

She stood, staring, turning this over in her head.

I'm on a timeline here, darling, Kearns thought. *Ideally you should have been dead two hours ago.* "Please?" he asked. "It won't take long. I'm so jet-lagged I'll probably fall asleep halfway through. I'll ask follow up questions via email, how does that sound?"

She sighed. "Okay, fine. There's a quiet coffee shop on Nebraska, about a ten minute walk away."

I know, darling.

"Yeah? Excellent. I hope they have tea. I'm not much of a coffee drinker."

She relaxed completely at the mention of tea. Clearly a tea drinker could never be a homicidal maniac.

"Shall we go?" He opened his hand and she turned and made for the door, Kearns keeping a step behind her, head down, shambling a little as he went through the front door with its video cam. Later, he'd wipe it out remotely, well before her body could ever be found. He watched with care but no one paid them the slightest bit of attention. Marcie Thompson wasn't a rock star the way Summer Redding was. Redding would never go unnoticed.

Out on the street, the day was cloudy, cold, with gusty winds. There was no one on Connecticut Avenue on this block. Excellent. The next security camera was on the next block. It had to be done before crossing the intersection.

He'd parked right next to an alleyway, a dirty white Transit van with mud on the plates, front and back.

"So," he said casually, "my editor is going to want to know *Area* 8's policy on the new NSA regulations. And I'll want to know your personal opinion, because I know the webzine allows its contributors to have a personal opinion that doesn't have to be in line with the editorial opinion."

She smiled faintly. "That's right. Summer is good that way, and—oh!" She looked at him in alarm as he jabbed her with the injector just as they were pulling up to the van. She rubbed her arm, frowning, but her eyes were already unfocused.

Kearns made it look quite natural. A couple reaching their vehicle, him opening the door for her, buckling her seat belt for her, getting into the driver's seat. He pulled out slow and steady, following the speed limit exactly.

He knew where to take her where she wouldn't be found for fifty years. An hour away on the I-495. Laurel, Maryland. Outside Laurel were the ruins of the Forest Haven Asylum, set in two-hundred acres that had been closed amid scandal in 1991. There were twenty-two buildings in the compound, all ruins. Ownership was contested and no one had claimed it in twenty-five years. Even better—there were plenty of bodies buried there. Some were of inmates who'd died under mysterious circumstances while it was a working asylum, some dumped by the mob.

No one went there, no one asked questions.

She'd be one more decaying stiff, identifiable only by DNA or her teeth, if they ever found the body.

She was slumped forward against the seat belt and he nudged her back with his forearm, checking the time. He'd be back in DC well before dusk.

All in all, a very good day.

En route to Portland, Oregon

SUMMER HAD FALLEN into a deep sleep that looked like a coma. Not even her eyes stirred as she lay on the comfortable seats. Joining the Mile High Club would do that to you.

Jack rose from his lie-flat seat and covered her with a blanket. It was a plane so the blanket was made of a non-flammable material, but it was soft and comfortable, gray and cream, the colors of the ASI logo.

He smoothed the blanket over her carefully but she was out for the count. It was a miracle he could stand up himself. That had been the most intense sex he could ever remember having. He had blacked out for a second there at the end. He had a feeling he'd fucked her too hard but he'd been completely unable to stop. It was one of the few times he'd ever been out of control during sex.

He stood and looked down at her, something weird going on in his chest. She was so pretty and he appreciated that. There hadn't been much of anything pretty in his life these past years. But she was so much more than just pretty. She was smart and had a kind of resilience he recognized in himself. That ability to bend but not break. She'd been through a traumatic twenty-four hours—she'd lost her home, her business and knew that bad people were after her. He hadn't heard a peep of a complaint out of her.

This was her new reality and she was facing it head on, without a whiff of self-pity, which she'd have been perfectly justified in feeling. She'd also have been justified if she wanted to blame him, because trouble followed him around and had rubbed off on her.

But no. She was holding it together and he admired the shit out of that.

He rubbed his chest where there was something warm, that hurt. Weird mix of feelings. Intermixed with the strange was something it took him a whole minute to identify, it was so rare. He was feeling...happiness. And hope. For the first time since the Massacre, he was looking forward to something.

He'd mourned his family for six months, heartsick and grief-stricken. Lying awake at night, tears seeping out of his eyes, feeling the oppressive weight of darkness inside and out on his chest.

Isabel had survived but he'd kept away from her.

But now he was reunited with Isabel. He'd connected with a great group of guys, even if they were squids. They'd worked instantly as a team when setting the trap for Hector and he and ASI and Nick were on the same wavelength. Not like those last years in the Clandestine Service where there was something rotten in the CIA and the only person he could trust was Hugh.

But above all, the reason he was feeling this absolutely strange and new happiness thing—if that's what it was and not heartburn—was lying down on the comfortable jet seat, sleeping.

Jack was having sex again after a very long dry spell, so that was great and newfound hormones were part of why he felt so good. But mainly it was because the sex he was having was with *Summer*. Sex with anyone else wouldn't be anything like it was with her.

There was this great flow to being with her, so smart and so alive. The future was dark—whatever these fuckers were planning it was going to be bad. Worse than 9/11. But Jack had an alternate view of the future that revved him up and Summer was front and center in that picture.

He had no idea how they could make it work, all he knew was that he was going to do his damnedest. Her life was back in Washington and even if they were able to unmask the conspirators and stop the disaster that was coming, Jack didn't want to go back to Washington. It was a political city, full of poison.

He would never work at the CIA again. If what he and Nick and the Director of the FBI suspected was true, the CIA would be disbanded and there would be a century's worth of Senate hearings. There was nothing left for him in DC.

Portland, on the other hand...

He'd been offered a job in an offhand way by John Huntington, one of the two partners. Then offered it again by Douglas Kowalski, the other partner. And man, was that tempting. The team was great, the work very interesting, the gear they had beyond cool. They had better gear than the government, that was for sure.

But Summer would be in DC. And now that he'd found her, he wasn't letting her go.

It made his head hurt.

Time for a shower.

The plane had a tiny shower, but still certainly better than the rusty showerhead back in the safe house. Jack felt better after a shower and a clean tee, clean shirt and clean briefs, all of which he had in his go bag.

Food was next, then work.

He went back out into the cabin, expecting to have to wake Summer, but found her sitting up, reaching for the blouse he'd thrown to the cabin floor at the end.

He checked inside himself to see if he felt guilty for throwing her blouse to the floor. At the time, he'd been wild to touch and taste her gorgeous breasts, so…nah. Some things you don't regret.

"Hey," he said gently, sitting down. She'd brought her seatback up, was searching for the blouse. He handed it to her, ran the back of his forefinger down her soft cheek. "How you doing?"

"Fine." She buttoned it, smiled. "Is that a nice way of saying I look like hell?"

Her hair was mussed, there was a small wrinkle in her cheek from the crumpled airplane pillow. She looked adorable. "Nope."

"Good. So—what's the plan?"

"There's a shower on the plane, did you know?"

Her eyes rounded. "A shower? Oh God, yes, please!"

"Thought so. Then we have coffee and breakfast—" He checked his watch. "More like lunch. Then we start going over our notes, what we have."

"But not Hector's laptop or his flash drives. Felicity has to check them first. They might be booby-trapped." Summer slid out and stood up, pulling her pants back up over her long, slim legs. Jack remembered those legs around his waist, tightening around him as he pumped into her...

He mentally checked the time they had en route.

"Jack." Summer snapped her fingers in his face. "We've had quite enough fooling around. Don't even go there."

He sighed. "There's no such thing as too much fooling around, but you're right. We have work to do. Oh! Forgot! You're going to love this." He pulled up his cellphone and showed her a sixteen digit number. "So I want you to log onto the Portland Macy's or Nordstrom or wherever it is you shop for clothes and order yourself a whole bunch of stuff from there online. Go to town, head to toe, and make sure you include a big down coat, lots of scarves and some floppy hats with brims. Use this credit card, in the name of Charles Iverson. I was told to tell you if you buy from Macy's to use either the Fifth Avenue Macy's or the Macy's at the Lloyd Center. Someone will pick the stuff up, so you'll have plenty of clean clothes once we arrive in Portland."

She took the piece of paper, looking uneasy. "I don't know, Jack. Who is this Charles Iverson? As soon as I can use my credit card I'll pay him back, but—"

"No need." Jack waggled his eyebrows. "Felicity— did I tell you she is a genius? She hacked one of Hector's many offshore accounts and found he had a whole bunch of credit cards in various names. So she gave us the number and identity of a couple. She said she was going to use it too except she was going to buy some gear. So, basically, you're spending a dead man's ill-gotten gains. The more you spend, the better. Isabel said she was buying ten cashmere shawls. Four ply. I don't know what that means."

"Expensive." She was grinning. "It means expensive. Good for her."

"Cool. Take your shower, then we'll have a bite to eat and we'll talk to the ASI crowd and come up with a plan." Jack swallowed. Slid his hand through her hair to cup the back of her head. It always surprised him to feel her hair cool against his hands. It looked like banked fire and he always expected it to be hot to the touch. "But not before you order a whole bunch of expensive stuff online, courtesy of that fucker, Hector Blake."

Summer laughed and moved to the back of the plane. A minute later, he heard the shower come on. The galley was well-stocked. All he had to do was haul stuff out onto the table. The laptops and tablets were all fully charged. There was a printer and he knew there was a secure comms system. They were good to go.

He sat down, plucking a grape from a fruit platter, and waited for Summer.

It felt good, waiting for her. Felt right. They'd had spectacular sex. Now that he was back to having sex in his life, after having that tap turned off for more time than he cared to count, he wanted more. Right now. But—he was also an adult and capable of deferring gratification. There would be more sex just like that in his near future, he'd make sure of it.

But more than the sex, it was great just sitting here waiting for her. She'd smile at him as she came out and he'd smile back. They'd eat together and start working together. He was really looking forward to that, almost as much as he was looking forward to the sex.

Summer was smart. Smarter than he was, for sure.

She understood human psychology and she had a strong grasp of geopolitics. The ASI guys had all looked at this from a military strategic point of view. Nick was all over the law enforcement aspect. The ASI team just wanted to smoke the bad guys. Nick wanted to put bad guys behind bars. Jack was more of the smoke-'em philosophy but above all, he wanted to understand what and why. Just like Summer.

Summer understood this stuff on a deep level. Not only her childhood in third world countries, but her education and her training gave her an ability to cut through smokescreens and grasp hidden patterns.

Jack wanted to sit next to her while they tried to figure this stuff out. He wanted to be with her as she did her thing.

He wanted to be with her, period.

Something profound was settling inside him, some sense of homecoming and it was all centered on Summer. He wanted to protect her but above all, he wanted her by his side.

He had his sister back. He had found his woman.

Now if he could only fuck the fuckers who'd fucked with him, his world would be complete.

"Food." Summer sat down next to him and he breathed in warm woman, smelling of airline soap and her own smell he'd recognize in a dark room.

"Glorious food," he replied. The summer she'd been around his parents had appeared in an amateur production of *Oliver* and they'd spent the summer singing "Food, glorious food!"

"I ordered about five thousand dollars' worth of clothes and I enjoyed every single second of it," she announced, putting cheese, a chicken wrap and apple slices on a plate. "Man, I'm hungry." She dug in, eating enthusiastically. "Like I said, I don't dare open Hector's laptop or his flash drives. Felicity needs to do that in case he installed a fail-safe, though knowing Hector, he didn't. He wasn't exactly what you'd call computer savvy. Though who knows? Maybe he improved these past years. But I am going to link to my cloud files and start going through them, putting some order in my notes from the past few days and adding what you know. Then I'll—" She stopped, looked at him. "What? Do I have lettuce in my teeth?"

He had to smile at her, he just had to. "No, sweetheart. No lettuce in your teeth. You look great. I'm just really glad you're here with me."

She sat back in her chair, unsmiling, food forgotten. Summer looked at him for a long time.

"You broke my heart," she said finally.

There it was. Jack had been expecting it. He met her gaze directly. "I know I did."

They stared at each other and Summer broke the link. Jack wasn't going to back down, make excuses. He'd behaved badly. He *had* broken her heart. He didn't have any excuse other than he'd been a dick. He'd been a kid. Okay, technically a man. Definitely of age. But considering what he'd been through since then, he'd been like a careless child who'd had fun with a toy but tossed it away when a newer, shinier toy came along. He deeply regretted it and if she wanted to scream at him, hit him, he had no objections. He deserved it.

"I was devastated," she said simply and he nodded.

"Why?" she whispered, and a long ago grief flitted across her face. For an instant she was the young Summer, barely eighteen, who'd had a tragic childhood and had fallen in love with him and he'd unforgivably walked away from her without a second thought.

"I don't have an answer for that," he said evenly. "Not one that makes sense. All I can say is that I was another person. Literally. They say that every cell in our body is renewed every seven years. I'm not that person, twice removed. I can apologize but it wouldn't mean anything, nor should it." Jack leaned forward, took her hand, placed it between his. Surreptitiously, he held his thumb across her wrist. She looked calm but her heart was racing.

Ah, honey.

Again, Jack opened himself to her, let her see his expression without concealment. He put everything he felt right there on his face for her to see.

"I behaved unforgivably. I have no excuses to offer, none. But the one thing I can say is this. I won't leave you again, ever." Her pulse gave a small kick under his thumb and speeded up. "Life has given me a second chance. Believe me when I say I understand what I would lose if I walked away again. Not going to happen. As a matter of fact it would take bolt cutters to get rid of me. And while you're in danger? I'm going to stick to you like glue. So get used to it."

Jack meant every word.

Under his finger, the surging heartbeat had slowed. Her breathing was calm and steady.

Hold that thought, sweetheart.

His cell rang. From Joe, his soon-to-be brother-in-law.

"I have to take this," Jack said.

She nodded. "Of course."

"Yo, Joe. Now's not really the—"

"Jack." Joe's voice was sharp. "You've got a TV monitor in the plane. Turn it on. Or link to USNews-Network on your laptop, whichever is quicker."

"What's wrong?" Summer asked. "What is it?"

Jack switched on the monitor hanging from the ceiling and turned on one of the laptops. The monitor showed a USNN talking head with helmet hair and a map of North Carolina in the background. A moving chyron read *Possible terrorist attack on Fontana Dam, tallest dam in the East.*

"For those who have just joined us," the talking head was saying, "we are receiving reports that the Fontana Dam, the tallest dam in the Eastern United States, situated along the Appalachian Trail, has been bombed. The dam holds over 630 million cubic meters of water. Early reports indicate there are heavy casualties down river. Here is footage that was posted on YouTube a few minutes ago."

Behind the news anchor was shaky footage of an explosion near the foot of the dam. There was no sound and at first it appeared nothing was happening. Then a crack appeared, snaked its way to the top of the dam, water leaking from the crack. A chunk of the wall came away and water spilled out like a small water-fall, then a big, powerful waterfall. The image grew shaky then stopped. Another image, tall and narrow, a cellphone image, showed the breach in the dam from the other side of the valley. The same sequence from another angle. The puff of smoke and debris, the thin line snaking up to the top, chunks falling away, the line becoming an open crack, the growing waterfall.

Summer watched, face pale, and reached for his hand. Jack held on tightly.

The screen showed the anchor again, wide eyed, speaking unscripted. "So far, ahm, reports are sporadic. There is a strong Twitter feed relating to the incident." The screen showed a feed—#AttackOnFontanaDam with thousands of tweets scrolling down.

"Joining us now by telephone is Dr. Alvin Norris of MIT, a structural engineer and considered one of the world's greatest experts on concrete dams. Dr. Norris, what could cause the breach in the dam's wall, other than a bomb? Is there a possible natural explanation?"

Jack switched channels, another news cable feed. But the backdrop was not the dam. Instead it was shaky footage from a helicopter of an overturned train, steam rising from the cars. Men and women in hazmat suits were approaching the center of the train. The helo was circling overhead, a more professional camera being used instead of cellphones.

Another anchor with helmet hair, this time male, with a very serious expression. "Reports are coming in of a train wreck just outside of Los Angeles. We have been told that the train was carrying barrels of highly toxic radioactive waste."

Jack switched channels, this time showing a smoking plane wreck, parts scattered all over a field. "—reports are of a loud explosion followed by the plane falling out of the sky just after taking off. We repeat, Flight 725 from Boston to Denver has apparently been brought down by an RPG, a shoulder fired missile."

Jack turned the tablet on, using an ASI proprietary Skype-like program Felicity had designed for them. Joe's face appeared. He looked drawn. "Christ, Joe, what's happening? Is this it? Is this what Blake was planning? A whole series of attacks, one after another?"

Jack could see a wall of big monitors behind Joe. Each monitor was tuned to a different channel or website and even without hearing the sound feed, it was clear that a series of disasters was taking place.

Besides the feeds he'd already seen, of the dam, the radioactive train and the plane wreck, there was a scene with hazmat trucks with flashing lights outside a hospital, with heavily-gowned medical staffers offloading patients from gurneys. The chyron at the bottom read: *Chicago: 123 cases of Ebola.*

Summer had the plane's laptop open and was scrolling. "Twitter's announcing even more disasters, Jack." She looked up at him, face pale. "Gas mains or a bomb took out twenty city blocks in Dallas."

The plane's intercom beeped. "This is the pilot. We're coming in to Portland International. We will land in twenty minutes. Please return to your seats and fasten your seat belts. The weather is rainy, ground temperature 45 degrees."

They were going directly in to ASI where they'd contact Nick and the Director. If this was the other shoe dropping, they were in trouble, because there didn't seem to be an end in sight to the attacks.

"See you on the ground, Joe."

"Yeah. Jacko will be at the airport to pick you guys up. He's leaving now, in fact."

"Roger that."

Joe reached out a finger to shut off the connection then frowned, looked behind him. In the background, Jack could hear a female voice. Joe's frown deepened.

"What's Felicity saying, Joe?" Jack asked.

"She's—" Joe shook his head. "She's saying these are fake attacks. Or at least the first one is. She says the dam breaking up and the water spilling out are CGI."

Summer's head jerked up. *What?*

"And she says she had an algorithm study the Twitter feeds and she can't trace the tweeters back more than a month. None of them."

Summer contemplated that for a second. "So they would be fake identities."

"Yeah." Joe stretched the word out. He turned his head. "You sure, Felicity?"

The high-pitched female voice in the background became agitated, indignant.

The tablet was picked up and Metal's face appeared. "Dude," Metal said calmly to Joe. "Please. We're talking Felicity here."

In the little time Jack had been around the ASI crew, he'd learned that Felicity, Metal's fiancée, was always right. She wasn't arrogant and she was fun and she beat the pants off everyone at video games. And she was always right.

"What, darling?" Metal got up and walked over to Felicity, looked at something on her computer then walked back.

Felicity's computer was like the magic dragons on *Game of Thrones.* A dangerous, mythical creature. It had been destroyed by Hector Blake and she'd had another one arrive from a secret lab in Hong Kong, more powerful than the last one. No one was allowed to touch Felicity's computer. They weren't even allowed to breathe on it. Jack had seen her work miracles with it. If Felicity and her computer said something was true, it was true.

"Dude," Metal said again. His normally super placid face was furrowed. "The Ebola case is fake, too. Felicity just, um, checked the records of all the hospitals in Chicago." By checked he meant hacked. "The footage is from the Ebola cases two years ago. And the train and plane wrecks—all fake. I think all of these disasters are fakes."

Summer picked up the tablet. Jack made the intros. "Summer, this is Metal O'Brien, Felicity's guy. Metal, this is Summer Redding."

"Summer." Metal dipped his head. "An honor. Everyone here reads *Area 8*. You do really good work."

"Did," Summer answered sadly. "Did do good work. For the time being, *Area 8* is down and I don't know when it will go back up again. So, Metal, these attacks, fake attacks. Someone's flooding the media with fake information, correct?"

"Looks like it."

She leaned forward, beautiful face intense. "It's a diversionary tactic. The media are kept confused. I have no doubt hazmat teams and SWAT teams and FEMA teams all over the country have been scrambled. If they have any smarts at all, these guys, the ones behind all this, will disable communications among them, just like they cut off cellphone and tablet connections during the Washington Massacre. Right now, all news teams are paralyzed. We're really dependent on news feeds and tweets and Facebook postings. This looks like a team has been working on this for a long time, if Felicity says the tweeters have an established identity. How many fake identities do you think there are, Felicity?"

Felicity's pretty face appeared, a hand on her guy's shoulder. Metal reached up a big hand and covered hers.

"All the ones I looked at. This is bad juju. Law enforcement agencies will be called out and they won't be able to tell the real thing from the fake. The entire country is on alert and I wouldn't be surprised if the Pentagon raised the DEFCON Level to III."

Metal and Joe nodded.

"How deep is this?" Summer asked.

"Depending on the prep time, which at this point I imagine is at least several months, it's pretty deep. I'm guessing tens of thousands of fake identities. It doesn't cost anything except in terms of manpower. I've followed some of the tweet identities back in time and they've got some generic responses to issues of the day and movies and music that have been retweeted over and over. Some of that can be done by bot, some was done by hand. Some of the responses were automated, didn't make much sense in the context of the discussion, but it looks like each identity has been around a while. Legit. They're mostly software."

"Someone's been planning this for a long time." Summer said softly.

"Scary shit." Joe turned to look into the camera directly. "Jack, whatever happens, I've got Isabel covered. She's in the house, I just talked to her and you know we've got a good security system there. I'm going home right now and I'll wait for you and Summer and everyone else. We're meeting at Isabel's for dinner." He dipped his head. "Summer, nice meeting you. See you tonight."

Summer nodded. "Joe. Nice meeting you, too. And

tell Isabel I'm really looking forward to seeing her again."

"Will do."

He disappeared and Metal spoke. "So Jacko will be picking you guys up at the airport. Felicity wants to see Hector's laptop and flash drives in the worst way. See you in about an hour." The tablet screen went dark.

"Something really awful is happening," Summer whispered. Her hand reached out for his and Jack took it. To give her comfort. To give himself comfort.

He nodded, kissed her on the forehead. "Whatever it is, we'll face it together."

ELEVEN

San Francisco
The Mission district

THE SOLDIERS ARRIVED in the dead of night. They infiltrated via two two-man submersibles launched from a stealthed submarine. It was the equivalent of an ASDS, an Advanced SEAL Delivery System, with a few extra bells and whistles. They landed at 4:00 a.m. at Kellar Beach where a van was waiting for them. They had fifty kilos each of gear in big bags they loaded onto the van. Weapons, fifty thousand rounds of ammo, night vision gear, flashbangs, IR and thermal imagers.

They could withstand a siege, but they weren't expecting one.

Zhang Wei and his men were technically PLA, of course. All of them had undergone training. But they were IT specialists and hadn't undergone rigorous commando training like the four soldiers had.

The van parked in the back of the building, in the alleyway protected from overhead surveillance. No one would ever know that four soldiers from the PLA, bristling with weaponry and gear, had entered the building.

A soft knock and the first of the soldiers entered the command and control room. He was still in his dark wetsuit, though he'd taken off the mask.

Zhang Wei stood up, saluted. The four men in wetsuits had all entered the C2 room, lined up neatly along the wall. They saluted back.

Zhang Wei addressed their team leader. "We have prepared meals for you. You will also find four cots. Until the op commences, you will stay hidden under-cover. Once we take down the grid, two men will de-ploy to the front and back entrances. There will be a sniper on the roof with night vision at all times. We estimate food and water in the city will run out in seventy-two hours but we are equipped for two months. By which time the PLAN ships will be moored off-shore. When our military lands, you will liaise with them and you will receive further instructions. But until then, your mission is to protect us and protect our equipment."

The soldier nodded, then his eyes drifted to the twenty big screens hung on the walls of the room. Each screen showed an emergency, with increasingly distraught newscasters trying to sift fact from fiction. The backdrop to each screen was a disaster—a downed plane, an explosion, emergency wards...

The soldier nodded to the screens. "Looks like the operation is off to an excellent start." He turned on his heel and with his teammates descended down to the basement.

So much could be accomplished through leverag-ing the power of computers, Zhang Wei thought. Only a class of soldier that had grown up with computers could understand this.

The old guard did not want war. Nobody wanted war. War was destructive, eliminated resources that had taken generations to build up, killed indiscrimi-nately. No. But by the same token, they didn't understand that you could conquer without war. Using virtual resources very intelligently, destroying very little.

That was the beauty of General Chen Yi's plan using Cyberwarfare Unit 61398. Using strength softly, with maximum sparing of infrastructure that would be used later, after victory. Takeover by stealth.

The General had already given the order to his opposite numbers in the navy. For the end stage, vast resources would be necessary. The officers would shift ships from the South Fleet and bolster the East Fleet. Two separate training maneuvers would be planned, both in the Pacific. So that when Zhang Wei turned the lights off all along the West Coast of the United States, the Chinese PLAN would arrive and keep a semblance of order, keep essential services running.

Zhang Wei could see it, picture it precisely. His would be the hand that pressed the button that started it all.

The entire West Coast electricity grid would go down. Irreparable damage to the breakers of generators, catastrophic failure of the generators and no spare parts available anywhere. The spare parts were all manufactured in China and the General had made sure that all generator spare parts were removed from the manufacturing process months ago. The West Coast of the United States would get its energy back when the People's Republic decided it could. Not one minute earlier.

The scenario had even been played out by the American authorities. The Aurora Project, which showed how even a minor cyber attack on vulnerabilities in the grid system could take it down. The Americans had even gamed it for him.

The experiment had been very clear, a sort of step

by step primer on how to take a country's electrical grid down. The test was a cyber-attack that opened and closed breakers in an unsynchronized fashion, placing immense stress on the generators. Torque literally tore the generators apart, throwing pieces as far away as twenty meters, leaving the generators a smoking ruin inside of three minutes.

Zhang Wei was certain he could do it in one.

America was an unruly nation. Not a nation of civil order. And it was a nation full of guns. After the first twenty-four hours without power, utter chaos would reign.

When it was clear that power was not coming back anytime soon, when the gas pumps stopped pumping, when the food stores were looted and no supplies were coming, when the water system stopped supplying water, when all communications except for the few who owned satphones were cut off…that was when the Chinese Eastern Fleet would come to the rescue on the greatest humanitarian mission ever undertaken. Three Peace Ark hospital ships, four Xu Xiake barracks ships, two Yantai-class supply ships, four Tang class destroyers and five Leizhou-class tankers would anchor offshore the major West Coast cities and start supplying emergency electricity to hospitals, select civic centers and water pumping stations. There would be food distribution to the hungry, rationed water would start flowing.

The sight of Chinese soldiers—disciplined, carrying essential supplies—would be the most welcome sight imaginable. Welcomed with open arms. Never to leave again.

Let the games begin.

Portland, Oregon

THE MAN WHO met them at the airport looked hard and dangerous. After they rolled to a stop in an empty part of the airport, Jack held up his hand, a sign to wait. He had already closed the window shutters and they sat and waited while the pilot opened the door that became a metal staircase. As soon as the staircase was open a man came up, nodded to the pilot, nodded to Jack.

He was dark-skinned, with a shaved head. He wasn't tall but was immensely broad with huge biceps. Despite the cold weather he was dressed in a T-shirt and jeans jacket. Summer could see part of a tribal tattoo where his neck met the collar of the tee and along both arms.

His face was closed, unsmiling. Not hostile, but not warm and fuzzy, either. Summer nearly took a step back when he entered the jet, but no one else seemed to find him disturbing so she forced herself to stay where she was.

He seemed very competent, so if he had been sent to kill them, he'd have done so already.

Jack slapped him on the back and though from his looks, Summer would not have been surprised if the man knocked Jack down with one blow, he didn't. He just nodded and turned to her.

God, he was scary-looking. Summer's skin prickled and she had to mentally nail her feet to the deck of the jet so she wouldn't try to run past him and escape.

Jack put his hand on her arm. "Honey, I'd like you to meet one of the great guys at ASI. Morton Jackman. Jacko to his friends."

His friends? This man had *friends*?

"Jacko, meet Summer Redding."

The man Jack called Jacko stuck out an enormous dark hand to her and said, "How do you do, ma'am? I'm a big admirer of *Area 8*."

His voice was the deepest she'd ever heard. Jack had a deep voice, a very pleasant one. This guy seemed to subvocalize, like a human woofer.

In an act of amazing courage, Summer offered her hand, trying very hard not to tremble. "P-pleased to meet you, Jacko. Thank you for saying that about *Area 8*."

Her hand disappeared in his and then an instant later he gave it back to her, none the worse for wear. Amazing.

He looked at both of them while he talked, which Summer appreciated. She hated it when men talked to each other over her.

"This is how it's going to work," he said in his *basso profundo* voice. "I've got an SUV with treated windows. I'm going to bring it to the bottom of the stairs. You guys stay here until I come back in to get you." He handed them two broad-brimmed hats and long scarves. "Hide your faces with these until you get into the vehicle." He turned to Summer and if she squinted, she thought maybe she could detect a hint of a smile in those black eyes. "Summer, I have about a billion bags from Macy's for you. I swung by. And Isabel ordered some clothes for Jack. Said she'd had enough of that homeless look."

He disappeared out the door and Summer waited obediently.

Jack took her hand. "It's going to be okay. No, wait. I can't guarantee that. But I can guarantee it's going to be better. We have a team now."

"I'm beginning to feel it," she said. "I miss my own team, though. Are you sure I can't—"

Jack shook his head sorrowfully. "No, sweetheart. A lot depends on you having disappeared. I'll have Nick or someone in DC contact them. Be patient."

Summer nodded. Jack had waited six months for justice. Was still waiting. She could wait a few days to contact Zac and Marcie.

Jacko stuck his head in the cabin then disappeared again.

Jack wrapped the scarf Jacko had brought around the lower part of her face, then put the felt wide-brimmed hat on her head. He stood back as if in admiration.

"You're beautiful," he pronounced.

Summer rolled her eyes. "I'm hidden beneath about a hundred pounds of material."

"I know what's under there. That's what counts." He wrapped his head so much he looked like the Mummy and put on his own hat over it. They were unrecognizable as they quickly moved down the stairs and into the SUV. Treated windows, Jacko had said. They weren't treated, they looked perfectly normal. Except... she peered more closely. You couldn't see inside. You couldn't see anything, not even if there were people inside or not.

Jack rode shotgun and slid the backseat door open for her. When she climbed inside it was very light. Most SUVs had tinted windows, but this one had perfectly clear windows. Though they weren't transparent from the outside.

Cool.

The third row seats had been lowered and she saw lots of huge white bags with the familiar red star. Their clothes. It would be nice to have clean clothes. She'd been wearing this outfit for over twenty-four hours. She'd been to Hector's funeral, to Hector's secret lair, Jack's safe house. She'd made love to Jack and been flown across the country in these clothes.

So much had happened in the past day, most of it centered around the man sitting in front of her, conversing quietly with Jacko.

If she asked, they'd clue her in on the conversation, she knew that much. Or at least Jack would include her. But she was all convo'ed out. They were going to figure out what horrible things Hector had planned. Secretly, the FBI was all over it in the person of Nick Mancino and the Director. Jack was on it as were the people he thought of as his team.

She could stop trying to puzzle this thing out for the moment and focus on herself. And on her feelings for the big man sitting in front of her.

Jack. Jack Delvaux. The man who'd broken her heart. She hadn't been kidding when she told him that. And to his credit, he'd understood.

But the girl whose heart had been broken had been a train wreck in waiting. She'd spent a miserable childhood under the uncertain protection of careless parents. Miss Darby's school had given her a solid structure and allowed her to grow but there hadn't been any boys to speak of and she'd had so little experience of them. They'd been like alien creatures to her.

That first week at Harvard, she'd been so lost and lonely. Boys had come on to her and she'd had no idea—no clue—how to respond. There seemed to be a code, a rhythm to it that escaped her completely. She'd been painfully aware of her virginity and unable to think of a way to overcome that handicap, how to date a man who'd understand and then, bam!

Jack had appeared right in front of her. Like magic.

Beautiful, kind Jack, who had immediately taken her under his wing, introduced her around, made her feel at ease around his friends.

And he'd seduced her. Yeah. She'd been so happy that Jack was her first lover. He'd been gentle and funny and tender. And oh so passionate. She couldn't possibly have asked for a better introduction to sex.

Girls talked and not everyone's first time was magic. If anything, the opposite.

She'd been so young and foolish and had somehow convinced herself that she and Jack were Meant To Be, when they'd been such *kids*.

Jack was right when he said he was a different person. He was. He and Jacko were discussing something quietly but every minute or so he turned slightly in his seat, as if to check to see whether monsters might have infiltrated the vehicle in the minute of time since he last looked.

He seemed more than willing to stay this time.

Was she?

He looked around again and this time met her eyes and smiled.

It wasn't the patented, brilliant Jack Delvaux smile that dazzled everyone he came across. It was a man's smile—someone who'd seen trouble and tragedy but could still smile.

Was she going to stick around afterward?

She smiled back at him.

Maybe.

"We're here," Jacko announced and Summer realized she hadn't even noticed her surroundings. Jack had knocked her off kilter because she was always aware of where she was—a legacy of her troubled childhood.

Even in the midst of trouble, Jack had managed to make her feel safe enough to get lost in her thoughts.

The area was gentrifying. Low rise brick buildings at least a century old. Some abandoned, some done up. Jacko rounded a corner of a building that was surrounded by a twelve foot wall, pressed on the accelerator and drove straight into the wall.

Summer caught her breath to scream but before she could, a section of the wall simply opened, Jacko drove in fast and braked hard, slewing the car so that it fit precisely between the lines of a parking space.

It was a remarkable piece of driving, though he'd nearly given her a heart attack.

Jacko looked back at her and again, there was a hint of a smile. "I love where I work."

Jack helped her down and she studied her surroundings. A low rise beautifully restored brick building surrounded by incredibly landscaped grounds. Healthy looking plants, a Zen garden, amazing teak and wrought iron benches strategically placed. An arbor that would be gorgeous come spring.

"I thought this was a security company," Summer said as they started walking along a brick herringbone walkway with inset lighting.

"It is," Jack said as they walked straight into a wall that, like the gate, opened fast at the very last minute. "One of the owners is married to a designer. This was her building and her business originally."

"Best-looking security company in the world," Jacko rumbled as they walked down a corridor with terra-

cotta wall sconces and thriving lemons in big enam-
eled vases. Turning into a door on the left—by this
time Summer wasn't surprised to see it whoosh open
as they approached and whoosh closed at their backs—
they were in a huge, posh space. Cool, neutral tones.
Elegant, not fussy. Prosperous but not over the top.

It gave exactly the impression a security company
should give—solidity and discretion with an extra dollop of beauty. If this was the work of one of the co-
owner's wives, she knew what she was doing.

They walked straight past the receptionist—Jack
gave the stern looking middle-aged lady a wink and
got a wry smile in return—into another huge room.

This was a command center. All business but still
somehow beautiful. Giant monitors everywhere, several work stations. The monitors all showed various
disasters as they were unfolding.

A big, lean man with black hair, snow white hair
at the temples, rose and walked toward them. He was
followed by a young blonde woman with her hair in a
ponytail, wearing blue sweats and a TARDIS necklace.

The big man took her hand. "Ms. Redding. John
Huntington. It's a pleasure to meet you, though I wish
it were under better circumstances. Everyone in this
office admires *Area 8* and we hope that when we find
those responsible for the Massacre, you will write a
full exposé."

"Count on it," Summer said, meaning every word.
If she had to go into hiding for the rest of her life, the
story would come out. "Traitors working against us.
It's monstrous."

Jack's hand fell on her shoulder, a warm, heavy, reassuring weight. "There's no one better than Summer to break the story."

The blonde girl peeped from around Huntington's shoulder. She held one hand out to shake Summer's and the other out for the laptop Summer was carrying. "Hey, hi! We met onscreen when you were on the plane. I'm Felicity, I belong to that big lug over there—" Metal twirled around in his office chair, sketched a salute then turned back to his monitor. "I'm the IT person around here and I can't wait to get going on Blake's laptop and flash drives. These people are driving newscasters and journalists nuts." She waved at the bank of monitors, each with its own personal disaster.

Summer recognized her. "You're the one who saw that the Fontana Dam footage was fake?"

"Sure am," Felicity said, pretty face sober. "But that doesn't mean they all are. Figuring out how many of these are false-flag digital fakes is taking a lot of band-width. The fake ones have been planned for a long time and some of the footage is real but old. These people are doing major damage—every single emergency service in the country is on alert. We're running through huge amounts of money, tying up resources, clocking up overtime on a vast scale."

"Do you think this is…it?" Summer asked. "What everything has been leading up to? What the Washington Massacre was about?"

They'd all drifted over to where Metal was manning a computer. What was on his screen was also up on one of the wall monitors.

Metal reached up a big hand, without taking his eyes from his monitor. "Summer. Nice to meet you in person. I feel like I know you from *Area 8*."

She clasped his hand. "Thanks. How many incidents do we have so far?"

"Twenty-one." One of the monitors switched images. The sound on all was off. Graphics were enough to give the important facts. The monitor showed a school—*Fairmont Elementary School* was carved in the stone of the façade. The feed showed little kids being rushed out of the school, masks being handed out, the kids and teachers being ushered into waiting medic vans. *Anthrax released in elementary school* was the caption. "Twenty-two," Metal said.

Summer clenched her fists. "That better be one of the fake ones."

The men all nodded soberly.

She looked at all of them. "Whoever these people are, we have to bring them down. Because I think they are showing us how easy it would be for them to create havoc in this country. How easily they can bring us to our knees."

John Huntington nodded soberly. "We're on it, though we don't have much to go on. You know, Ms. Redding—"

"Summer, please," she said.

He nodded again. He had a natural authority. Part of it was his physique and good looks. But most of it was something that just flowed from him, a leader's calm. The whole company had an amazingly reassuring vibe to it.

"Summer. As you know, we're working with an element in the FBI. Both of us have immense resources. It's just a question of time. Plus"—he indicated Felicity, whose fingers were blurring over Hector's keyboard—"we have a secret weapon. If there's anything to be found in Blake's computers, she'll find it. No question. Then we analyze it and go on the offensive."

"Yes, sir," Summer said. "You understand that both Jack and I fear that there is CIA complicity in all of this, don't you?"

"I do. We do. Which is why the FBI has set up a secret task force with only very trusted agents. Headed by Special Agent Nick Mancino. The operation is compartmented and there will be no leaks."

Summer stiffened at that. "I hope you're not implying that *Area 8* will leak anything? I would never do that. As a matter of fact, *Area 8* is offline for the moment."

He was already shaking his head. "I wasn't implying anything of the sort. It's clear from what you write that you are a true patriot. Though the whole story will have to come out some day and I hope you'll write that story once we have the leaders behind bars."

"Gladly." Oh yeah. She was going to write a series of exposés and then a book and then she was going to go on TV and report on the group of traitors who sold out the country and killed hundreds of people. For money.

And they weren't finished yet.

A dull ringing sound and Metal clicked on Skype. Nick Mancino's face showed. He looked pale and drawn. "Hey, man. Is Summer there?"

Her eyes grew wide and her heart thumped. What did Nick want with her? Had something worse than her apartment being blown up happened?

Metal rose from his chair, opened his hand. Summer sat, because her knees felt suddenly weak. Jack stood at her back, his hand still on her shoulder. She reached up to hold it, like a touchstone, something solid to cling to.

"I dispatched an agent to provide protection for your two editors, Zac Burroughs and Marcie Thompson."

Oh God! Summer's head swam. Zac and Marcie. So smart and so energetic. They'd help her make *Area 8* what it was. Her throat was so dry she had to take a sip of water to be able to speak. "And?"

"We couldn't find either of them. They weren't anywhere and their cells were off. My agent let himself into Burroughs' apartment and made a thorough search. One door was closed, and he was unable to open it. Some kind of liquid cement had been placed in the lock and the door was stuck in the jamb. Circumstances warranted his breaking the door down and it wasn't easy. This is what he found."

On the screen was a long plastic…thing. Several screenshots carouselled across the screen until she realized what she was looking at. A body bag. She gasped and Jack's hand tightened on her shoulder.

Nick nodded. "I won't show you the next pictures, but Zac Burroughs is dead, Summer. I'm really sorry."

Grief washed over her. Funny, smart Zac. Who'd had crazy parents like hers, only loving grandparents. Who'd studied his heart out at journalism school. Who believed in the power of the written word with every fiber of his being. Who'd fought alongside her to build *Area 8* to what it was. Zac, who'd had a secret crush on her but rarely let it show.

"So they're going to get away with this, too?"

Nick gave a grim smile. "Not quite. As a matter of fact we have a lead."

Everyone leaned forward. "Spill it, Nick," John Huntington ordered.

"Yes, sir. So we backtracked and Zac had had a latte at a corner bar."

"Trigo's." Summer blinked her tears back. "We met there a lot. He said his apartment was too messy to have meetings there."

"Yeah, Trigo's." Nick leaned forward too, though he was three thousand miles away. The picture and sound were so clear it was as if he were sitting across the table from them.

"So the guy left no forensic evidence, and the street cameras showed this."

On the monitor there was the photograph of a man with a baseball cap on and white fuzz where his face would be.

"IR lights in the bill," Jack said. Summer glanced at him. He was all business, face gone completely cold. The man on the screen was linked to the people who'd destroyed his family. His eyes travelled as they took in every detail.

"Put that up on the wall," John Huntington said, and the photograph showed on the wall monitor. It was very clear. She could see every wrinkle in the man's jeans, every zipper on his backpack. They just couldn't see his face.

"Later, the fucker must have worn latex gloves," Nick said. "But on the street he was glove-free."

"What did he touch?" Jack asked. "Please let him have touched something."

"He touched Zac's body when he injected him with what the autopsy showed to be ketamine."

Summer's eyes widened. "Isn't that used on *animals*?"

"It is," Nick said grimly. "Kid didn't have a chance. And the fucker sprayed the kid's upper body with bleach so there aren't any prints or any DNA we can pull. However…" He held up a forefinger. "Our entire forensics lab is top flight, of course, but we have a particular forensic scientist who is off the charts brilliant. He lost his wife in the Massacre and he's pledged to work day and night without sleep if he has to until we bring those responsible to justice. And to tell the truth, he's already done something amazing. Now pay attention."

Everyone was practically quivering with attention, except Jack, who was as still as stone.

"Watch this photo," Nick said. It was another shot of the man with the blurred face, in mid-stride, one hand reaching for his backpack, open palm facing the lens.

Nick manipulated the photo, bringing the hand into close-up. It was slightly pixelated. Then another manipulation, some kind of magnification, and the close-up showed the open palm in incredible detail. Summer could even see the calluses.

"Shooter's calluses," Jacko murmured and the other men nodded. Jack had told her that Jacko was the "designated shooter" of the group—a gifted sniper. If anyone could recognize shooter's calluses it was him.

"So our genius guy sent this photo to an experimental 3D printer he's been working on with a private sector company, and they manufactured a hand out of polymer and took its prints."

"I want that printer," John Huntington told Nick. "Right now. I don't care what it costs."

"We'll see," Nick answered. "But the important thing now is that we had prints and we found a match."

A match! The man who'd killed Zac! The man who probably killed Marcie.

"I want to see his face," she said but before she finished a face was up on the monitor. It was an ID card and it bore the seal of the CIA.

Summer brought a hand to her mouth. The blood drained from her head, she saw spots. Her lungs wouldn't work. A loud buzzing filled her head. She couldn't read the name her head swam so hard.

The man who'd killed Zac, who'd probably killed Marcie, who was after *her*, worked for the CIA. It was official.

"Wait!" Jack studied the photo. "I know him."

"Yeah. I imagine you do, though he was recruited while you were stationed in Singapore. Philip Kearns. In the Clandestine Service from 2010 to 2014. Fired for inappropriate use of Agency resources and blackmailing a CI. Corruption, in other words. But our forensics guy found a couple of bank accounts that are linked directly to Marcus Springer's black funds. It'll take a warrant to pull the files and we might have to go to a higher court, but by God we've found a smoking gun here."

"Springer is mine," Jack whispered and the hairs on Summer's arms rose at the ferocity in his voice. "I want him."

Nick shifted in his seat. "Totally get you, big guy, and I can't fault you, but the Director's not on board with personal vengeance. But I promise you, Jack, I *promise*, that when we get through with him, Springer will do life in solitary confinement at Leavenworth.

And we'll make sure what remains of his life is miserable."

"So, this man—" Summer waved at the screen. "This guy killed Zac." Her eyes welled over. "And Marcie?" she asked through a tight throat.

Nick shook his head. "Missing. We can't find her. She's not in her apartment. We can't pull out all the stops, not yet. Can't put out a BOLO, that would blow the op. Springer's got eyes and ears everywhere and we're trying to keep under the radar, but we have several men working on finding her."

Summer wiped her eyes. "I'm so afraid you'll find her body."

"So arc we." Nick apparently wasn't a guy to mince words. "But we will find her and we're working fast. I still hope we can find her alive." On camera, his gaze shifted. "Hey, Delvaux. I'm counting on you keeping Summer alive."

Jack's grip on her shoulder turned painful for a second, then he eased up. "I will. You can count on it."

"Plus us," John Huntington added.

"Yeah," Metal growled. "She has a team. She'll live to publish everything and expose the fuckers. Every single one. We'll aim for the needle for every single one of them."

"How's Felicity doing?" Nick asked. "We're hoping for leads."

"Felicity's doing fine," she called out without taking her eyes off the screen. Summer was fast with a computer but Felicity was another order of magnitude fast. Her fingers were a blur and images changed on the monitor so fast Summer couldn't follow. "However, Felicity has been on the job exactly twenty two minutes and forty seconds and not even Felicity can work miracles. There's some heavy duty encryption here, by pros. It's going to take a while to unpack."

Metal sighed. "She's not going to sleep or eat until she starts cracking this."

"Look," Jack said quietly and everyone's heads swiveled to the bank of wall monitors. A skyscraper was smoking and, as they watched, started tumbling to the ground, shards of concrete and glass falling through the sky like shiny, heavy rain. The top twenty stories tilted and wrenched away from the base, exposing beams and office furniture, like a doll's house with the walls cut away.

Everyone stopped, including Felicity.

Someone turned the sound back on.

"—hoaxes all day but this is real," a shocked newscaster was saying. She was dressed in a parka and the wind blew her hair around her face. At the end of the street behind her was the tumbling building.

She looked familiar to Summer. A journalist she'd watched before. *Hathaway Building in Boston Destroyed* slid across the bottom of the screen. "I'm standing not three blocks from the building and I can feel the heat of the fire. Four thousand people work in the Hathaway Building."

9/11 was on everyone's minds.

"Goddamn it." Metal's normally super cool expression turned ferocious, narrow-eyed with rage. Jack told her Metal had lost his entire family in the Twin Towers. His father and brothers on the day itself and his mother a week later, dead of a broken heart.

"These are *Americans* doing this," Nick said. His

face and voice were cold, too, the skin of his nostrils white with stress. "They are going *down*."

Summer looked around the room. All the men stood stock-still, icy rage on their faces, bodies stiff with tension. After looking up, Felicity had turned back to her computer, pretty face pale and hard, fingers blurring even more quickly.

Whoever the shadowy forces arrayed against them were, they were powerful. But Summer felt something even more powerful in this room, a great spirit rising. Some combination of the intelligence, training, toughness and will of the people in the room. She counted herself and Nick in this. Something greater than the sum of its parts. Something strong and invincible was taking shape.

Power was right here with them, and was projected by Nick from the monitor. A common will was forming, made of strength and intelligence. A desire for revenge and a thirst for justice. Everyone was pulling together for a common goal—bringing monsters to justice.

This was exactly what *Area 8* was about. And though *Area 8* was gone and might never return, its spirit was right here in this room. And it was formidable and it would prevail.

TWELVE

SHE WAS THE best-dressed fugitive ever, Summer thought, standing on the steps of Isabel's new home. She and Jack were going to stay in Isabel's fiancé's house, next door. Joe and Isabel had been next door neighbors but apparently Joe had all but moved in with Isabel. Joe gave Jack the keys, said, "Don't burn it down, otherwise do what you want," and disappeared into Isabel's home.

They were invited over to dinner so they both showered and changed. Jack changed into something that looked exactly like what he'd been wearing before, only clean. She on the other hand had ordered a green cashmere sweater with matching cashmere bolero, heavy silk trousers and soft Gucci boots. She had five bags of this stuff.

Isabel opened the door and rushed into Summer's arms, hugging her tightly. Summer hugged her back, incredibly moved. Isabel had been so nice to her the summer she'd first returned to the US.

Isabel pulled back, smiling and crying. She swiped impatiently at her face. "Summer, it's so good to see you and so good to know you're safe." She turned to her brother and reached up to hug him, too. Like Summer, she had to stand on tiptoe to do it. "And you too, you big lug. You're definitely too mean to kill." The tears were falling freely now and Jack didn't answer, just hugged her tightly, rocking them back and forth.

They'd been through the wringer. Their family lost, Isabel grievously wounded, Jack forced into hiding for six months. They deserved every moment of happiness they could wring out of life.

Isabel pulled away from Jack, smiling through her tears. "I'm really glad you ditched the homeless look." She wrinkled her nose. "You *smelled*."

"Good old stink of piss." Jack's voice was light, but Summer could tell he was moved at seeing his sister again. "Don't knock it, it saved my life. No one gave me a second glance. Otherwise I'd probably be a floater in the Potomac."

Isabel shuddered.

Joe ambled up behind Isabel, put an arm around her shoulders. "Hey, Jack. Good to see you again. Summer, nice to meet you in person. Honey, is the pork roast *supposed* to be black?"

Isabel's eyes rounded and she rushed into the kitchen with a cry.

Joe shrugged. "Be prepared to be amazed at the food," he said to Summer. "I'm responsible for the drinks, though, so we'll start with cocktails. Scotch or Prosecco?"

"Prosecco, definitely."

"Great. More Scotch for me and Jack." He poured two scotches in whiskey glasses and some Prosecco in a flute for her.

The guys started discussing something to do with security and Summer wandered into the kitchen. It was well-organized with amazing smells coming from it. Several platters were on a counter, the contents looking incredibly tempting. Summer reached out a hand then pulled it back.

Isabel pulled some meat out of the oven—no traces of black at all—and put it on the stove top. "Go ahead," she said. "I don't mind previews. And Joe and Jack will demolish everything as soon as it's on the table, so go ahead and grab your share."

Summer used a small fork to pick up something and put it in her mouth. It was small, round, fried. And delicious.

"What was that?" she asked.

"Olive ascolane," Isabel replied. "Homemade, not the frozen variety. Meat-filled fried olives. An old recipe from Abruzzo. Try the special bruschetta." She held out a thin slice of roasted bread with a white cream on top and Summer nearly moaned. "Oh, God."

Isabel smiled smugly. "Yep. Homemade sourdough bread and a ricotta mousse with truffle on top." She bit into her own slice, placed her elbows on the island countertop and leaned toward Summer. "So. You and Jack."

Summer fought a blush and coughed as the sip of Prosecco went down the wrong way. "Well, uh…"

A dollop of the incredible mousse had dropped onto the counter and Isabel scooped it up with her finger which she put in her mouth. "You know, Mom and I were just delighted when we got word that Jack was dating you in college."

Well, Summer had a response for that. "We dated for a week, Isabel. Then Jack dumped me."

Isabel sighed, lifted her eyes to Summer's. "Yeah. Because that's what Jack did back in the day. But that's not Jack anymore. Trust me, Jack is an entirely different person now."

Summer nodded. She didn't know what to say.

"And I can tell he's in love with you."

Summer *really* didn't know what to say to that. No words were possible. Though her heart gave a treacherous thump in her chest.

"Honey?" Joe's plaintive voice came from the living room. He stuck his head in the kitchen. He was a remarkably tough-looking man. Thin—he was still recovering from battle wounds that had nearly taken his life—but very muscular, he was one of those men who looked like he could withstand more or less anything short of a nuclear bomb. So it was a miracle that he somehow also managed to look like a starving homeless waif. He even batted his brown eyes at them. "We're starving out here. Any hope of sustenance soon?"

Isabel's face lit up when she saw him. It was amazing to Summer. Isabel had been very kind to Summer but she was an upper class woman through and through. Summer had never seen her unnerved or embarrassed. She'd never seen Isabel taken with any particular man, either. Isabel had always been cool and collected and even a bit unemotional.

It was astonishing to see her so open and affectionate with Joe. He walked into the kitchen, kissed her when she lifted her face to his, and stroked her cheek.

Summer looked away. Nobody should intrude on their private happiness. Isabel so deserved this. She'd lost her entire family except for Jack in the Washington Massacre. She'd been so wounded she'd been in a coma. It was hard to think of what she'd been through.

But it had brought Joe into her life. He loved her. And she had not only Joe but a whole group of incredible people around her.

Summer was only tangential to the group yet even to her it felt like warming cold hands at a big bonfire. She could only imagine what it was like inside the circle.

Jack stuck his head in. "Hey, you two, stop locking lips and start taking care of us. We need food!"

Isabel broke away from Joe, falling back down on her heels. He was a tall man, almost as tall as Jack.

"Food, glorious food!" Isabel sang and she started ferrying out platters of the stuff. Summer helped and soon the dining table was groaning with food.

Thin slices of roasted pork with a strawberry reduction glaze. Grilled zucchini with olive oil and balsamic vinegar. Roasted pepper couscous.

A reverent silence descended as they started eating. Everything was amazing. Peak experience after peak experience.

"I can't believe you get to eat like this every day," Summer said to Joe.

"I know." He smiled smugly and cut himself a slice of gratinéed chard. "I'm even eating greens now. And liking them." He turned to Isabel. "I will never leave you," he intoned solemnly. "You can lose your hair and your teeth and gain three hundred pounds and I will never, ever leave you."

Isabel cleared her throat, ran the tines of her dessert fork over the tablecloth. "Speaking of eating like this every day…" She looked at Summer then at Jack. Her heart was in her eyes. "There's a house for sale just down the block." Her voice was hoarse. She waited a moment, sipped her wine. "It's really nice. The moment you're declared living, Jack, what's left of the sale of the family home is yours. I could—I could never bring myself to take what would have been your share. I simply couldn't do it. It's still in the bank and it's yours. And it would cover more or less the cost of this house I'm talking about. A really nice family lived there, it's got to have good vibes. Portland is a great place to live. We could be a—a *family* again."

Isabel's voice broke as tears fell down her face.

Joe put his hand on Jack's arm. "Much as it pains me to say this, I actually look forward to having a lunk like you as my brother-in-law. And if you lived close by—" He looked away for a second, jaw muscles clenching. Joe looked so amazingly rough, the kind of guy who wouldn't show emotion, but now he was clearly moved. "If you lived close by, we really could be a family. I've never had much of a family myself, so I wouldn't mind trying it out. Can always toss you away if it doesn't work." His eyes were suspiciously moist. "And Midnight and the Senior have said several times they'd like you to come work for them. They have too many hard-working former SEALs, they said. They need some sneaky slacker former CIA pukes."

Jack was frozen. Why wasn't he saying anything?

Isabel glanced at Summer. "And Summer can run *Area 8* from anywhere, right? I mean, I know she reports on a lot of DC stuff but that's why God invented airlines, right? And she's going to write a book about this anyway, might as well write it here in Portland."

Wait a minute. Were they including *her* in this? Why? This was a Delvaux thing, she wasn't involved in any way. How could she just up and move to Portland? And she and Jack weren't—weren't whatever it was Isabel thought they were.

Summer opened her mouth and Jack's cell pinged. For a second he didn't move. Summer was about to answer for him, when he thumbed his screen. He looked—stunned. As if he'd received a huge shock and still wasn't over it.

"Metal," he said. "Hey. Is Felicity making any progress?"

Metal's face appeared on the cell's screen. "Yeah. Felicity is sending the entire contents to Summer's laptop and yours. You guys know him better than we do and you might be able to pick up things that won't ping our radar. But Felicity's got one important thing. You got a bigger screen?"

"Yeah." Joe hauled out a big tablet. "Send it to me."

"Okay. Sending now. While your system is getting it, let me tell you that Nick says a lot of stuff is going on in DC. The Director is about to come out in the open about Marcus Springer. He's about ready to file for a warrant for Springer's arrest, but he's waiting for more evidence. The FBI accusing one of the heads of the CIA of treason is not going to be easy and the Director knows he might lose his job over it. But he says it would be worth it to take Springer down. Okay, I'll pass you over to Felicity." The screen changed and Felicity's pretty, angry face came on.

"This guy had candy-ass security," Felicity said, frowning. "I take it almost as a personal insult. So I sent the contents to Nick and to the Director of the FBI because there are several interesting bank account numbers and figures and there's some interesting email correspondence from an anonymous IP. He also talks a lot about an Event, capital E. He doesn't say when the event will occur or what it will be. We don't know if by Event he means these fake attacks today plus the real attack on the Hathaway Building. So I'm going to keep going through his files as will the FBI. But I did discover one very interesting thing." Onscreen, she showed a tablet with a big number on it.

37.8267N 122.4233W

"What's that?" Summer asked. "Wait! That looks like—"

"GPS coordinates," Jack, Joe and Felicity said at the same time.

"What does that correspond to?" Jack asked.

"It corresponds to here." A Google map came on-screen with a teardrop. "San Francisco. A tiny alleyway off Brannan Street. Not far from the big new Google headquarters."

Summer traced the teardrop. "Could that be it?" she wondered. "An attack on Google? God knows if we lose it, we'd be in a sad state."

Felicity cocked her head, considering. "No, it doesn't compute. Because the building isn't completed yet and it will be just an admin building. Google's diffuse, it's got server farms everywhere. Even blowing the Mission street building up wouldn't take Google down. It would be a tragedy for the loss of life and there would be a huge loss of property but…it wouldn't be a dev-astating blow."

"So…what?" Summer asked.

Felicity just shrugged.

"Well, we're going down tomorrow morning, do

some recon," Metal said. "Nick's alerting a few guys from the SF FBI office. We need intel. The special agents will have to stay on the perimeter until the Director gets warrants but we can get in close. You in, Joe? Jack?"

Before they could answer, she got her voice in. "I'm coming too," Summer said crisply. Determined. They weren't going to leave her behind.

"Sweetheart…" Jack said uneasily.

"This story needs to be told. And it needs to be told right. There are a lot of different threads and I have no doubt that Springer and whoever else is working with him have a team that can obfuscate the truth. My job is to get to the bottom of this and explain it to people in a clear fashion. Get the truth in before their lies start. To do that, I need to be with you guys in San Francisco. I'll stay out of your hair."

Metal had been talking off screen. "Nick says you can't go near the infil team."

"The what?"

"The team that will try to infiltrate the building," Jack explained. He was still frowning.

That made sense. "That's fine. I'm not an operator. I'd just be in everyone's way. But I want the right to debrief the team as soon as they come back."

"We're booking rooms at the Marriott on 3rd Street, which is only a few blocks away and Summer can just stay in the hotel. Unless they're planning to set off a nuke along the San Andreas Fault, she'll be safe, Jack."

It was the exact wrong thing to say. Jack's face showed extreme alarm.

"That was a joke." Summer put her hand on Jack's

arm and looked at Metal. "A very bad one, in extremely poor taste. Wasn't it, Metal?"

Metal's mouth took on a mulish cast and then Felicity's face appeared. "My guy sometimes suffers from foot in mouth disease. Pay him no mind. ASI's jet will take off tomorrow morning at 9:00 a.m. from the general aviation section. Jacko will swing by at 8:15 and pick Jack, Summer and Joe up. You'll find all the tac gear you need on the plane. Nick's guys will be based in a suite at the Marriot from 7:00 a.m. on. They'll text you their room number en route. You will have four connecting suites—Joe, Jacko and Jack and Summer and the FBI team. Tomorrow's going to be a big day, so stop stuffing your faces—Isabel, I want boxed leftovers from tonight's dinner, including dessert—and get some rest."

Isabel waved at Felicity. "You got it. Are you overnighting at ASI?"

"Yeah. I'm doing all the hard work here, so I'll need sustenance. You dig?"

"I do. I'll send Joe over right now with the leftovers and I'll be over early tomorrow morning with some fresh croissants and a slice of your favorite cheesecake. If you ask nicely."

"Asking nicely."

"You got it. Thank you for this, Felicity."

She looked blank for a second. "Oh. Yeah. Ah." Felicity blew out a breath. "Don't thank me, it's what I do." Her head cocked again as she listened to something offscreen. "Nick says for everyone to get to bed and sleep comfortably for him. He's catching the red eye and he'll be in SF around dawn."

Isabel rose and shooed Summer and Jack from the

table. "I can't help you guys but I can certainly take care of cleaning up. Go to bed the two of you. You're going to need to rest." Isabel stood on tiptoe to kiss her brother goodnight. She whispered something in his ear and he nodded soberly. Then she hugged Summer tightly and whispered in her ear. "Take care of him, Summer. He's been through so much. Take care of him, bring him back and think about staying here with us. Staying here and being a family."

Summer hid her face against Isabel's neck and simply clung to her.

Family.

A powerful surge of emotions she had no idea how to handle pulsed through her.

Family.

Jack.

Family.

She stuffed all those emotions into a tight box and nailed the lid shut. She couldn't deal with this, not now. They were in the middle of a national emergency. She'd elected herself a chronicler of historic events. Her writing would shape the way people looked and talked and understood what was happening. Maybe, with some luck, her writing would attain historic status.

She couldn't think about this, about Jack and Isabel and Portland and family, not in any way.

But it was a long time before she could let Isabel go.

JACK WAS QUIET as he opened the front door of Joe's house and ushered Summer in. Isabel's words had affected him deeply. Buying a house nearby, settling down here. Seeing Isabel and Joe nearly every day.

Working at ASI with men he already considered friends and teammates.

But the thing that made it gel in his mind was doing all this with *Summer*. Isabel had nailed it when she'd asked Summer to stay here, in Portland. Instinctively, Isabel had understood that Summer was the one for him.

Isabel had always been smart when it came to the human heart.

When he'd felt Summer inhabit a Summer-shaped space in him that he hadn't known was there, he'd been right. Only that space was permanent.

Jack had had a lot of women but he had never had this sense of partnership that he felt with Summer. Like they were a team, working toward the same goals.

Right now that partnership was centered on unraveling a dangerous conspiracy, but he could feel that that partnership could extend to building a life together, a family together.

A family.

If he was ever to find a family, it could only be with the woman whose back he was touching.

He hadn't ever really thought about kids, but once the idea was put in his head he couldn't dislodge it. Kids here, in Portland, with his sister and Joe and the other guys from ASI and their women. Kids who would have cousins nearby because Joe and Isabel were already talking about having children.

Kids with a woman who was strong, with an iron moral core. A woman he desired more than his next breath, but also a woman he could count on, just as his mother had been.

He didn't need to accompany Summer over a threshold with a hand on her back. She was perfectly capable of that all on her own. She was an amazingly capable woman and didn't need his help in anything.

But he needed to be touching her right now, had to be touching her or nothing made sense in his life.

Summer looked around with a sad smile on her face. "Isabel wants you to move here."

What the fuck was up with that sadness? Like he was going to leave her or something?

"She wants *you* to move here, too."

The sad smile grew sadder. "That's because she somehow thinks I would be an incentive for you to move here."

Fuck yeah, she'd be an incentive.

Jack herded her into the bedroom. He wanted to talk to her but he also needed to touch her naked skin, he needed to be kissing her, he needed to be inside her, because that was where he found peace.

"I wouldn't think of moving here without you," he said harshly and when she turned a surprised face to him, he kissed her.

And kissed her.

And kissed her.

He walked her backward into Joe's bedroom, half carrying her, half breathing for her. She'd gone to town with the clothes shopping. Everything he touched was either cashmere or silk, but it was the silk of her skin he was after.

He undressed himself and then her, very slowly, his present to himself after these past six awful, lonely months. This was his prize.

Slowly. He had to go slowly, because he'd behaved like a starved beast on the plane. Something about the disasters unfolding had been like a burr under the skin. Many were fakes but some were not. Even the fake disasters had shown him—as if he needed to learn that lesson—how fragile life was. You build and you build and then some cruel monster comes along and swats it all away with a careless hand.

Look at his family. The most solid family in the world, they lived in a structure of love, unbreakable and untouchable and in the space of a few minutes, his family was gone.

Bad things were coming and for some reason, Summer seemed to be in the crosshairs, too.

He could lose her. He could hold her lifeless body in his arms and weep his rage to the sky and the sky wouldn't care. She would still be gone.

He had to bind her to him. He had to make sure she stayed with him, because he would keep her safe. He'd keep her safe because his own life depended on it.

When she stood naked before him, looking up at him, he could see her heart in her eyes. She'd deny it, but he could see it. She was his. And he was hers.

They belonged together. They would have a family together. After all that he'd seen, Jack ached to bring children into the world who would be loved as he and Isabel had been loved. Children who would grow up strong and fight the evil in the world.

Jack reached out to touch Summer. He cupped her breast, warm and heavy in his hand. He turned his hand so his palm ran over her flat belly, where someday a child of theirs would grow.

His cock swelled at the thought.

Summer's eyes grew round. "Wow. Whatever that thought was, hold it, because it worked."

He smiled. Oh, yeah.

His hand lay over her womb as he bent to kiss her breast, the breast that would nurse their child. His dick jerked at the thought. His breathing sped up.

Before he lost control again, he stood up, looking at her face.

He'd watch that face age, he'd watch lines of good humor etch themselves into her skin. Lines fan out from those beautiful eyes. But he knew, beyond a shadow of a doubt, that she would always be beautiful to him, just as his mother had always been beautiful to his father.

Words jostled in his throat. He had so many things to tell her, he had so many things he wanted to learn from her. But there was one thing above all he had to say. More important than anything else.

He eased her on her back and took a moment to look at her. Her legs were slightly parted, a sign of welcome. He felt that welcome in every cell of her body. She opened everything to him. When her arms came up, he smiled and slid his body over hers, slid into her body, saw her close her eyes and smile.

Her body was his.

When he didn't move, just stayed inside the warm clasp of her sex, she opened her eyes. "Jack?"

He nodded, but made no move to start making love. Summer's smile faded as she saw his serious expression. "Is something wrong?"

He picked up her hand, looked at it for a long time then looked up at her face.

"Summer Redding, will you marry me?"

THIRTEEN

San Francisco
The Mission District

TODAY WAS THE DAY. Zhang Wei went over his checklist again, but it was a pure formality.

There was already chaos in America. In all, over the course of the last twenty four hours, there had been fifty seven perfectly plausible yet fake attacks that had flooded the airwaves and three real attacks, which Springer's men had taken care of. The news organizations had still not separated the fake from the real.

Springer had sent in encrypted data on the state of play of the US Government. The entire security apparatus of the United States was in full blown panic. All leave had been cancelled for all law enforcement agencies and every single police officer in the country was clocking in overtime. No excuses. The only police officers not on duty were in the hospital. The National Guard had been called out, quite uselessly, in all fifty states. Every resource FEMA had was in the field. Homeland Security was in a state of high alert.

Every single news channel was in disarray. There weren't enough reporters in the world to cover the fake attacks, some of which had been planned for remote, hard-to-access areas. The Fontana Dam, for example, was hundreds of miles from the nearest big city. Helicopters had overflown the area for hours, looking in vain for the bombed dam. By the time they got the news that the dam bombing was a fake, the airwaves had been filled with the other attacks.

Zhang Wei followed all the news networks on his monitors but he was also following Twitter feeds and news blogs. The more intelligent bloggers were speculating that yesterday was one huge hack but Zhang had several more fake attacks and one real one planned— a bomb that was going to go off in the Port of Savannah at 3:00 p.m.

An atmosphere of havoc and disorientation ruled, and emergency services and law enforcement services were being chewed up. By tonight, police officers, hospital staff, medics, members of the National Guard would have been on continuous duty for twenty-four hours. Exhausted and disoriented, they would be unable to face a complete blackout in six western states.

A blackout that would be real, and would last forever. Or until China released the generator spare parts.

When the electricity came back on, there would be no doubt who had turned it back on. The PRC, which had been supplying water and food and medicine for the previous six months.

The blackout was planned for 5:00 p.m. today. An hour before sunset, preceded by massive cellphone jamming all along the West Coast. Then the lights would go out. By dawn it would be clear this was no rolling brownout. Electricity companies would have to start telling the truth. The generators were broken. There were no spare parts. They would *stay* broken until the spare parts could arrive.

When would that be? There was no answer to that.

The Politburo had quietly bought all the companies that manufactured spare parts. They would arrive when China said they could arrive.

When asked when the lights would go back on, the electricity companies would give a huge shrug. Because the answer was—*we have no idea*. And frantic orders would be sent out, except computers and cells wouldn't be working to place the orders. Everyone would go back to the use of landlines, which would work—for a few days.

Landline phone power came from telephone companies, from internal generators that feed into a battery bank. But the battery banks would fail in a few days.

And in a few days, the entire West would be in complete upheaval. Zhang Wei smiled as he thought of eight million Angelenos trying to escape via the freeways. The freeways would become ribbons of metal as passengers deserted their vehicles and set out on foot. Travelling by day because there was no light by night. Not even the light of the moon. Today was the new moon.

Grocery stores would receive no supplies, freezer contents would melt, hospital generators would run down, water pumping stations would stop working and whatever trickled out of faucets would be gravity-driven from cisterns and untreated.

Anyone dependent on insulin, blood pressure medication, anti-depressants, anyone who had infections and needed antibiotics—they would be out of luck.

Whoever survived the first week of panic and violence, would start dropping dead. Third world diseases like cholera, typhoid, diphtheria would quickly make a comeback.

He and his men, on the other hand, would be safely closed up in this building, snipers on the roof with suppressed rifles protecting them if anyone thought to break into an abandoned-looking building. They would have ample electricity, food and water. All they had to do was stay hidden until the PLAN arrived.

And the PRC would emerge victorious, having defeated the strongest nation on earth, without firing a shot.

All of this would begin at 5:00 p.m. when Zhang Wei pressed "enter."

"STAY HERE," JACK said anxiously. For about the billionth time.

It was only because Summer could clearly see how frightened he was for her that she didn't roll her eyes. There was an entire team marshaling in the living room of their suite. The ASI men—Jack, Jacko, Joe—and three FBI special agents from the San Francisco Office. They hadn't been fully briefed but yesterday's fake attacks, which were still ongoing, had them spooked. All they knew was that maybe the people who were behind the attacks were in an alleyway off Brennan Street in the Mission.

Jack had been fine discussing tactics with the ASI guys and the FBI special agents, cool and calm. They stood around a big tablet in their bulletproof vests, going over a surveillance plan and Jack was good. And then his eyes showed the whites all around when it came to her.

"Jack," Summer said patiently, hand on his arm. He was so stiff his muscles practically hummed. "I know the drill. As I've said time and again, I am not an operator. I know I'm not an operator and I have no desire to be one. My role here is to gather intelligence, put together the facts. Which I can do from the comfort of my hotel room." She swept her arm to indicate the amazingly lush suite. "So, in essence, while you and your teammates go out in the pouring rain and freezing cold to examine what's probably an empty building, I'll stay here in the comfort of this room, going through the contents of Hector's laptop and ordering room service. Did I make an adequate summary of the situation?"

But irony bounced right off Jack and everyone else on the team had had a humorectomy.

He stood a moment, staring at her, breathing heavily, like a bull.

He finally broke eye contact, rotated his index finger in the air—*let's head out*—and the six men left the hotel room.

Summer sat with an exhausted sigh on the very comfortable burgundy sofa. She'd been uneasy with the men in the room. They sucked up all the oxygen. Well, Jack did, anyway. They hadn't had a moment alone since waking up this morning in Portland, after he'd asked her to marry him.

She hadn't said yes. She hadn't said no, but she hadn't said yes, either.

It wasn't that she didn't want to marry Jack. It's that she wanted to marry him too much. Her heart had taken a dangerous leap at his words, a leap of joy so intense it scared her. This was it for her. He was it for her, always had been, since she was twelve. It was why she'd never really fallen in love with anyone else, why she'd never even been tempted by any other man, except for an occasional night of sex, when she was feeling particularly lonely.

Jack was it. Jack had always been it.

He'd asked her to marry him and she wanted to with all her heart. But all of this was happening in the heat of danger, with emotions running high. He'd just been reunited with his sister, thoughts of family were on his mind, particularly after spending six months alone, on the run.

Maybe he'd built some kind of fantasy in his head of forming one big happy family back in Portland, living close to his sister, recreating his happy childhood. Great. If it were like that, Summer was all in. Happy happy, forever.

But Jack's family had been unusual. Everyone said so. Almost a freak of nature. She'd never seen anything like it before or since. Summer's own experience with families was darker, not happy at all. Being tied to someone you hated, like Aunt Vanessa had been tied to Hector. Life with her parents had been hell on earth. She never visited her memories, but they were almost all bad, shot through with the kindness of neighbors who felt sorry for the little girl with the terrible parents.

But even without the horror stories of her own family, she'd seen enough to know that huge pain could follow a bad choice. Poor Zac had come from a terrible family background—a violent father, alcoholic mother—and he'd become almost asexual, terrified of relationships.

Of course Jack was fundamentally kind and not an alcoholic. But Jack, for all his worldliness, for all that he'd gone through as an agent, a spy, was an idealist.

She knew that to him, the nastiness of the world existed, but it was kept at bay by family.

What happened if the family went sour?

What happened if Summer found she couldn't be open enough, loving enough, for Jack? Nothing in her background and nothing in her life had prepared her for being a loving wife or—God!—mother.

Jack had taken it badly when she hadn't said yes. He thought it was a reflection of him. It wasn't. It was a reflection of her.

This was getting her nowhere. She wasn't being useful and furthermore, she was depressing herself. As always, the best tonic for any down thoughts was work. Work had always uplifted her.

She didn't have an answer for Jack. Not now, anyway. She was too troubled, too unsure of herself. Her life was in turmoil. How could she think of a lifetime commitment when she didn't know where she'd be tomorrow?

Work, she thought. The ultimate tonic.

Felicity had copied all of Hector's files and put them on a brand new laptop for her, while she continued working on the flash drives and the original laptop. When Summer asked her whether she was sure that everything of Hector's was in the cloned computer, Felicity had merely looked at her.

So. She essentially had Hector's computer with her. She opened the laptop on a desk near a window looking out over the Financial District of San Francisco. She'd never been to San Francisco before and had only seen the streets as they drove in from the airport.

Someday, when all this was over, when no one was trying to kill her, when she had her life back, she was coming back. It had always been a city she'd wanted to visit.

Maybe she could come with Jack…

Focus, Summer!

Okay. She looked at the files on Hector's laptop. Felicity had flagged the encrypted files so Summer concentrated on the non-encrypted files. No use in duplication of effort.

The hard disk was full. It was going to be a task lasting several days, carefully going through everything. She called room service for coffee and a club sandwich and got to work.

Hector's computer files were compelling, though she had to force herself to look at some of the photos of Hector's partners.

It was a little like wading through mud, though. A walk around Hector's mind was not pleasant. It was filled with vindictive bile, money obsession, soulless sex. She was about ready to give herself a break when a name caught her eye in a file in a folder dedicated to investments.

Aurora.

Could be anything, really. The name of an investment company, a new corporation, a hedge fund. A woman. But it could also be the chilling experiment run in 2007 on the safety of the electricity grid. Testing the grid, it had been proven it was vulnerable to hacks. Summer had done a series on the safety of infrastructure and had been appalled at what she'd found out. She'd interviewed twenty scientists and four experts from Homeland Security and had come away with the clear feeling that it was a disaster just waiting to happen.

The Aurora file didn't talk about cybersabotage. Rather, it was a series of investments, to the tune of almost a hundred million dollars. She wasn't an expert, but looking at the files carefully, Hector was selling short stocks in power companies. Which would only make sense if he knew there were going to be major power outages which would make those stocks plummet.

It was the Aurora scenario. Her heart thudded. And the date those stocks fell due was today. All the sell orders were dated today. At 2:00 p.m. Eastern Standard Time. 5:00 p.m. Pacific Time. In half an hour.

Heart thudding, Summer called Jack's cell and got no signal. She frowned and called again. And again. Crazily, she hadn't taken anyone else's cellphone number. She wasn't supposed to have emergencies, she was safely in a suite at the Marriott.

This was the biggest emergency she could think of.

In twenty minutes, if she was right, the electricity grid would go down. Maybe forever. And the United States would be plunged right back to the Middle Ages in a couple of seconds.

She grabbed her coat and rushed down the stairs and out the door and started running as fast as she could toward Brennan Street.

JACK TAPPED HIS EAR. They had an excellent comms system, provided by ASI. Even the FBI guys had taken one look and ditched their FBI-issue set. Unfortunately, Jack had to wave away the thick locks of hair of his wig—a dark haired one, a big bushy prof's do. He hated this one, too.

They'd all been in place for hours. He and Joe took

turns sitting in a nearby coffee shop, the two FBI guys, Hank and Mike, and Nick were in a van a block away. Jacko was where Jacko could do the most good. On high.

"What are you seeing, Jacko?"

Jacko had set up a sniper's nest on the roof of a building several blocks away but with no tall buildings in between. He had a clear sight of their target with his Leupold Mark VI rifle scope that could see the balls on a fly. Knowing Jacko, he could probably shoot those balls off, too.

"Jackshit, Jack," Jacko answered in his deep bass. Then, unusually, a chuckle. Not too many chuckles from Jacko. "Nothing. Oh, they have stealth film over their windows. The kind I have. You can barely tell, but I have it at my place and I can tell."

Jack felt a slight shiver. The building was old and probably slated for demolition. But the door and window frames were new. And now the window panes had a very expensive film that let in light but did not let out light. Jacko had gone to the roof of two other buildings and reported that there was a very effective camouflage netting in the back alleyway. The kind of camouflage netting Jack had put in the alleyway of his safe house. The kind that fooled drones. You'd need a drone with a laser rangefinder to tell that they weren't looking at the ground but at something eight feet high.

The van had directed an IR gun at the building and seen four warm bodies on the first floor and four on the second floor. Eight heat signatures, eight men. But they were more or less staying put and no one had ventured outside.

One good thing the FBI guys had confirmed—no

radiation leakage. They'd all heaved a sigh of relief at that, because, well, a nuclear bomb was always a fun possibility.

He and Joe had quietly made the rounds of the corner grocery stores in the area, but without knowing who or what they were looking for, without a photo of a possible perp, nothing was gained.

Stalemate.

Nothing was happening.

Jack checked his watch. 4:40 p.m. There were quite enough eyes on this place. He'd like to take a break and walk the couple of blocks to the Marriot and see Summer. Surveillance could last all night. It could last forever, actually. He'd argued for a warrant to enter the premises but Nick and the Director were both in agreement that might spook whoever was in there.

This was an open-ended op. He didn't have to stay 24/7. He wanted to see Summer. Now. He wanted to make sure she was okay, see it with his own eyes.

Also because…well, he'd proposed and she hadn't accepted. That was burning a hole in his head. She had feelings for him, he knew she did. If there was one thing Jack understood, it was women. He was out of practice, sure, but women hadn't changed in ten thousand years, there was no evidence they'd changed in the past couple of years. She cared for him. Secretly, he thought she loved him, but unfortunately he couldn't put his hand to the fire on that. But he could make her love him. He was going to be the most devoted husband on the face of the planet.

He'd grown up with his dad, who'd been the most loving husband possible. He had an excellent example.

Summer, on the other hand, had had awful examples

of husbands. Her own father who must have been a real prick, and high most of the time with it, and Hector. Who'd hated his wife. Wives.

No wonder she was hesitant. That was it, wasn't it?

She couldn't be rejecting *him*, could she?

That thought drove him a little crazy.

She obviously couldn't see what he could see, because she had no experience of it in her world. But what he could see, so very clearly, was the two of them in that pretty town, Portland, surrounded by friends who would become like family, with Isabel close by. With every day that passed, he came closer and closer to the decision to accept ASI's job offer. It was an amazingly cool company and he was ready for the private sector. He'd had enough government bullshit. ASI's bosses were real clear on what they did and did not want and they stood by their employees, always. Hugh had been like that, but Hugh was gone. Even when he was no longer a fugitive, even when this mess was cleared up, he knew he'd never go back to the CIA. The CIA was probably going to disappear anyway.

He and Summer could have a beautiful life together. A life of meaning. Their children would grow up in a loving family, surrounded by good friends.

Summer could do whatever she wanted, and whatever she wanted to do, he'd support her. She could commute back and forth to DC if she wanted to continue *Area 8*. She could found another webzine. She could write books. He didn't care as long as she spent some time with him and they could create a family.

A family.

The feeling of yearning that evoked nearly brought him to his knees.

He had no business thinking these things while he was on an op. Which was why he had to ask for an hour off and go see Summer. Reassure himself she was okay, was safe. To see if she loved him.

Because God knows, he loved her.

He checked his watch again. 4:43. At five he'd leave for an hour, go see Summer. He missed her already. He could almost see her before his eyes, in that incredibly pretty and probably amazingly expensive forest green outfit that suited her coloring. He could see her…

Fuck. He could *see* her!

She was supposed to be safe and warm back in the hotel.

What the fuck was she—

"Yo," Jacko growled. "Girlfriend at your two o'clock."

4:45.

She was running, not caring that people were looking at her. Summer reached him, panting.

"Whoa." Jack caught her. "What are you doing out of the hotel? I thought I told you—"

"Jack," she gasped. "I know what they're going to do!" She stared up at him wild-eyed, trembling. "They're going to wreck the electricity grid! Trash it! No power for years! The Aurora scenario! Scheduled for five! In a quarter of an hour!"

"Fuck!" Jack tapped his earbud. "You guys hearing this?" He turned to Summer. "Why didn't you call me?"

"Your cell isn't working! I tried but I couldn't get through!"

He checked, and goddamned if it wasn't dead. "You guys—your cells working?"

"Negative." Joe.

"Negative with us." Nick, from the van.

"Mine does," Jacko said. He was the farthest away.

Terror prickled up his spine. This was exactly what happened just before the Massacre. Everyone's cells went dead. The ASI system worked on a separate radio frequency.

"Nick!" he shouted, but he didn't have to because Nick, Hank and Mike were already out of the van. "We have a quarter of an hour," he said.

They were around the corner from the building and Nick started hauling out gear.

"Summer, get away!" Jack was sweating. Not from the op but from having Summer anywhere near here.

"Summer, can you shoot?" Nick turned to her.

"Yes," she replied calmly. "A little."

He handed her a Glock 19. "It's got a full magazine. Get back to the hotel but keep that with you."

She nodded and took it. "You guys have got to hurry. You've only got a quarter of an hour."

Jack nodded. "The hell with a warrant. We have to go in fast, weapons hot."

Summer turned a pale, frightened face to him. "Do you have your vest on?"

"I do." He checked his weapon, looked at the gear Nick had. Joe had arrived and was sorting through the explosives for breaching the door. Hank and Mike were holding flashbangs. Jack bent to kiss her quickly. "Get out of here, Summer."

"Go," she said and they took off at a run.

Jack had never trained with any of the men but they worked together smoothly, as a team. They were all equipped with MP5s, besides the rest of the gear. In a minute, Joe had placed carefully calibrated amounts of C-4 around the front door and detonated it from around the corner. As the door exploded, Hank and Mike held a box with cylinders inserted in it. A flashbang launcher, Jack knew, though he'd never seen one. They launched two into the front window, raced to the side, launched two more, then stood back and launched two more into the second story window.

Nick, Joe and Jack waited for the flashbangs to go off, grenades emitting enough light to blind for several minutes and enough noise to deafen a person.

"Go go *go*!" Nick screamed and they ran into the building, weapons up.

Three Chinese men with the build of soldiers lay on the ground, stunned, unable even to reach the weapons on a table. "I got this," Joe yelled. "Get the computer!"

Jack and Nick rushed up the stairs and into a room that was the control room. Monitors everywhere, thick cables covering the floor. Four thin men, different from the soldiers downstairs, were groaning on the ground. One sat up, holding his head, watching them wide-eyed. Stunned, but coming to his senses.

Hank and Mike came up and started restraining them. The one sitting up shot to his knees, then feet, reaching out—

"*Jack!*" Jacko screamed. "Out back! One's escaping! And oh God, Summer's there! Get out there!"

Jack had never moved so fast in his life. He tore down the stairs, made his way to the back of the building, crashed through the door into an alleyway covered with netting.

And there she was! Summer. What the fuck was she doing? She had the gun he'd given her, pointed at the ground. She looked up, then back down to the ground, a determined frown on her face. She was looking at a piece of iron pipe. She pulled the trigger and shot it, shot it again and again.

"Jack!" Jacko yelled again. "Your six!"

And everything went into slow motion. Summer, a determined look on her face, shooting at the pipe, not looking up. The pipe severing. A man at the other end of the alley, raising a gun aimed straight at her head, Jack flying, tackling Summer and taking her to the ground just as he felt a blow to his arm, followed by hot pain.

But there'd been two shots…

He lay on Summer, frantically touching her, only one arm wasn't working. At the end of the alley, a man lay on the ground, face up, unmoving.

"Summer!" Jack shouted, only it didn't come out as a shout, it came out a cough. His voice was weak. Something red soaked the asphalt. She was bleeding!

No, he was bleeding.

"Oh God, Jack!" Summer was kneeling over him, stuffing a scarf against his wound. Jesus, it hurt. Heads appeared above him. Nick, Hank, Mike. But he only saw Summer, crying.

"You took a bullet for me," she whispered.

Jack nodded. Then tried to talk. "Yes."

"Yes," Summer said, though her tears. "Yes, I will!"

Had he hit his head? "Yes you will?"

"Yes." She leaned down and kissed him. It hurt. "I'll marry you."

EPILOGUE

Portland
A month later

"TO SUMMER AND JACK!" Isabel raised her glass and everyone else did, too. The entire crew of ASI and of Suzanne Huntington's company drank to them.

Jack had to drink left handed because his entire right arm was still in a sling. The bullet wound had required surgery and some rehab which Metal—who had turned out be quite a sadist—was overseeing. Getting shot sucked, but it had tipped Summer over into accepting his proposal, so there was that.

The engagement was being celebrated in a beautiful lodge on Mount Hood and Isabel catered. It was a rowdy crowd but everyone grew silent each time a new course came out.

There was a lot to celebrate. Their engagement. Jack's new job with ASI. The founding of Summer's new blog, *Natura*, dedicated to environmentalism. She said she was sick of politics and that the environment was more important. She ran the blog out of their new home, on the street where Isabel and Joe lived. They were celebrating the day, two weeks ago, when the Director of the FBI went to visit the Deputy Director of the CIA, Marcus Springer, and presented him with a warrant for his arrest for 720 counts of conspiracy to murder—the Washington Massacre—and high treason. The plan to bring down the electricity grid over half the United States had been found in Hector's files and no doubt would be found in Springer's files.

Summer had shattered the fiber optic cable just in time. Another two seconds and they'd be in the dark, surrounded by chaos.

There was another big thing to celebrate. Jack had found out via an old Harvard friend. He'd asked him to keep him advised and he had just gotten word.

Summer smiled wryly at him, looking at her left hand ring finger. She complained about how big her engagement ring was and how much it bothered her when she worked. But she never took it off. Jack had bought the biggest diamond he could, just to show the world who she belonged to.

But the fact was, Summer belonged to the world.

Even staying by his side day and night in the hospital, Summer had written hard-hitting articles on the conspiracy that had knocked the political world off its axis. A dope of a man, John London, was supposed to be the next president, but when she wrote about the deal he'd made with Hector and Marcus Springer—to do the bidding of the Chinese once he was president—he was out of the running and retired to his country home. A new wind was sweeping Washington because it turned out many politicians had been complicit in the plan.

The Chinese denied any knowledge of the plan, blaming it on rogue elements and executing General Chen Yi, the head of the cyber unit of the PLA. New trade agreements were in place, all favorable to the US.

Summer's articles, all dedicated to the memory

of Zac Burroughs and Marcie Thompson, had made history.

And she was going to make history once again.

Jack stood, tapped his knife against a glass. The room quieted.

"I think all of you know that I am the luckiest man alive. I don't know how, but I managed to get Summer to agree to marry me. Of course I had a bullet in me and she couldn't know that I'd survive and hold her to her promise—" He waited for the laughter to die down. "But being a woman of her word, Summer has agreed to marry me and we have decided to have a June wedding. You are all invited."

The room broke into an uproar, everyone grinning. Jacko took the opportunity to grab the last piece of blueberry cheesecake and winked at him.

"But I have more news," Jack went on. "Of the good variety. I have just received word from a good friend of mine that my beloved Summer Redding, soon to be Summer Delvaux, has just been awarded the Pulitzer Prize for Investigative Reporting. She'll be getting the official call in a minute or two. So help me raise a toast—"

Jack smiled down into Summer's shocked face, knowing he was going to be looking at that face for the rest of his life, and that she would be winning award after award. And that he would love her all his life.

"Help me raise a toast to Summer, the woman I love more than life itself, the most amazing woman in the world."

* * * * *

Go back to the beginning with
Lisa Marie Rice and Carina Press
MIDNIGHT VENGEANCE
(*Men of Midnight Book 1*)
Available now, wherever
Carina Press eBooks are sold!

*Morton "Jacko" Jackman isn't afraid of anything.
He's a former Navy SEAL sniper, and he's been in
more firefights than most people have had hot meals.
Lauren Dare scares the crap out of him.*

*Gorgeous, talented and refined, she's the type of
woman who could never be interested in a roughneck like him. So he's loved her fiercely in secret,
taken her art classes, and kept a watchful but comfortable distance. Until now.*

*Lauren had finally found a home in Portland, far
from her real identity, far from the memories of
her mother's death, and outside the reaches of the
drugged-out psycho who's already tried to kill her
twice. One tiny misstep—a single photograph—has
shattered it all. She has no choice but to run again,
but this time she'll give herself a proper farewell:
one night with Jacko.*

*Their highly charged emotional encounter changes
everything. In Jacko's arms there cannot be fear,
there can only be pleasure. Anyone wishing her
harm will have to pass through him, and Jacko is a
hard man to kill.*

ONE

Portland, Oregon
"Inside/Out" Exhibit of Suzanne Huntington's
interior designs

"GIRLFRIEND ON YOUR SIX."

A hard elbow jabbed into Morton "Jacko" Jackman's hard side. It would have knocked a lesser man down. Former senior chief Douglas Kowalski wasn't known for his gentleness or delicate touch. But then neither was Jacko. He was a former Navy SEAL too, just like Senior. But both of them were out of the service and working in the same company, Alpha Security International, so Jacko could knock Senior on his ass and not be court-martialed.

Except, well, Senior was a good guy.

Senior's elbow couldn't knock Jacko down, but his knees nearly buckled at the thought of the woman behind him.

"Not my girlfriend," he mumbled, hoping the tan he'd gotten over his dark skin this past week teaching Mexican *federales* in Baja the fine art of fucking with the enemy hid his red face.

Senior shifted his eyes sideways, a hint of a smile on his big ugly mug. "No?" He shook his head and jabbed him again. "So why the chubby every time you lay eyes on her?"

Fuck. Busted. Jacko pulled his tuxedo jacket lower.
He'd learned to control his dick at fourteen. What was
he—back in high school? Why couldn't he be in jeans,
like he was most times he saw her? Tight stiff ones
that kept the hard-on down because it didn't have anywhere to go.

Except you don't wear jeans to a fancy art exhibit.
Particularly not when your boss's wife's works were
on show.

"Bravo red, moving fast," the chief murmured. Anyone farther than a foot from them wouldn't have heard
a word and wouldn't have understood anyway. The
orientation clock. "Bravo red" meant she was moving
behind him to his right. Man.

Lauren Dare.

Oh. God.

Jacko thought he could smell her but that was crazy.
Still, why not imagine he could smell her, because she
drove him crazy in every other way? Though smelling Lauren in a room full of hundreds of people, every
single one—man, woman and other—wearing perfume
or cologne, with caterers walking around with hot food
on platters and glasses of wine everywhere…well, that
stretched even Jacko's sense of his own craziness.

He wasn't known for this. He wasn't what Suzanne
Huntington, the big boss's wife and the star of the show,
would call a fanciful man. He was known for being
hardheaded and hard-hearted and hard-bodied. He was
a roughneck from Texas who'd be in jail if he hadn't
signed up for the Navy. They'd pounded self-discipline
and a sniper's focus plus a dozen lethal martial arts
into him. He could handle any type of weaponry, explosives, hand-to-hand combat.

Not one ounce of his very extensive and very expensive training gave him a clue about how to handle Lauren Dare.

There she was! Alone and lost-looking against the wall across the room to his right. For such a beautiful woman, she was doing her best not to attract attention, though for Jacko that didn't work. Couldn't. It was like the roof opened up and the sun shot a beam straight down onto her like a spotlight. Jacko was surprised people weren't gasping and turning to watch her.

She was doing everything possible to keep a low profile. She didn't even want her name on the program, though all of the works on the wall were hers. Suzanne insisted she take the credit for them, but Lauren had insisted right back. Very few people knew this entire show was all hers. He had no idea why she didn't want credit. Most people were happy to receive it for things they didn't do; few refused it. But who knew why women wanted anything, anyway? Lauren didn't want anyone to know, and for him, that was that.

Lauren was moving through the crowd like a ghost, nodding and smiling and never stopping to talk to anyone. Jacko couldn't understand how the men managed to avoid staring at her, but then he'd always known deep down that most men were assholes. You'd have to be an asshole and blind to boot not to realize that Lauren was the most beautiful woman in a room full of them.

Two of the beauties were married to his employers, John Huntington and Senior.

Lauren moved gracefully, not speaking a word to anyone, accompanied by notes from heaven. It took Jacko a full minute to realize that angels weren't sending down a sound track for Lauren Dare to move to. It was Allegra Kowalski, up on a dais, playing her harp. The notes morphed into a recognizable tune he'd heard Senior's wife play a million times.

Senior's wife was a talented musician—a harpist and singer. Jacko remembered the first time he'd met her, sent to be a bodyguard while Senior hunted down the fuckhead who'd attacked Allegra and blinded her. She'd had to have tricky experimental surgery to get her sight back, which had added years to Senior's life. Jacko would have done his duty, even lain down his life, for a snaggletoothed banshee girlfriend of Senior but as it happened, Allegra Kowalski was beautiful and sweet and had played her harp for Jacko for a couple of hours while he sat in a chair facing the door, .22 on his lap, finger along the trigger guard.

Allegra's music had fucked heavily with his head and changed him forever.

But Lauren was the one who messed with him the most. Those long, white delicate hands of hers created things he couldn't even begin to imagine existed and yet became stone hard reality for him the instant he saw them.

He'd seen her drawings and paintings first. Suzanne, the wife of his other boss, John Huntington, aka Midnight Man, designed places where you walked in and felt like you were in some kind of stylish fairyland. Suzanne had sent him to pick Lauren up in her workshop to talk about creating images of Suzanne's designs. Jacko had walked into a big airy room and had frozen because he was surrounded by the most beautiful things he'd ever seen in his life. He'd simply stood stock still and gaped, mouth open like some raw recruit watching SEALs in training.

And then Lauren had walked into the room and even her gorgeous watercolors and drawings vanished from his head like smoke.

Suzanne and Allegra were beautiful women. They were known for being beautiful, though they never used those coy tricks most good-looking women did. But Lauren—it was like she was another species. A cloud of shiny dark hair surrounding a heart-shaped face with silver-gray eyes on top of a body to make men weep. It had been a hot late summer day and she'd worn a sundress that showed delicate pale shoulders, slender arms and a tiny waist, and when she spoke Jacko didn't hear a word she said.

His head was buzzing too loud.

She tried twice. He got that much. He saw her full mouth open and close and all he could think about was that mouth on his while his entire body buzzed and he got the first of many, many hard-ons that sprouted whenever he was around her.

At the third try, he tried hard to focus and managed to grasp that she was asking him a question. *Morton, right?* He simply stared at her. *Suzanne said she'd send someone called Morton?* And at the end there was this little inflection, making it a question. And fuck him if he didn't forget his own name was Morton.

He was an asshole and blown away by her, but in his defense was the fact that only the Navy ever called him Morton, and that was only on official occasions or when he was being chewed out. He'd been Jacko forever.

It was only when he saw the first glimmerings of fear in her eyes and she took a quick instinctive step back that he pulled his head out of his ass. And felt ashamed. Having a 240-pound thug who lifted weights daily and had spent the last fifteen years training to kill people stare at you was probably not a good thing. Particularly if you were a beautiful woman with a slender build, alone in a space with the thug.

So he'd used every single ounce of self-discipline the Navy and particularly SEAL training had beaten into him and nodded and said—*Yes, Morton's my name—most folks call me Jacko. Suzanne Huntington sent me to pick you up.*

She'd just stood there, staring at him. Well, he could do something about her unease. He'd tapped his cell and called Suzanne. When she answered he simply handed the phone to Lauren and watched as some color came back into her face.

And when he complimented her on some of the artworks she actually blushed.

And Jacko was lost.

He drove her to Suzanne's office in Pearl, which was also the headquarters of Alpha Security International, where Jacko worked. He thought driving under eighty miles per hour was for dead men but he kept it at a steady forty and would have driven at twenty miles an hour if he could, just to stay in the vehicle with her. He waited for her as she and Suzanne talked, then drove her back. At thirty miles per hour. When he dropped her off at her house, he drove around the block and stopped the car and waited for his hands to stop shaking.

When he found out that Lauren taught drawing at a community center, he enrolled immediately and got another huge whack to his system. He was *good* at it. Damned good.

The past four months of his life had been work, thinking of Lauren, attending her classes, sitting in his empty apartment drawing maps and drawing Lauren. There hadn't been room for much of anything else. No cycling out to the boonies and letting his Kawasaki Vulcan Voyager motorcycle rip. Megadeth, his favorite band, came through Portland, one night only, and he didn't go. It was a Tuesday and Lauren taught on Tuesday evenings. So no Megadeth.

No fucking, either.

That was a shocker. He didn't even realize he'd stopped fucking chicks until three weeks after meeting Lauren. It hadn't even occurred to him. When it did, he made a point of going out that evening to his usual hole, The Spike, and picking someone up because Jacko Jackman didn't do abstinence. Nope.

A couple of chicks he'd hooked up with before stopped by and made interested noises and to his enormous surprise, his dick said no. Fuck no.

As a matter of fact it felt like his balls tried to crawl up into his body.

He never tried that again and so he might as well have been a tattooed and pierced monk these past four months for all the tail he got.

And the reason was right in this room.

Jacko tracked Lauren as she made the rounds, speaking briefly with a few people when they spoke to her, then moving on. In the room full of trendy women dressed in bright peacock colors tottering on stiletto heels, she was low key in a midnight-blue dress with ballerina slippers. Jacko couldn't even see the other women while she was in the room.

They all seemed overblown and shrill. Sharp laughing voices crackling. Lauren's voice was never sharp. It was soft, with an underlying tone like music, only not.

She was sweeping the room with her eyes and Jacko felt a change in the air when she saw him. Her face went from slightly sad to joyous in one second, and his heart nearly exploded out of his chest when she veered course immediately, making a beeline for him. He could feel himself stiffening in every sense.

"Incoming," Senior muttered. "You're on your own here, son. I'm going to my own woman."

Palm Beach, Florida

"Go on in," the muscle said, waving toward the door with his .44, a weapon that probably cost more than he did.

Frederick Rydell stifled a sigh. The quality of Guttierez goonhood had declined sadly since the death two years ago of that thuggish, though stylish, mobster Alfonso Guttierez. The organization had fallen to his moron nephew, Jorge Guttierez. Alfonso had had discreet, well-dressed security at the gate. Frederick passed through a metal detector and that had been that.

Jorge's muscle had actually frisked him, rumpling Frederick's Hugo Boss jacket, and had taken entirely too much pleasure in touching his private parts and between his buttocks.

Really.

Alfonso would never have hired this outlandish man-child with a backward baseball cap and oversized jeans with the dropped crotch.

Morgan, Alfonso's personal bodyguard, had always been impeccably dressed, able to serve tea or shoot you between the eyes without breaking a sweat. This goon looked incapable of thought, let alone style.

Frederick opened the door to the suite of rooms Alfonso had used as a study and had to work hard to hide his shock. The two rooms were high ceilinged and elegantly decorated. Alfonso's late wife had been a bitch of the highest order but a bitch with exquisite taste. And Alfonso himself was a thug with social ambitions. It didn't really make any difference in Floridian high society if you made your money running drugs and arms and trafficking in humans. As long as you made a lot of it, you were in. Alfonso had had a lot of it and Chantal, the new wife, knew how to spend it.

Alfonso's study wouldn't have been out of place in a lord's palace. It had been filled with superb antiques, exquisite rugs, decent art on the walls. And Chantal managed the staff like a general. Frederick had never seen the mansion less than perfect. Never even a fallen petal from the numerous floral arrangements.

Now it looked like pigs had rooted through the rooms, followed by the Huns.

After the deaths of Alfonso and Chantal, the staff had kept things going but Jorge had let the staff go, one by one, replacing the maids with the girls he fucked and who had no desire to pick up after themselves.

Frederick stopped on the threshold, willing his stomach not to rise. This was the worst he'd seen the rooms, a physical manifestation of the disintegration of Jorge's personality.

The rooms smelled of sex, expensive whiskey and overwhelming perfume. Someone had vomited and someone had shat and not flushed, so there was an overlay of that coupled with disgusting smells of fast food. The French chef had been the first member of the staff to go.

Two of the sofas had been pulled askew, cushions on the ground. Pizza and takeout boxes littered the marble floor. One of the antique mirrors—fashioned by the same craftsmen who'd made the mirrors in Versailles, Chantal had told him—was cracked.

Frederick schooled his face to blandness but his mind was racing as he crossed the room. He stepped on a used condom and his throat quivered as his stomach shot up his gullet.

Jorge was sitting with his back to the huge two-inch-thick bullet-resistant windows that gave out on to a flagstone terrace that ran the width of the mansion.

"Party last night?" Frederick asked, keeping his tone light.

Jorge grunted. He was sitting in Alfonso's chair, forearms on the surface of the Chippendale table that had served Alfonso as his main desk. A satchel sat next to Jorge's right hand. As Frederick walked closer he could see that Jorge was keeping himself upright by his arms on the table. Frederick checked Jorge's eyes, overly bright with pinpoint pupils. Christ, the man was wasted.

Jorge was going to talk business stoned out of his mind.

With an inner sigh, Frederick felt a pang of pity for himself pulse through his system. He'd earned a lot of money off the Gutierrez machine and now it was coming to a close. Like most good things, he supposed.

"So," Frederick said, sitting down on one of Chantal's antique chairs, noting with a repressed shudder that the seat cushion was stained. He couldn't bear to think of what might have caused the stain. "Here I am for my monthly report."

He'd had a not-unpleasant monthly appointment with Alfonso, to deliver ongoing reports. Frederick was the Gutierrez family's computer expert and the confidential conduit for communication with the various international…dealers Alfonso had business with. Alfonso owned two hotels, three nightclubs and four restaurants in Florida, which, being Alfonso, were exceedingly well run and turned a tidy profit.

But they were fronts for what earned Alfonso the real money — drugs, prostitution, people trafficking. All activities Alfonso managed at a remove with Frederick's help. He never got his hands dirty, directing everything via secure computer, which was Frederick's lookout. Vast amounts of money exchanged hands via bitcoins on the darknet, and every month Frederick visited Alfonso, he was treated to a superb brandy while delivering his report, and watched as 25K was deposited in his account in the Caymans.

Everyone was happy.

Since Alfonso's death, the businesses, legal and otherwise, had been going to hell. Very quickly. Frederick would have left long ago if it weren't for the fact that Jorge was desperately looking for Anne Lowell, Chantal's daughter, Alfonso's stepdaughter. Right after Chantal and Alfonso's wedding, Anne had fled from her family, disliking everything about her mother's new household. Anne had come from an upper crust family in Boston and hadn't mixed well, to put it mildly.

She'd been gone years before Frederick's association with Alfonso, and no one would have given Anne Lowell a moment's thought if it weren't for the fact that

Chantal had died an hour after Alfonso, as his main heir. And then Anne had been Chantal's main heir.

So she had inherited most of the estate, the above-ground one anyway, and Jorge had gone wild. Alfonso's brother had sent his only son up to Miami to learn the business, and Jorge thought he had it made for life. But Alfonso soon understood his nephew's weaknesses and had made sure to leave everything to Chantal. Who would probably have wisely put Frederick in charge.

Alfonso had never said a word to Frederick about his succession. Alfonso had been a very healthy self-disciplined fifty-year-old and Frederick had looked forward to many more years of happy association with an empire efficiently run by Alfonso. But that happy scenario had come to a crashing halt when a drugged-up teen slammed straight into Alfonso's Porsche.

Frederick often wondered whether the teen had been hopped up on Alfonso's product. Alfonso had had a great sense of irony and would have appreciated it.

Frederick had been sorry for Alfonso but above all, sorry for himself. Alfonso's death had put a serious crimp in Frederick's plan to sock away five million in the Caymans before forty.

"Give me your report," Jorge said sullenly, slurring the words. With a sigh, Frederick complied, knowing that Jorge understood one word in ten. Concepts such as bitcoins, Tor, arbitrage, currency conversion flew right over his head.

Only one thing mattered to Jorge—Anne Lowell.

Jorge had somehow got it into his head that if Anne Lowell died, everything would become his. Magical thinking, of course. Anne Lowell would certainly never leave anything to Jorge in a will. Jorge had no concept of the legal issues pertaining to estates and succession. Somewhere in his drug-addled mind, a dead Anne Lowell equaled a magical return to prosperity.

Frederick did nothing to disabuse him of the notion. An obsessed Jorge was going to pay the monthly retainer forever, though he had no clue how to do that online. It was strictly cash, in a satchel. Frederick had upped his price to 50K a month and had stopped looking very hard. He'd found Anne Lowell. Twice. It wasn't his fault Jorge was an idiot.

In college, majoring in computer programming, Frederick had had to take a course in creative writing and had been unexpectedly good at it. He loved movies and often thought he had the makings of a decent scriptwriter in him. Lately he'd been observing Jorge and his antics, thinking he could turn the situation into one of those tragicomic TV series everyone loved so much, like *Breaking Bad*.

Jorge and his minions trying to be crime lords, but fucking everything up. Frederick even had a title for the series. *Code Name: Moron*.

It was so annoying, being paid in cash. The bills were probably all laced with cocaine. Jorge pushed the satchel of cash over to him and then fixed baleful bloodshot eyes on Frederick. "You find the bitch yet?"

"I've found her twice for you," Frederick said, as he'd said many times before. "And both times your goons botched it."

Either she was very, very clever or very, very lucky. Twice they'd killed the wrong girl. Now she'd completely disappeared.

And he'd stopped prioritizing her. Let Jorge stew in his juices.

Jorge pounded a fist on the desktop. He was sweating like a pig. The side of his fist left a sweatprint. "Find that bitch! Find her now!" Jorge's attempt at being tough was beyond pitiful. "I'll give you a bonus if you find her before May 1."

Yeah, right.

Still, something was very wrong. Frederick had heard rumors that Jorge was deep in the hole with some very bad guys. Alfonso had left some well-run businesses but Jorge was crapping all over everything around him. He couldn't get it out of his head that finding Anne Lowell and killing her would—poof!—make all his troubles disappear.

Jorge was a cretin who wanted to run with the big boys and was in way over his head. Not that Frederick gave a fuck. He planned on cashing in 50K a month until someone smoked Jorge.

A dead Anne Lowell was not going to solve any of Jorge's problems. But Frederick wasn't about to say that.

Frederick would find Anne Lowell again, sooner or later, though he wasn't putting any effort into it. Who cared? As long as he was being paid, Frederick would keep at it on a low-level priority basis. Nobody could hide forever in a country with fifty million surveillance cameras.

Pity. Anne Lowell was, by all accounts, a charming, kind young woman who didn't deserve getting whacked by a lowlife like Jorge.

But hey.

TWO

Portland

THIS IS A BIG MISTAKE, Lauren Dare thought. A huge, potentially disastrous mistake.

The show was as terrifying as she'd thought it would be. Why oh *why* had she accepted Suzanne's invitation?

Lauren sighed. She knew why. Because Suzanne had insisted so strongly and just wouldn't take no for an answer. Because Suzanne had threatened to simply cancel the show if Lauren wouldn't at least show up. No matter that the show was important to Suzanne's career.

The drawings, pastels, gouaches and watercolors up on the walls were Lauren's. She'd illustrated Suzanne's brilliant interior designs, that was all. Lauren didn't want—couldn't have—her name on the program in any way and had made that abundantly clear, without explaining why. Suzanne had reluctantly accepted. But Suzanne had been adamant—if Lauren's name couldn't be on the program at least she'd attend the opening.

Suzanne was across the room, signaling her to come over, but Lauren didn't dare. Suzanne had a gleam in her eye and there was no guarantee she wouldn't let slip who had actually made the illustrations to someone she thought might be important to Lauren's career.

Suzanne was almost visibly vibrating with the need to praise Lauren in public.

She didn't understand that Lauren didn't have a career. *Couldn't* have a career.

Bless her. Suzanne meant well but it could cost Lauren her life.

She shouldn't be here at all. Being here was insane, a gesture crazy beyond belief. She was still alive at twenty-eight against all the odds because she didn't *do* things like this. Hadn't put herself in the public eye in any way in two long, dangerous years. She'd stayed alive for the past two years by being invisible. And her Portland life for the past year was supposed to be all about keeping her head down.

So *why* was she here?

Affection, that was why. Her downfall. She had simply been embraced by Suzanne...

Glorious harp music began playing, notes beamed straight down from heaven.

...and Allegra. Both charming, lovely, talented women who hadn't taken no for an answer when it came to becoming her friends. A stone heart would have crumbled and Lauren's heart wasn't made of stone. Oh no.

Her life would have been immensely easier if it were.

And it wasn't just Suzanne and Allegra who had bound her in silken ropes of affection. No, there was also Claire Morrison, their friend and the wife of a homicide cop. She'd horned in too. Friendly and smart like the others, warmhearted and funny. Simply irresistible.

And Lauren hadn't resisted much, had she?

It was unforgiveable. Lauren was alive because she kept her head low; she didn't make friends; she wasn't noticed in any way.

So she shouldn't be here, at a big social and media event. It was insane, and dangerous.

A trick to not making an impact, to not being noticed, was to keep moving. She'd arrived deliberately late by taxi, rebuffing offers of all three women to pick her up, and slipped in unnoticed, dressed in a dark, simple gown she could move easily in and ballerina slippers, no heels.

Because you never knew when you might have to run.

And that's when she met his eyes and broke out in a smile because she simply couldn't help it. Another reason she'd stayed on in Portland way over her new life's sell-by date.

Morton Jackman. Jacko.

He was her star pupil in her weekly drawing classes, though there was little she could teach him beyond the basics. He was a natural. Somehow he was always around, giving a hand in closing up at the community center, offering to drive her to the supermarket when her car broke down, fixing her leaky faucets and cleaning out the grout. Putting in fancy new locks in her doors.

She had no idea why he stuck around her so much when she clearly made him uneasy. Spooked him, even.

Though she should be the one spooked. And she had been, the first time they'd met. Suzanne had sent Jacko to pick her up for their first business meeting. He worked for Suzanne's husband, who ran some kind of fancy security company, though Jacko looked precisely like the kind of guy a security company was designed to protect against.

He was pierced, tattooed, his head was shaved and his muscles had muscles. He looked like trouble. Your worst nightmare, come to life. And yet…

Morton "Jacko" Jackman had the soul of a poet, though he'd probably punch in the face anyone who said so.

Lauren had never seen anyone respond the way he did to fine art and classical music. As if they had been designed precisely for him. He understood and reacted to art instinctively, in a way no education, however advanced, could teach.

And though not an untoward word had been spoken, though they barely ever touched beyond a handshake, Jacko had somehow become part of her life, too.

Well, she was going to stick with Jacko because sticking around Suzanne was dangerous. At any moment Suzanne could spill the beans over who had created the artwork on the walls and there would be a fuss, the spotlight of attention would turn to her and blood would be spilled. Hers.

Jacko could be counted on not to say anything, simply because she'd asked him not to. Jacko wasn't the kind of guy to accidentally spill anything.

She swerved and walked straight to him, happy to see a friendly face.

Well…friendly. That might be going a bit far. He wasn't *unfriendly* around her. He was just stiff and formal. But she liked him in spite of himself and he made her feel safe.

No one would touch her—could touch her—while Jacko Jackman was around. He didn't do it deliberately but there was a definite *don't mess with me* vibe around Jacko that was like a protective force field. Lauren recognized that she liked having him around partly because she relaxed in his presence. No need to be tense or worry about the outside world. He did that for her.

As she walked toward him, she could see white all around his dark eyes. She smiled at him, placed a hand on his big arm.

"Hi, Jacko."

He swallowed. "Ma'am."

Lauren rolled her eyes. Being with Jacko was always interesting. He was fun to tease, like pulling the tail of a dangerous tiger you knew wouldn't bite. "*Lauren*, Jacko. Not ma'am. I've told you a thousand times. Unless you want me to call you sir. Do you want me to call you *sir*?"

"No, ma'am."

She stepped closer and his eyes opened even wider. "Jacko, how long have we known each other?"

"Four months, three days and seven hours. Ma'am."

Wow. That was actually…true. She had to think about it for a minute but he was right. "So don't you think you could bring yourself to call me *Lauren*? Considering the fact that we've known each other four months, three days and seven hours?"

"Yes, ma'am."

"Lauren."

"Lauren. Ma'am."

She sighed again and looked around the room. No one was paying her any attention at all, which was precisely what she wanted. Nobody was paying much attention to what was on the walls, either, which was cool. Everyone was completely taken up with the hot hors d'oeuvres making the rounds on platters and the excellent champagne an army of servers was pouring into glasses. Allegra's music made for a gorgeous backdrop to the sounds of happy people drinking and eating and gossiping.

She hadn't really had a chance to see her work up on the walls. The work was hers but Suzanne had framed and hung the drawings and watercolors, and Suzanne had a wonderful eye for color and balance. Now that everyone was eating, drinking or listening to Allegra would be a good time to look at what was on those walls.

She leaned close to Jacko and was surprised to find that he smelled really good. It wasn't something as overt as a cologne. It didn't have alcohol overnotes. So it must be soap. Citrusy and fresh. And his own smell. Mmm.

"Jacko, will you walk around with me while I look at the drawings? I haven't had a chance to see them framed and hung."

"Yes, ma'am," he said and stuck his elbow out at an odd angle. She stared at it—was he going for a gun under his jacket?—and after a long moment realized he was offering her his arm.

Such an old-fashioned gesture from such a rough man, she hadn't even recognized it at first.

She took it and she relaxed another infinitesimal amount. There was just something so incredibly reassuring about Jacko. Holding his arm felt good. Really good.

She looked up at him and smiled and he flinched. Okay. She was relaxed, but clearly he wasn't. Somehow she made him uneasy. But still, he wasn't running away screaming, so she tugged him toward the west wall. She knew it was the west wall because it was painted blue with gilt letters in cursive writing on the top—*West Wall*. The east wall was taupe, the north wall salmon and the south wall mint. Gilt letters proclaimed each wall. Suzanne had chosen the frames according to the colors of the walls.

They walked. Walking with Jacko in a crowded room was a very interesting experience. She'd bumped shoulders with about twenty people before. The room was full of people and everyone was intent on something else—food, drink or someone more interesting than she was. She'd been jostled and stepped on and shouldered aside.

Instead, now, it was like Moses parting the Red Sea. Everyone somehow made way for Jacko, shifting out of his way as if that were the natural order of things. Those who didn't instantly move got a glare that—once they saw it—made them scramble. No one jostled her; no one stepped on her toes; no one crowded her.

"Have you seen the works already?" she asked.

Jacko had been scrutinizing the crowd as if they were enemy insurgents, carefully and coldly. He looked down at her. "Yes, ma'am. Lauren. I helped hang them."

"So which ones do you like?"

His dark eyes met hers. "All of them. Every single one."

She faked a smile. Wrong answer.

"But the Morgenstern series is amazing," he said. "And so is the Lachland residence. Never seen anything like it."

Okay. Right answer.

"I'd really like to see up close what she did with the frames."

"Sure thing." He looked down at her and if she didn't know better she'd say that was a *smile* lurking in his eyes. Jacko smiling? Nah.

But he walked her to the appropriate wall, people parting for them. Jacko snagged a couple of flutes of champagne off a passing silver tray and held one out to her. It was very deftly done, considering the size of his hands.

It had amazed her during drawing lessons, too. The number 2 pencil looked like a stalk of straw in his huge hands, yet that hand sketched the most delicate images imaginable. He was an expert on hand-drawn maps, and his own were exquisite.

They stopped in front of the Morgenstern series. Suzanne had gone all out in the presentation. Over the series was a long acrylic rectangle with *Morgenstern residence—24 hours* laser-etched across the top. The watercolors were framed with a gold passé-partout within an elaborate wrought iron frame holding the entire ensemble together. She'd had the idea of the Morgenstern series as she sat on a park bench across from the façade of the home. It was a Belle Epoque building and by some miracle of light and shadow, each part of the day—sunrise, noon, late afternoon and dusk—highlighted different parts of the façade.

So she'd done watercolors of the four parts of the day, each a slightly different hue, each shift of the sunlight highlighting different aspects of the ornate façade.

"Suzanne did a really good job framing them."

That earned her an odd look. "The works are yours. Not hers."

There was nothing to say to that.

She sipped the excellent champagne, holding the flute up so it caught the light. The crystal felt good in her hand, catching the light of the overhead chandeliers, so fine it was almost as if the bubbles were caught in air instead of glass.

She twirled the stem. Her family had had flutes just like this in Boston. Fifty of them. Three lifetimes ago.

For just a fleeting second sadness descended over her. She'd trained herself, *schooled* herself against it. Thinking of the past not only did her no good, it was actively dangerous. She had to be present, fully in the moment, every second, because danger could come leaping out of the darkness at any time.

The only way to survive was to be on her guard and to be grateful for every second, because every second could be her last. No past, no future, only the present.

And if it hurt her, just a little, not to be able to claim the watercolors and drawings she'd worked so hard on, if it hurt her, just a little, to remember her charmed childhood in Boston that could never come back, too bad.

That was life.

"Let's go look at the Agarwal house sketches over on the east wall." She tugged at Jacko's arm.

"Sure. They're beautiful. My compliments." They were crossing the big room and he looked down at her and she thought she saw...again, could that be a *smile* in the depths of his dark eyes? Jacko was the most serious man she'd ever been around. His emotional tones ran the gamut from sober to grim and back again. Even the hint of a smile was extraordinary.

"Well, it was thanks to you." She gave him a sunny

smile, straight up at him, and his face froze. It looked like something hurt.

The sketches of the Agarwal house had come out well, she had to admit. It was thanks to Jacko that she'd been able to sketch the house at all. The Agarwal house was an extraordinary structure built by an Indian venture capitalist heavily invested in green energy. The house was built on a remote vast plot of land on the foothills of Mount Hood and had been designed to blend into the forest.

Lauren had sketched it in fall and deepest winter and had extrapolated what it would look like in spring and summer. She'd spent three full days filling ten notebooks with sketches.

When Jacko had heard through Suzanne—who'd received the contract to design the interior décor—that Lauren intended to spend a lot of time on the isolated estate he had insisted on accompanying her. The first time, Lauren had balked. She liked—no, needed—to take her time. She didn't want to draw hasty sketches with a bored guy tapping his size 14 boot waiting for her to finish up. But it hadn't been like that, not at all. Jacko seemed to have enormous reserves of patience. He found a bench where he sat quietly, simply waiting for her. Five minutes after she arrived in the morning, Lauren had forgotten Jacko's presence and only came up for air in the early afternoon after an orgy of sketching to find him waiting in the exact same spot in the exact same position she'd left him in.

Something told her he'd be able to do that for days and maybe even weeks, not just hours.

And, truth be told, the fact that he was there, watching over her, allowed her to lose her sense of time and do it right. Without him, there was a bit of her that would have remained tense and alert.

"You were very kind and very patient with me. I appreciate it." She looked up and met his eyes and again smiled sunnily at him. He blinked and his face became even more wooden.

"My pleasure, ma'am."

She rolled her eyes at him. "Lauren."

"Lauren," he repeated dutifully.

God it was fun teasing him. She tugged at the massive arm under her hand. "So come on, let's go over to the blue wall." They turned. "From what I can see of the frames, she did a magnificent—"

And then it happened.

And it cut her life in two.

Copyright © 2014 by Lisa Marie Rice

ABOUT THE AUTHOR

Lisa Marie Rice is eternally thirty years old and will never age. She is tall and willowy and beautiful. Men drop at her feet like ripe pears. She has won every major book prize in the world. She is a black belt with advanced degrees in archaeology, nuclear physics and Tibetan literature. She is a concert pianist. Did I mention her Nobel Prize? Of course Lisa Marie Rice is a virtual woman and exists only at the keyboard. She disappears when the monitor winks off.

Check out her website at lisamariericebooks.com and sign up for her newsletter.